PASTURES NEW

PASTURES NEW

J.M. Gregson

This first world edition published in Great Britain 2008 by
SEVERN HOUSE PUBLISHERS LTD of
9–15 High Street, Sutton, Surrey SM1 1DF.
This first world edition published in the USA 2008 by
SEVERN HOUSE PUBLISHERS INC of
595 Madison Avenue, New York, N.Y. 10022.

British Library Cataloguing in Publication Data

Gregson, J. M.
  Pastures new
  1. Peach, Percy (Fictitious character) - Fiction 2. Blake,
  Lucy (Fictitious character) - Fiction 3. Police - England -
  Lancashire - Fiction 4. Murder - Investigation - Fiction
  5. Detective and mystery stories
  I. Title
  823.9'14[F]

  ISBN-13: 978-0-7278-6593-9   (cased)

All Severn House titles are printed on acid-free paper.

Typeset by Palimpsest Book Production Ltd.,
Grangemouth, Stirlingshire, Scotland.
Printed and bound in Great Britain by
MPG Books Ltd., Bodmin, Cornwall.

To Pauline Hogan, who once had the best tennis backhand in Manchester and who remains a lady of spirit and beauty.

One

'Successful businessman. Late fifties but vigorous, well preserved and open to new ideas. N/S. Interested in the arts, theatre and local history. Seeks lady of similar interests for companionship and outings.'

It looked entirely unremarkable in print. Unmistakably dull, in fact. When he looked at it among the scores of more attractive and ingenious offerings in the local and national papers, Geoffrey Aspin couldn't believe that this turgid offering would excite any interest at all.

Everyone else seemed to assert GSOH, or even VGSOH. But despite the advice of the helpful lady at the newspaper, he had chosen not to include these mystic letters. Somehow Geoffrey felt that people who had to insist in print that they had a very good sense of humour might be either cackling bores or severely deficient in the humour department.

He hadn't even wanted to put N/S: it seemed such a priggish assertion of virtue. But probably if you didn't say that you were a non-smoker, all those anonymous and rather scary women out there might assume that you were a forty-a-day man, with nicotine-stained fingers and an advanced carcinogenic wheeze. In the same way, the many men who insisted that they were 'tactile' suggested to him sexual predators bent on the most unspeakable physical experiments.

For the same reason, he had reluctantly crossed out the fact that he was interested in various sports. He'd looked at it for a long time, and tried various ways of re-phrasing it, but 'sportsman' still seemed to him to invite women to arrive with the wrong expectations, demanding all sorts of impossible sexual gymnastics, which he would be both unwilling and unable to provide.

Even after he had settled on this singularly dull summary of his qualities and requirements, it had taken him three weeks to pluck up the courage to insert it in the *Lancashire Telegraph*. Advertising for female companionship, even of the most innocent kind, wasn't the kind of thing people like him did. He'd never dared to discuss such things with his male friends at the golf club, even when they were at their most affable and sympathetic at the nineteenth hole. He'd heard a programme on the radio in which people claimed confidently that such columns attracted people from all walks of life and provided a valuable service, but he'd never known anyone who used them.

At least he'd never been aware of anyone who used them. He made that sturdy correction to himself, told himself again that you never knew what went on behind closed doors, but he still didn't find it convincing. For a man who had begun and developed a highly successful printing business, Geoffrey Aspin was still a touchingly naive person.

He stared once again at his innocent and humdrum contribution, glanced through its more exotic companions, and shook his head sadly. Although he professed himself to be in touch with modern society, it still surprised Geoffrey Aspin that there was a long column of men openly seeking other men. Most of these seemed to offer 'great personalities'; they also proclaimed variously 'excellent equipment for all sorts of frolics' and 'interest in bars, pubs, theatre, horse riding and any other activity which offers fun'.

Whilst modesty seemed conspicuously absent from the way people in the column described themselves, 'fun' seemed to be a favourite word: Geoffrey wondered for the hundredth time whether this word was a key cipher in some elaborate code which only those familiar with the rules of this arcane game understood. If 'fun' was the chosen noun, then 'bubbly' must surely be the favourite adjective. Even the women seeking men, in that section he had read and re-read over the months with increasing desperation, seemed to be quite determinedly bubbly.

Geoffrey Aspin hoped he wouldn't get one of those. He was sure that a bubbly fifty-five year old would be more than he could cope with. He found himself wishing yet again that he had not put his advert in the paper at all. It had taken several whiskies and an evening of television dominated by the inanities of *Big Brother* to induce the despair which had finally spurred that leap into the darkness.

In the cold grey light of a Wednesday morning, his aspirations for female company seemed even more pathetic and ridiculous. During those long winter evenings, which had been the preludes to nights of disturbed sleep and even more disturbing dreams, his loneliness had seemed overwhelming, dominating his life like a physical pain that would not go away. Now his yearning for company seemed pathetic; a lack of perspective which should have been summarily dismissed; a defect of character which would excite first derision and then condemnation in anyone who discovered it.

He stared yet again at his modest, unambitious, three-line entry to the columns of DATING POINT, and found comfort in its very inadequacy. Amongst all the more lurid protestations of excellence around it, his contribution must surely be dismissed by those anonymous armies of females whom he suddenly found so fearsome. He shut the paper firmly and addressed himself with relief to the realities of life.

It was high time he was off to work and the welcome challenges which awaited him there. No doubt there were decisions to be taken, and he would act with his usual firmness and confidence. Thank goodness that Mrs Green, his friendly, efficient and unfortunately very happily married secretary, would never know anything of the agonies of his long and lonely evenings.

It was at that moment that the phone rang. An impersonal, distinctly uninterested voice from the newspaper told him that he had four responses to his entry waiting for him on their confidential voicebox line.

Detective Chief Inspector 'Percy' Peach, scourge of the criminals of North Lancashire, was almost equally feared and respected by the team he commanded in Brunton CID. He was trying hard to be patient.

The man who was testing his resolve was not one of the local thugs but his superior officer, the bland and self-satisfied Chief Superintendent Thomas Bulstrode Tucker. The man in

charge of Brunton CID section, universally known among his
workforce by the name allotted to him some years ago by DCI
Peach, Tommy Bloody Tucker.

Tucker was quite a handsome man, if you favoured suavity
in features and expression. He was now in his mid-fifties,
with one eye on the fat pension which awaited him and the
other on keeping his nose clean at all costs so as not to
jeopardize that end-of-career Holy Grail. He was a trifle
florid and running just a little to fat now, but his full head
of hair, silvering becomingly at the temples, and his regular,
heavy features gave him the gravitas for set-piece occasions.
Tucker regarded public relations as his forte, and he was duly
trundled out in times of crisis to assure the sceptical Lancashire
public that the police had the situation well in hand.

Those above as well as those below Chief Superintendent
Tucker in the hierarchy knew that in the task of solving
serious crimes which was officially his job, he was hopelessly out of his depth. But rank carries its own defence, and
Tucker held an elevated one. No one in the higher echelons
of the police service wished to expose him as a phoney: that
might raise questions as to who had promoted him to the
rank at which he was so patently inefficient.

Percy Peach understood all of this, knew how the system
operated, knew that Tucker had only campaigned for his
inspector's elevation to the rank of chief inspector because
solely by that means could he secure his own promotion to
chief superintendent. But he knew also that Tommy Bloody
Tucker depended on him, that the impressive crime clear-up
rates of Brunton CID on which Tucker rode were wholly the
work of Peach and the officers he had hand-picked to support
him.

Although he would never acknowledge it openly, Thomas
Bulstrode Tucker knew that too. Although he intensely
disliked the bouncy rubber ball of a man who was sixteen
years younger than him, he had long since realized that he
was dependent upon him. He knew Peach took liberties,
though he was seldom quite sure when he was taking them.
But Tucker had to tolerate a certain amount of insolence,
because he needed Peach far more than Peach needed him.

Percy Peach was a thief-taker, a man who worked at the

crime-face and refused to be removed from it and sat behind a desk. He had no aspiration to the higher rank which would have taken him away from the squalid, sometimes violent, world where he excelled. Peach was happy in the company of working policemen and villains, where he knew exactly what he was doing. He was proof against any threats from the figurehead who needed him so desperately to see him through to his pension with a spotless proboscis. Consequently, he took liberties, and Tucker could do little about them.

Peach was making his mid-week oral report to Tucker, who had never mastered the advantages of e-mail communication. 'The former Mount Zion Methodist Chapel in Clitheroe has been attacked by vandals,' Percy announced carefully.

'Ah!' said Tucker sagely, buying time to digest the implications of this.

'Windows were smashed in. There was quite a lot of damage.'

Tucker decided that he could now see how matters stood. 'Really, you shouldn't be bothering me with this, you know. It's petty crime. I have much more important things to worry about.' He gestured vaguely with his right arm over his massive but entirely empty desk.

'Very good, sir. I'll tell the newshounds that it isn't worth a statement from you. They seemed to think the attack might be racially motivated.'

'Oh, I think you can rule that out, Peach! Take it from me, the Methodists might get a passing sneer from the drinkers in our society, but they don't excite sectarian or racial passions any more. Not in the twenty-first century.' Tucker shook his head sadly that his DCI should be so out of touch with modern trends. 'I should leave it to uniform – tell them it's not a matter worthy of CID attention.'

'If you say so, sir. Just so long as you're prepared to take full responsibility with our Asian community. I'll assure them that you see no sign of the National Front violence they're mentioning. I expect you know best, with your overview of these things.'

Tucker paled visibly – always a welcome phenomenon for Percy Peach. The chief superintendent was fond of claiming for himself a detached overview of the society in which they operated, which was denied to the more limited and lesser-ranked mortals beneath him. It was always a danger signal for Tucker, however, when Peach quoted this Olympian command of things back to him.

Tucker said uncertainly, 'Our Asian brethren have a strong affiliation with those of the Methodist persuasion?'

'*Former* Mount Zion Methodist Chapel, I said, sir. It's many years since our Methodist friends worshipped there. It's been a factory in more recent years. I thought you might have remembered that, sir, with your unrivalled knowledge of our patch.'

'It's Clitheroe, Peach,' said Tucker dismissively. He spoke as if the ancient small town, ten miles from where he sat, was Bangkok or Shanghai.

'The place where the *former* Methodist Chapel still stands has been approved as the new site for a mosque in Clitheroe,' said Peach, with the air of one instructing a rather dim child.

Tucker's face set grimly. It was time to put this upstart in his place and dismiss the matter. 'It's petty vandalism, Peach. There's no more to be said about it. End of story.'

'It's very disappointing that with what seems to be a racially motivated crime, no one is prepared to conduct a dialogue with the Asian community.' Peach stared neutrally at the ceiling.

'Don't give me that claptrap, Peach. It's rubbish and you know it. You're wasting my time.'

'I see, sir. Sorry about that. It's not my rubbish, though. I was quoting Mr Sheraz Akmal, Secretary of the Medina Islamic Education Centre. However, you have made things splendidly clear, in the decisive manner which is such an admirable feature of your direction. I shall be happy to relay to Mr Akmal that you think he is wasting your time.'

'I didn't say that, Peach.'

Tucker was visibly as well as mentally deflated. He shrank to a smaller size in his huge executive chair. It was a physical process which Peach was always happy both to initiate and to study in detail.

Peach said, 'The local police have been dealing with it, but perhaps I'd better get over there and put this Akmal fellow in his place. Tell him that Chief Superintendent Tucker doesn't want him wasting our time.' He nodded his satisfaction at the prospect of such firmness.

'You won't do any such thing, Peach!' A major public relations disaster rose like an awful vision in Tucker's normally inactive imagination.

'It would please the far-right people in the National Front Party,' said Peach persuasively.

'Of course it would! And therefore we must tread carefully.'

'They're a powerful political force in the town, since they won the Mill Hill seat in the local elections. Going from strength to strength, their spokesman says.'

'You should pay a damn sight less heed to these bloody spokesmen, Peach. They're a waste of bloody time!' said his chief fiercely.

'Ah!' Peach frowned, as if attempting to cement a difficult new concept into his memory. 'I should ignore Mr Akmal then, sir, shouldn't I? As spokesman for the Muslim community in Clitheroe, he says we should have a discussion and a dialogue with him. He says that would be the British way of doing things.'

'You must *not* ignore him, Peach. Race is a sensitive issue in these parts, in case you hadn't noticed. We must treat this Mr Akmal with—'

'Thirty-seven-year-old father of three, sir, according to the *Lancashire Telegraph*. He says that they're trying to develop something for the whole community with the new mosque and youth centre in Clitheroe, whilst a few individuals are trying to damage this landmark building. Still, I'll be happy to tell Mr Akmal that you think it's claptrap and that he should go away and stop moaning. It's good to hear such a firm line being taken with these spokesmen who waste such a lot of our time. Bold, I must say, even perhaps daring, in today's context.'

Thomas Bulstrode Tucker sighed the heavy sigh he always sighed when he saw work coming his way. 'I think you'd better leave this matter with me, Peach. It seems to require diplomacy.'

'Not my strong suit, sir, I agree. If diplomacy and a bit

of soft soap are required, the situation would be much better
in the hands of someone with your overview of things.'

Peach smiled benignly at the drab Brunton world outside
as he looked at it through the window on his way back downstairs. A couple of broken windows, a hundred and fifty
quid's worth of damage, and the matter already being efficiently dealt with by the beat coppers at Clitheroe. Tommy
Bloody Tucker would no doubt get a flea in the ear from his
opposite number in charge of the uniformed branch. But it
would keep him out of Percy Peach's hair for the rest of the
day.

Two days later, Geoffrey Aspin sat staring at the steam rising
from his untouched cup in the town's busiest coffee house.
He had never been to Starbucks before, but he hadn't cared
to confess that to the woman who had suggested this venue
from the other end of the telephone line.

His own priority as a prominent local businessman was
privacy. But the women who had responded to his advert
seemed to have quite different requirements for a first
meeting. They apparently wanted it to be as public as possible.
Geoffrey would have gone for the protection of darkness;
they had insisted on the bright revealing light of day. He had
thought to meet out in the country, well away from Brunton,
home, and the prying eyes of those who knew him; they had
insisted on the town and the crowds they seemed to think
implied protection. He had suggested a quiet back-street pub;
they had insisted on places like Starbucks, with its busy,
brightly lit interior and its constantly changing clientele, any
one of whom might be able to recognize Geoffrey Aspin.

He selected the only alcove he could see and huddled
himself like an inexperienced private detective at the end of
it. He had agreed to bring with him a copy of *The Times*,
wear a blue handkerchief with the corner displayed in the
top pocket of his jacket, and to carry the cap he hadn't worn
for years. He felt not only an idiot but also a conspicuous
idiot.

The worst element of all was that the embarrassment was
of his own making. He'd been taken aback when the woman
wouldn't give him either her name or her address. This cloak

and dagger stuff seemed a waste of time to him, but the patient female voice on the other end of the line had explained that it was standard practice. He'd had to confess he was new to all of this; that he'd had to have the mysteries of 'voicebox' explained to him by the newspaper; that he found the whole of this introductory process both bewildering and disconcerting.

He'd thought, during the prolonged clumsiness of these voicebox messages to each other, that such unfamiliarity with the mechanics of meeting would have left him impatiently dismissed. Instead, the as yet anonymous female who was initiating him into these arcane rights had seemed to think his inexperience quite a plus factor in the dossier of his qualities which she was apparently assembling.

For his part, he had found the friendly, incredulous laughter which greeted his naivety both refreshing and attractive. In his working life, Geoffrey Aspin was very sure of himself, very decisive. Now he found his first tentative steps towards a new relationship perplexing and alarming, but also rather exciting. His instructor had put him on the spot when she had said he must wear items which would clearly identify him. The handkerchief and the cap and *The Times* were all his ideas, culled he was sure from some cheap thriller he had read thirty years earlier and thought to have forgotten. It had seemed rather amusing at the time.

Now, in the harsh white lights of Starbucks, these trappings seemed an utter disaster. He hadn't just quietly identified himself for the woman he was to meet, but had made himself stand out as a complete prat. Geoffrey felt like a fish floundering on a very public river bank, unable because of the assignment he had undertaken to flop himself back into the anonymity of the waters of swiftly moving humanity in the street outside.

The suit was a mistake, for a start. Everyone else in the coffee shop seemed to be casually dressed. The cap, which he had set like a badge of identification upon the table, seemed a garish red rather than the quiet russet he had remembered. And the flamboyant light blue silk handkerchief in the top pocket of his jacket was an even bigger mistake. It might match his tie, as he had planned, but it must make

him look like an ageing homosexual in need of company, to
judge by the curious looks he was getting as people passed
the end of his alcove and decided to sit elsewhere. He sipped
the froth on his cappuccino without enthusiasm, extracted his
silver ballpoint pen from his inside pocket, and pretended
an intense interest in the crossword he had never been able
to master.

The whole thing was a mistake. He hadn't arranged a date
for himself for nearly forty years; in the days of his youth,
he would never have dreamed of the elaborate efforts which
had landed him here. The crushing loneliness which had
made the nights so desolate in the years since Jill's death
had unhinged his judgement. He had never dreamed that he
could be so inadequate, so bored with his own tedious
company, so lacking in the interests which should fill his
life without a close companion. Well, he had learnt his lesson
now. He was sitting here in a place he didn't want to be,
drinking coffee he didn't want to drink, waiting for a debacle
which he could not avoid. This was one new experience he
was certainly not going to—

'You must be the man I'm looking for.'

A blonde woman with a becoming, pleasingly uncertain
smile. Holding the brown leather handbag which she had
suggested as her own mark of identification a little self-
consciously in front of her. Looking taller than she was,
because she stood close to him as he sat, shutting out some
of the light, making the alcove seem suddenly a more intimate place, where they might conduct their negotiations with
a degree of privacy. Running just a little to fat – no, he
corrected that ungracious thought immediately: without the
skinniness which would have made her look gaunt now that
she was in her fifties. Buxom, that was the word. Somewhere
from that distant past which he thought had gone for ever,
the phrase 'comely wench' surfaced. He banished it; the
expression was surely sexist, though Geoffrey had only the
vaguest idea of what that dangerous modern word comprehended.

He shuffled awkwardly and he feared a little arthritically
to his feet and held out his hand. 'Geoffrey Aspin.' She took
his hand in her own much smaller one, widened her smile,

set down the coffee she had brought from the counter on the table beside that ridiculous cap. 'I won't give you my name yet. That's the usual procedure, for a first meeting. We should both err on the side of caution, in case we wish to proceed no further.'

He nodded earnestly, feeling it odd to sit down with someone without even knowing her name, but grateful for any guidance he could get about the way this strange social ritual had to be conducted. He was surprised to find that he was sweating. He pulled the silk handkerchief from his top pocket, drew it quickly across his brow, and banished it thankfully from sight into the side pocket of his jacket.

'Have you got a partner?' she said.

It was the first time Geoffrey Aspin had ever heard himself associated with that word. He wasn't sure whether he was pleased or irritated; his brain was racing too fast for him to be sure of anything. 'No.'

'You're divorced?'

'No. My wife died three years ago. Cancer.' He was going to enlarge on that, but realized just in time that this wasn't the moment to do it.

'Family?'

'Two daughters. They live in this area, but they're both married. They—'

'It's best we don't give each other too many details at the moment. All that can follow later, if we decide to proceed.'

It sounded very clinical, but he supposed that was the way these things had to be conducted. He didn't know what he should ask her. He said rather woodenly, 'You've obviously done this before. I'm sorry, but it's my first time.'

'Don't apologize. You're not shop-soiled, like some of us. It's an advantage being new to this.'

'It didn't feel it, while I was waiting for you. I'm sorry for suggesting these trimmings, by the way.' He gestured at his suit, the newspaper and the pocket which held the handkerchief. 'I suppose I wanted to pose as some kind of ageing matinee idol – though I'm not sure the cap fits in with that.'

She grinned, her first natural, spontaneous smile. 'I think I pictured someone out of a spy thriller. But at least you didn't come up with the carnation which most men seem to suggest; that makes you look as if you've slipped out of a wedding reception. Anyway, I've nothing against matinee idols. They always seemed impossibly out of reach when I was a girl.'

He smiled back. 'They're just as out of reach now, I'm afraid. I'm more your nuts and bolts than your morning or evening suit man. It was just a disguise.'

'I think morning dress might stand out a bit in Brunton. Especially in Starbucks.'

They had their first little giggle together on that thought. He removed his cap from the table and made it invisible on the seat beside him. Then, as he wondered what to say, he was grateful to see her retreating into sips of her drink to punctuate her statements. 'Another coffee?'

She smiled again, and he realized, as he shuffled to his feet, how she understood the release that physical movement provided for him. She said, 'We should really go Dutch in our first meetings, so that there are no obligations on either side. I sound as though I've been round the block a few times, don't I? I haven't, actually, but I had one bad experience and been given a lot of advice. Yes, another coffee would be most welcome, thank you. I scarcely noticed the first one in my anxiety.'

As he went to the counter, he was filled with an absurd elation that she should have confessed to some of the nervousness which had almost made him bolt from the place. They chatted, guardedly but happily enough, for another twenty minutes, feeling increasingly relaxed in each other's company. For the first time since he had placed his advert in the DATING POINT section of the newspaper, Geoffrey Aspin felt glad that he had done so.

'You can call me Pam,' she said eventually, and he felt that she had made a great concession to him. 'I still won't give you my telephone number or my address yet, though. We can pick up anything we have to say to each other through the voicebox system. I think it's best to observe the protocol in these things.'

He nodded almost eagerly, anxious to show her that he was not offended by her caution. He wondered about her bad experience.

'You already know my name, though, because I didn't know the rules. Would you like my phone number?'

'That's up to you, Geoff. I've already forgotten your second name, by the way. Maybe that was Freudian – or more likely I didn't register it in the initial embarrassment of meeting.'

They had a final rueful grimace together at the futility of human aspirations, and then he said, 'I'd like to give my phone number to you. I don't feel threatened, you see.' Rather than feeling resentful because she had denied him her own particulars, he was grateful when she did not rebuff his offer to confide more of himself.

'I'll ring you then, if I want to have any further contact. Let's say within three days, so that we both know where we are. Don't be offended if you don't hear from me. And please don't feel you have to be polite to me, if you don't want to take this any further. It's much less messy to knock these things on the head at the beginning than later on, believe me!'

He almost forgot to pick up his cap, then folded it firmly in his left hand rather than put it upon his head. They went out to one of those cheerless days of low grey cloud which showed the battered old cotton town at its worst. Yet to Geoffrey Aspin the world now seemed a brighter place. They turned away from each other and walked briskly in opposite directions down the busy street. Neither of them looked back.

Geoffrey thought he would remember nothing of this strange meeting by that evening. After all, he had been more nervous than he could remember being for at least forty years. But he found that he could easily picture the fullness of the woman's lips and her humorous blue eyes and the way she held her head a little on one side as she looked at him, as though assessing him and approving what she saw. She hadn't worn much make-up, he thought, but perhaps she was just very skilful; the mystique of the female toilet was an area which had never excited his curiosity. Her neatly cut dark blonde hair had been quite beautiful, and he was sure owed nothing to artifice.

For all his experience of life, Geoffrey Aspin was still an innocent in some aspects of it.

He remembered also, with a quite disturbing vividness,

the appealing curve of her breast beneath the soft wool of her sweater, the well-turned calves above the expensive leather shoes, which had heels which were high but not too high. It would be a pity if he never saw her again; the woman who he was surprised to find seemed to have made quite an impression upon him.

Nevertheless, he must prepare himself for disappointment. He had lived life long enough to know that it held far more disappointments than delights. If Pam didn't want to see him again, it was far better to know it at this stage, as she had so sensibly told him. He passed two rather bleak evenings telling himself this, and was unwontedly tetchy with his staff at the works during the days.

At nine o'clock on the third evening, his phone bleeped only twice before he reached it. 'Geoff, it's Pam. I would like to see you again. How do you feel about that?'

Two

Things moved quickly for Geoffrey Aspin, more swiftly than he had imagined was possible when he had placed his tentative toe into the swirling waters of DATING POINT.

He suggested a theatre excursion to Manchester as their first outing together, and Pam accepted, with due caution but without any argument. If she noted that Manchester was thirty miles from Brunton and therefore offered a degree of anonymity to their enterprise, she did not comment. Perhaps anonymity suited her too. Perhaps she wanted to be sure that if this adventure led nowhere, she could terminate it without anyone else knowing that it had even been undertaken.

He picked her up where she suggested, on the road behind the bus station. She had probably arranged that so that she could get the bus into town, he thought. He knew it was pointless, but he could not help speculating about which bus she had used to get there, which part of the town or its suburbs or the country around it she had come from. She knew his name and his phone number; probably by now she had checked his address. He understood perfectly why there was this imbalance of information between them: she had explained the rules of this strange new game to him at their initial meeting in Starbucks, and it was he who had thrust his unasked for phone number upon her. But he found as he drove the Jaguar into the centre of the town that he resented the wall of silence which she had seemed so concerned to erect around herself.

She was waiting for him, as he had hoped she would be, an umbrella held at an angle to hide her head from the March air, which was cold but scarcely damp. It was more a conceal-ment than a protection, he felt. She slid swiftly into the car, gave him a quick smile of recognition and appreciation, and they were away. For a few minutes, he was self-conscious about his driving, as he had not been for years. Should he show her how eminently safe he was, or should he be a little more flamboyant, as a young man anxious to impress on his first date might have been? Then, on the open road over the moors towards Bolton, the familiar thrust of the big engine seemed to take over, and they surged swiftly towards the city without the need for such consideration.

The tickets he had booked were for a routine thriller. He had considered that a neutral choice, not too demanding and not entirely banal – he had no idea yet what her tastes were. It was a production on its way to London, well directed and well acted, and not overburdened with philosophical discourse, as he had foreseen. It held their attention, or at least as much of their attention as either of them wanted to give to it.

Geoffrey was intensely conscious of the woman beside him. Her attention was apparently unswervingly upon the brightly lit stage, yet he was sure she was conscious of the male presence at her side. He could feel the warmth of her, smell her perfume, catch the glint of her hair as the stage lights rose and fell, sense the soft curve of her breast only inches from his arm.

Geoffrey Aspin thought inevitably of his dead wife and of times long ago. Jill had always insisted during her last illness that she did not expect him to become a monk when she was gone, that he would need the close company of women to carry on his life. Women, she had said: not a particular woman. But he did not feel guilty, did not feel any presence overseeing him from beyond the grave. His mind raced through a turmoil of widely differing emotions.

He could not remember when he had last been in a theatre. At the interval, he rose awkwardly to his feet, realizing that they were going to be at the back of the queue for the dress-circle bar. 'What would you like to drink?'

'Quite honestly, I think I'd prefer an ice cream, if that's not too juvenile for you, Geoff. But you get what you want for yourself.'

'You shall have the best ice cream that money can buy! I might even forsake the alcohol and join you, Pam.' It was the first time he had used the name she had given to him, and he felt the blood rising to his face: surely you couldn't blush when you were approaching sixty?

He was curiously pleased that she wasn't much of a drinker. He decided that he must be a very old-fashioned man. His children had always told him that he was, but didn't all children say that about their parents? The pair stood rather self-consciously with their tubs of ice cream in the corridor outside the bar, studying photographs of famous former productions, feeling their way into a relationship, experiencing the paradox of working hard to be relaxed with each other.

After the performance, they applauded enthusiastically, trying to pretend that their attention was entirely on the stage and not on the profile and reactions of the person beside them. They discussed the play and the performers on the way back to the car, each learning all the time small facts about the other from the desultory, apparently irrelevant comments. The Jaguar ate up the miles of the largely deserted motorway swiftly at that hour of the night, so that they were back in Brunton surprisingly quickly.

'You can drop me by the bus station,' she said determinedly.

'Your last bus will have gone.'

'I don't think so. If it has, I'll get a taxi.'

He glanced sideways, then directed his gaze back to the road. After the warmth he had felt growing between them over the last four hours, her face had set into an unrevealing mask. For an instant he wondered whether he should risk offending her.

Then he said, 'This is silly. I don't want to know where you live until you choose to tell me. But let me at least drop you at the end of your road.'

She moved into the explanation she had been planning for the last twenty minutes, but dropped it before it was properly under way. 'All right. You can drop me at the end of my road. I'll be quite safe from there.'

She gave him directions, and he drove out to the west of the town as she told him, stopping as she directed at the end of a well-lit road. She sat for a moment after he'd braked the Jaguar, then said, 'I've enjoyed tonight. Really. I'm not just being polite when I say that.'

'I enjoyed it too. Give me a ring if you want another outing.'

'I will. And I do.' She leant quickly across the car, pressed warm lips against his cheek, and then slipped from the car. Just as she was about to close the door, she stooped and leant briefly back into the warm male cave of the vehicle.

'By the way, Geoff, the full name's Pam Williams!' she said. And then, with the briefest of goodnight smiles, she was gone.

On the same March evening when Geoffrey Aspin and Pam Williams were enjoying themselves in the Manchester theatre, Detective Sergeant Lucy Blake was concluding a day off spent at home with her widowed mother.

In the familiar cottage at the foot of Longridge Fell, she had enjoyed her mother's cooking after wandering round the small, immaculately tended garden which held so many childhood memories for her. These were the two things she missed most when she was in her cosy modern flat in Brunton, which otherwise met her requirements admirably.

Sitting comfortably beside the open fire in the low-ceilinged sitting room, allowing her mother to bring her up to date on the village gossip, she thought of the days when she had wandered around the garden with her father. She remembered learning the names of plants, feeling the cool smoothness of daffodil leaves and the velvety softness of pussy willow catkins, sniffing the heady perfume of crimson rose petals and hearing her father's laughter at her delight in these new sensations. Dear, dead but not forgotten days.

'The crocuses are finished now, but the daffodils are beginning to bloom. I never think spring is really here until the daffodils are trumpeting it for us,' said Lucy. She wondered how the words for such a simple thought could sound so pretentious. She stretched her toes luxuriously towards the flames in the hearth and settled a little lower in her armchair, feeling pleasantly drowsy.

Her mother's response had her alert and sitting bolt upright in an instant. 'Spring's here now. It's high time we were fixing a date for this wedding,' said Agnes Blake determinedly.

'There's no hurry.' Lucy's automatic, defensive response. 'I'm sure Percy wouldn't say that.' Agnes looked towards the two photographs on the mantlepiece, sharing pride of place in the house. The black and white one of her husband, sweater over his shoulder, looking shyly at the camera as he walked off the field after taking six wickets at Blackpool in a Northern League cricket match forty years ago. The more recent one of Peach was in colour, with a dark blue cap concealing the shining bald head above his immaculate white cricket gear, so that he looked younger and more innocent, almost boyish. The inscription beneath was in Agnes Blake's small, immaculate script: 'Denis Charles Scott Peach, after another dashing half-century for East Lancs in the Lancashire League'.

Agnes was the only woman who insisted on remembering the full forenames of the man universally known in the Brunton police service as 'Percy'. She knew as only a few others did that he had been christened by a cricket-mad father after Denis Charles Scott Compton, the 'dashing cavalier of Lords' who played in the era after the Second World War, and in Agnes Blake's formidable opinion, the finest English batsman who had ever lived. Those magical forenames had been an immediate bond between her and the man who was now her prospective son-in-law.

Lucy had taken Percy Peach home to meet her mother with great trepidation. She knew that his shining bald head and black moustache were an acquired taste; more importantly, he was a man who was not only divorced but almost ten years older than her. The fiercely direct chief inspector and her doting mother had struck up an immediate bond and were very quickly mysteriously at one with each other, so that Lucy now found herself outflanked and defeated whenever she opposed this formidable alliance.

She was sure now that she loved Percy, but marriage had not been on her agenda until her mother had got busy on the theme and Percy had proved unexpectedly and treacherously responsive. They were now officially engaged and she had a ring on her finger to prove it. But Lucy enjoyed her CID career and was doing well in it: she saw no need to interrupt it with marriage and a family until some as yet undetermined time in the future.

That wasn't how her mother saw things. Engagement meant marriage, as far as Agnes Blake was concerned, and the sooner the better. She would be seventy this year: it was high time she had grandchildren. That she should still be without them seemed to her almost to set a question mark over the respectability which was still so important in a country area. She was fond of reminding her daughter that other, younger women in the small local supermarket where she worked part-time had teenage grandchildren.

'Percy Peach is a taker of villains,' said Lucy firmly. 'He's more interested in my performance as a detective sergeant than in fixing a date for a wedding.'

'Detective sergeant,' Agnes Blake contrived to ooze a massive contempt into her pronunciation of the rank she was usually so proud to proclaim to her friends in the village. 'It's time you got yourself a proper sense of priorities, my girl!'

Lucy remembered how there had been no arguing with that 'my girl' when she was an eight-year-old. Twenty years later, she still found it difficult. She sought desperately for some diversion from her mother's drive towards the wedding. 'Percy and I couldn't work together if we were married, Mum. It's only because our chief superintendent is too stupid to realize that we're "an item" that we're able to operate together at the moment.'

'An item!' Mrs Blake's fierce curl of the lip on the heel of the innocent little word comprehended all the decadence of twenty-first-century life. 'In my day, we called it "living over t' brush" when you hopped into bed together without the benefit of wedlock.'

Lucy had cursed her fresh complexion and her freckles for as long as she could remember. She cursed them anew now, as she found herself blushing at this maternal intrusion into the intimacies of sex. 'Things have moved on since your day, Mum. And anyway, we aren't living together.'

'As good as, I'm sure. I'm not as daft as you think I am, our Lucy, and don't you forget it.'

Lucy Blake shot suddenly from the familiar armchair, glanced at the clock on the sideboard, and said, 'Time I was off to bed, Mum. I have to make an early start tomorrow. I've to be at the police station in Brunton by eight o'clock.'

She stooped and planted her lips affectionately on her mother's forehead.

Agnes Blake did not move. 'You're running away again, our Lucy. I shall need to have a word with Percy, since I can't get any sense out of you on the matter.'

'He's very busy at the moment.' It wasn't really true. The really serious crime in which Peach revelled, and in which she was delighted to be involved, seemed to be in the midst of a spring lull. But a small white lie was surely justified against this insistent and masterful parent.

'He can usually make time for me,' said Agnes with a small, confident, threatening smile. 'He has a proper sense of priorities, your Percy, even if you haven't.'

Twenty minutes later, in the familiar low-ceilinged bedroom where she had slept as a girl, Lucy Blake tried and failed to read the paperback she had been looking forward to starting. Instead, she fell to wondering why she should so fear a pincer movement by the two people whom she loved most in the world.

You couldn't really wish for a homicide. But a murder was what she needed at the moment to defer any fixing of this marriage date.

Two weeks later, Geoffrey Aspin drove Pam Williams out into the Ribble Valley.

He had booked an early dinner at an inn at Whitewell, in the hope that the place would still be quiet at that time in the evening, which would reduce the chances of their being seen together. Now this secrecy irritated him: why should he be ashamed of being seen with this attractive woman at a table for two, or even out in the town with her hand through his arm? He was a free man, and she was a free woman. He would be proud to be seen publicly with Pam. Perhaps he would tell her that tonight.

It was still only the beginning of April and there had been showers earlier in the day. But now they had a perfect spring evening, with a quickly darkening blue sky and a crimson sun dropping low over the invisible coast, twenty miles away to the west. The long line of Pendle Hill, lit by the setting sun, revealed the detail of its slopes and the fissures of its streams as they drove alongside it. On the other side of the car, there were glimpses of the bright surfaces of the Ribble and the Hodder rivers as the Jaguar moved comfortably along the quiet roads.

It was a majesty which made Geoffrey uncharacteristically reflective. 'I did a lot of hiking round here when I was a boy. You got the bus out to where you wanted to start, and then spent the whole day on the hills or the fells. That was before we got motor bikes and went to the Lake District. I think you're always most at ease in the countryside you knew in your youth. I am, anyway.'

At his side, Pam Williams smiled a small, private smile, happy to hear him reminisce, preparing to break down the barriers she found so difficult to abandon and reveal a little of herself. 'I grew up in the Black Country. We didn't see much real country, except on holidays or coach trips.'

It was an unremarkable sentence, but each of them realized that she had made a small but significant move towards him.

The food at the pub was good and for quite some time they had the dining room to themselves, with the window beside them. They looked out over trees and a small stream, which slowly disappeared as the twilight became darkness and the stars began to glitter over the fell.

As they waited for the dessert, Pam Williams told him her full address. Looking for some answering piece of information in this strange bartering, Geoffrey confessed that the 'late fifties' phrase he had used in DATING POINT actually signified that he was fifty-nine. She gave him a tight little answering smile and told him after a minute's silence that she was fifty-seven.

Then, as they savoured the coffee and petit fours whilst a noisy family party began their meal beside them, she slid a small card she had prepared earlier across the table to him. Beneath the address which she had already confided, the card listed her telephone number and her mobile number in small, clear, black lettering.

Things were moving faster than Pam Williams had planned, but she found she was gratified rather than alarmed to find it so. An hour later, she invited Geoffrey Aspin into her home for the first time.

*   *   *

The shaven-headed thug was new to him, but the lawyer at his side was an old foe of Percy Peach's.

The young man had dark hair and small, neat hands. He handled all the National Front legal business. He would defend this muscular bully as stoutly and as proudly as if he had been the most innocent victim of circumstances. Peach hated the lawyer more than the moron he was here to protect, who at least had the excuse of limited intelligence for his actions. But Peach wouldn't let his anger overrule his intellect; there were certain rules you had to obey in the interview room, even in the face of the vilest conduct.

He regarded the young hoodlum on the other side of the small, square table with steady malevolence, taking in his coarse features, the dried blood on the tee shirt which stretched tight across his torso, the tattoos of Union Jack and rather somnolent lion upon his bare forearms. He watched the brown eyes try to hold his own unflinching stare of assessment and fail, watched the truculence oozing away from the formidable physical figure in front of him, as the man slid glances at the lawyer beside him and waited for proceedings to commence. Silence was always a good weapon: few people enjoyed delaying an exchange about which they were apprehensive. They became more nervous, and nervousness was something which he could usually play to his advantage.

Peach eventually said quietly, 'You're not under caution yet, but I think we'd better have a record of this conversation. People like you have a habit of remembering things differently when it comes to the crunch. And the crunch is certainly coming.' He grinned his satisfaction at that thought and reached across to set the cassette recorder in silent, menacing motion. The young lawyer looked for a moment as if he was going to object, then thought better of the idea.

'I never done nothing,' said the young man sullenly.

'Need to watch your language, son. Your lawyer could tell you that that means that you did do something.'

The hoodlum looked uncomprehendingly at his lawyer, then back at Peach. 'I never hit no one.'

'If that's going to be your defence to a charge of Grievous Bodily Harm, I look forward with interest to the sentence you will get.'

'You got no evidence. I never 'it no one.'

Peach beamed. It was a sight which would have sent a collective shudder through the experienced criminal fraternity of the area. 'We have the baseball bat, son. With blood and hair on the business end. And your dabs neatly and firmly on the handle end of it. I call that evidence. Exhibit A, that will be in court. I doubt whether we shall need Exhibits B and C.'

'He 'it me first.'

'Not what your victim says, Mr Utting. Not what the two independent eye witnesses say either.'

'Paki bastard 'ad it coming to 'im.'

The lawyer at his side nudged him sharply and pointed at the silently turning cassette in the recorder. 'My client will maintain that he was provoked,' he said. 'If you are unwise enough to take this to court, Mr Utting will provide witnesses to that effect.'

'Who will no doubt be his friends who were also involved in this affray. Whereas we shall be able to produce independent witnesses who were merely appalled bystanders. I defer to your knowledge of the law in forecasting which way the verdict will go.' Percy Peach turned an even wider and more pugnacious smile upon the sallow features of the young lawyer.

'Your fucking witnesses will never come to the bloody court,' said the young thug, irritated because he suddenly seemed to be no longer the centre of these exchanges.

'Very serious charge, intimidating witnesses,' said Percy with satisfaction. 'Another Crown Court charge. Judges don't like any interference with witnesses. Send you down for several years for that, I shouldn't wonder.'

Peach leant across the table so that his face was no more than a foot from the coarse features of his hapless adversary. He could smell the stale breath, see the dirt on the scalp under the stubble of short hair. 'Don't even think about it, sunshine. If I hear you've even been near one of those witnesses, your feet won't touch the ground.'

Like most of these bullies, Utting was a coward under pressure. He flinched back in his chair. 'All right, I thumped the bastard. 'E 'ad it coming to 'im. Now 'e can bandage 'is bloody 'ead and fuck off back to 'is own country.'

The lawyer said hastily, 'Detective Chief Inspector Peach, I need to talk to my client in private.'

'Indeed you do,' said Percy contentedly.

He switched off the recorder and left them, taking with him the young constable who had sat silently through this. In three minutes, they were called back. 'Mr Utting will plead guilty to the lesser charge of assault,' said the lawyer.

Peach nodded without expression. Assault was all they would ever have gone for: the Crown Prosecution Service would never have taken on Grievous Bodily Harm with the evidence available. And the young girls he had as terrified witnesses wouldn't need to come to court if this bruiser pleaded guilty. 'All right.' He nodded to the young constable. 'Get him charged. If he changes his mind about that guilty plea, come back to me immediately.' He addressed his last words to the man at the table. 'If you go anywhere near either of your victims, or the witnesses, you'll be back in here and we'll throw the book at you. And there won't be any question of bail. Understand?'

Utting gave him a sullen nod of acquiescence. Peach didn't trouble to disguise his contempt for either the man or his lawyer as he turned on his heel and left.

Three

'Things can move on very quickly in a month.' Geoffrey Aspin stated the obvious with great contentment.

'I never expected things to move as fast as this.' For some reason she could not fathom, it seemed important to Pam Williams that she should assert that. 'It's only nine weeks since we made the first contact with each other. Until a month ago, I was still giving you as little information as I could about myself. Now you know everything there is to know.'

'I doubt that. But I intend to go on exploring your mysteries.' Geoffrey grinned down happily at her, enjoying sending himself up with the cliche, feeling totally at ease with the woman who strolled by his side. It was early May and they were in the middle of a four-day break in Cornwall, staying in the Tregenna Castle at St Ives. The clouds were flying high above them, driven across the intense blue of the Cornish sky by an exhilarating spring breeze.

'This is the kind of light which made St Ives into an artists' colony,' said Pam Williams. She breathed hard on the clean air, looking over the fresh new green of the cliff-top's short grass and down upon the intense blue and the glistening white horses of the sea, hundreds of feet below them, enjoying the rush of the wind in her hair, feeling years younger than she had two months ago.

Geoffrey lengthened his stride and said suddenly, 'I feel years younger than I did before we started all this!' He was amazed when the mature woman at his side dissolved into girlish giggles. When she explained how he had voiced her own thoughts, the two of them were rent by a mirth which was wholly out of keeping with their mature years. A moment later, as the laughter died, she tumbled clumsily into his arms and he kissed her, unhurriedly and without embarrassment.

For a full minute they held each other, revelling in the fresh wonders of the world around them and their own new place within it.

That evening, full of good food and mellowed by an excellent Shiraz, she said suddenly, 'I'm glad we came here.'

'It's an excellent hotel.'

'It's not just that. I thought it was a long way to drive for a few days, but now I'm glad that we did it. It must be psychological, but I feel that I'm in a completely different world down here.'

Geoffrey knew exactly what she meant, but he chose to interpret it more narrowly. 'St Ives couldn't be much different from an old cotton town.' He couldn't resist adding loyally, 'Though I still say the country of the Ribble Valley takes a lot of beating.'

She grinned at him, appreciating his foibles, but without the irritation which might have accompanied her sympathy if they had been married for forty years. 'I didn't just mean that. I was thinking it's good to leave behind all the complications of the families and friends who might wonder what we're about.'

Geoffrey didn't want to say that he had himself spent the early weeks of their relationship wondering just what it was going to be about. They left the dining room and went to have coffee and mints in the adjacent lounge. He looked appreciatively at the pictures on the walls and settled back into his armchair with his cup.

'This was a railway hotel originally,' he said, 'The old Great Western Railway was the grandest of all the lines, in its heyday. Isambard Kingdom Brunel didn't do anything by halves. And the Tregenna Castle had to match his ideas.'

'You're not going back into the age of steam again, are you?' said Pam with a grin. She had already found that the vanished age of steam locomotives was one of his enthusiasms. It marked a new and welcome stage in a relationship when you could tease each other.

'With you around, I wouldn't dare. But I'm brave enough to steal your mint, if you're going to leave it again.'

They wouldn't need to go through the tiresome stuff about diet again, thought Pam. She liked a man who didn't repeat himself – though it had been nice to hear him say with such ringing sincerity that she didn't need to watch her figure last night, and even to have his assurance that he would do that for her. Conventional humour was quite reassuring when you liked the man who offered it.

She said suddenly, 'You seem to know all about this place. Did you come here with Jill?'

He smiled, and she thought how much better and more relaxed he looked now that he had caught the spring sun. 'No. I've never been here before. I knew quite a bit about Brunel and the Great Western, and I picked most of the rest of it up from the hotel brochure.'

She was relieved not to be competing with a ghost. 'You've no need to be frightened of talking to me about Jill, you know. We can't change the lives we've lived, and she was an important part of yours. It's different for me, having divorced a man I've no wish ever to see again.'

He was pleased with her for that. Nevertheless, he had more sensitivity than to dwell on his memories of his dead wife. He might talk about her to Pam at some time in the future, if things continued to go as well as this. In the meantime, he had more serious worries: his family knew nothing about this new relationship, and he was now sure that he was going to have to tell them all about it.

On the next morning, Geoffrey looked rather longingly at the golf course which was attached to the hotel, but didn't venture on to it: Pam didn't play, and on this first outing together, he wouldn't leave her. He wasn't silly enough to think that such self-denial would survive for very long, but from what he'd heard from Pam so far, he was sure that she'd eventually encourage him to pursue his passion for that infuriating game. Instead, they swam together in the hotel pool, walked again on the cliffs and visited the dramatic outcrop of St Michael's Mount. On the next day, they spent happy hours at the National Trust garden at Trengwainton, where Pam proved unexpectedly knowledgeable and enthusiastic about the plants. 'Some of the hardy Japanese camellias will even grow in Brunton, nowadays,' she informed him. It sounded like an assurance for the future.

It was on the last evening of their four days in Cornwall

that Geoffrey Aspin told Pam Williams that he wished to marry her.

Back in Lancashire on the same evening, an entirely different union was under discussion in one of the recesses of the almost deserted Brunton CID section.

'It's time you were making an honest man of me,' declared Percy Peach to Lucy Blake. 'I have serious qualms of conscience about the way you take me into your bed and make use of my body. I defer to your urgent physical demands, because I realize that you have certain needs, but my conscience tells me that we should have the benefit of wedlock. Because of my unselfishness, you do not appear to realize that all the time I am exploring the recesses of your bottom I am wracked with ethical doubts.'

'You've been talking to my mum.'

Percy's eyes grew round with wonder, a phenomenon denied entirely to the criminal fraternity of the Brunton area and intensely irritating to his prospective bride.

'You mean that your mother thinks we should get married? Well, there you are then. Haven't I always said that Agnes Blake had a very sensible perspective on the world in general and the lives of her loved ones in particular? She talks such sense because she has the benefit of much experience: she can stand back from these things and take a detached overview.'

'Like Tommy Bloody Tucker?'

'Wash your mouth out, my girl! Not at all like Tommy Bloody Tucker. I don't understand how a young woman I've always thought had a certain sensitivity could link her own mother with that affront to humanity. I'm shocked.' He walked over to the filing cabinet in the corner of his office and shook his head sadly at its smooth grey surface, demonstrating the depth of that shock.

'I'm not your girl! I get enough of that from my mother, without you joining in. And I'm busy getting on with my career. I don't need the complication of marriage at present.'

Percy Peach walked with difficulty back to the chair behind his desk, apparently just making it before he slumped into its welcome support. 'I'm deeply shocked. Really I am. Deeply shocked. I didn't think that even a thoroughly modern young woman like you would ride so cruelly over both the conscientious scruples of a partner wracked with moral doubts and the views of an ageing mother. May I remind you that Agnes Blake's dying wish would be to see her only daughter married to the man of her dreams?'

Lucy Blake considered this unlikely scenario for a few seconds. Sometimes the scale of Percy's effrontery and baroque imaginings took aback even her, who should have been most prepared by experience for his wiles. 'Firstly, I do not recognize this picture of a man torn apart by conscience. My recollection is of a man who seems to have as many hands as an octopus and who uses them to explore the most intimate recesses of my overworked body, without any inhibitions at all and with the maximum of lusty enjoyment, and—'

'Just because my natural altruism makes me hide my pangs of doubt, you shouldn't just assume—'

'And secondly, my mother is in perfect health and still working two days a week in her local supermarket. She is nowhere near making dying wishes yet, and even if she were—'

'I'm glad you're able to reassure me of that. All I can say is that when we met on Easter Sunday, your mum seemed very anxious to progress our nuptials.'

Lucy had thought she had kept them apart when Percy had come over for tea on Easter Sunday. She had spent several hours preventing collusion between the two of them on this. Perhaps even the brief toilet break which nature had forced upon her had been enough for them. Or perhaps he was merely chancing his arm, and her mother and he hadn't talked at all about this. Percy was good at chancing his arm, and he was always saying that you should play to your strengths.

She said stubbornly, 'It should be my wishes that count in this, not my mother's.'

'Ageist, that is. I'm surprising to hear the sentiment voiced by one whom I have striven to make the most sensitive DS in the—'

'As sensitive as you, you mean?'

Percy stretched his neck in an attempt to secure maximum

dignity, an effort curiously reminiscent of a toucan on cocaine. 'I do not demand or expect the impossible. I merely presume that the members of my team will be conscious of the moral issues involved in any decision.'

'You demand and expect that the members of your team will carry out your bidding without question, as a matter of fact. I'm merely trying to point out that you can't carry this attitude into your private life.'

Percy shook his head despondently. 'You're saying that an elderly lady who has been most kind to me should have her dearest wishes thwarted. I have to be honest and declare that your attitude saddens me.' He cast his eyes to the carpet and hung his head; he did sadness rather well, he thought immodestly.

Lucy looked at her watch and said in desperation, 'I need to get to the shops.' She tried not to be conscious of Percy's black eyebrows arching impossibly high towards the baldness above them.

Percy's smile said that he saw through such transparency. 'I think we should fix a date. I'm tired of living over t'brush, our Lucy.'

Perhaps it was his use of that old dialect phrase which her mother had used which finally caught Lucy off guard. She said uncertainly, 'What did you have in mind?'

'I thought August.'

'August of next year. I suppose that might be possible, but we'd need to—'

'This August.'

'This August? Three months hence! That is totally impossible.' She sought desperately for a reason why, and hit happily upon one immediately. 'Everywhere will be booked up, long ago, for this August. My mum will want somewhere decent, you know.'

'And I shall want somewhere decent, to please my mother-in-law, whose daughter is so cruel about her mother's wishes.'

'And there are dresses to organize.'

Percy flung himself absurdly on to one of his sturdy knees. 'I shall take you without a dress. Without a stitch, if necessary.' He brightened with a sudden inspired thought. 'We could have a rehearsal tonight, if you like.'

'Not just a dress for me, you wazzock! There'll be bridesmaids' dresses to think of, and a best man, and—'

Still on one knee, he flung his arms wildly around her hips. 'I may be a wazzock, Lucy Blake, but I'm *your* wazzock. You may take my proud body and do with it what you will.' He buried his face in her fascinating stomach and began to explore the contours of her backside with the expertise of a very determined wazzock.

Despite her decision to be firm with him, she dissolved into giggles, which increased his excitement and doubled his activity levels. He moaned softly into the roundness of her belly and said with searing sincerity, 'With my body, I thee worship, Lucy Blake. Twice nightly, with encores.'

She shook him off and backed away. 'Arise at once sir, from that semi-recumbent posture! There, you've brought out the Lady Bracknell in me. That should be a warning to you, Percy Peach.'

'I'm heedless of all warnings and all dangers, where you're concerned, lass. September, then?'

'What? Oh, no, certainly not. It would have to be next spring at the earliest.'

Percy smoothed his trousers and nodded slowly. 'So that's fixed, then. You drive a hard bargain, lass, but so be it. Spring it is, then. Will you tell your mum, or shall I?'

Lucy Blake wasn't sure how it had happened, but she knew she'd been outflanked again, by the mother who wasn't here and the man who emphatically was.

Four

'You've kept this a secret.'
    Geoffrey Aspin heard his daughter's voice hiss on the sibilants. He tried to firm up his resolution. 'Not a secret, Carol. We just thought we should be discreet, in the early stages.'

'And now that the early stages have gone, you don't care who knows?'

'I don't, as a matter of fact. I don't mind if the whole world knows about Pam and me. Of course, I don't expect the whole world will be very interested, but—'

'You can't just make a joke of this, Dad.'

'I wasn't trying to make a joke of it, Carol. I was trying to make you see it from my point of—'

'So your eldest daughter only gets to know of this at the same time as all the world. I see.' Carol's lips set in a thin line and she looked past him, out of the window of the house, to where the bedding plants she had put out three weeks earlier were showing an early brightness which now seemed to her quite inappropriate. She flicked a strand of her dark hair impatiently off the left side of her forehead, in that gesture which her father had found so fetching in her when she was a girl and an adolescent. 'I should have thought you could at least have told your family about this before it became public knowledge.'

She was still a striking woman, tall and with the brittle elegance of a model. But a meanness had grown about her face in these last few years. He wanted to tell her how much better she looked when she smiled and how infrequently he saw her smile nowadays. He wanted to ask her to give him the benefit of the doubt, perhaps even to give the world at large the benefit of the doubt occasionally.

'Pam and I wanted to be discreet about it. Surely you can understand that? Our relationship might never have gone anywhere, and if it hadn't, no one need have known about it.'

'I told you. A secret. Hole-in-the-corner stuff that you didn't want your eldest daughter to be aware of. So how did this "relationship" start? How did you meet this woman?'

'Her name's Pamela, Carol. She likes to be known as Pam.' Geoffrey heard the anger pressing against his clipped monosyllables.

'And how did you meet her?'

He was tempted to lie. But he didn't want to lie, not to his daughter. More to the point, he could not think at this moment of any lie which would be convincing. 'I advertised. You put a tiny bit about yourself in the paper and—'

'Advertised?' She managed to force a wealth of outrage and contempt into the seemingly innocent word, and he again wondered irrelevantly how the pretty, lively young woman he remembered in her graduation robes could have grown into this thirty-six-year-old harridan. 'You mean that you touted yourself about in the media like a—'

'It's quite discreet, Carol. It's called DATING POINT. There's a similar page called ENCOUNTERS in *The Times*.' He had an obscure, hopeless wish that the mention of that august organ would dignify and justify his conduct to her.

'I see. And how exactly did you trumpet your attractions in the national press?'

'I can't remember. And it doesn't matter.'

For an instant, he thought she was going to begin a tirade about how much it *did* matter, how little he cared for the feelings of herself and the rest of her family. But she controlled herself and merely said through tight lips, 'And did you have many replies to this curriculum vitae of your achievements and your personality which you paraded through these columns?'

'A few. Actually, I didn't say much about myself, so that—'

'You played the field, did you, before settling on the delights of this – who was it – Pamela?'

Geoffrey wondered why families should make their own

rules of conduct. How could he be so dominant and in control at his factory and yet so much at the mercy of his eldest daughter in this exchange which was going all wrong?

'As a matter of fact, I didn't play the field, as you choose to call it. Pam was the first and the only person whom I met.'

'Ah! Love at first sight, was it?'

He wanted to fly into a rage, to ask her what she knew about love, to tell her that she should be glad that it was coming to him at his time of life. He was obscurely aware that this would make him only more ridiculous in her eyes. 'I'm not going to talk about love, Carol. I just hoped that you might be glad to see—'

'Dad, have you any idea how this looks from the outside? Have you any idea how it looks to the world at large to see a man making a fool of himself?'

'I know what it feels like from the inside! I know how lonely I was in the two years before I met Pam. You and Louise have your own families and your own lives to live, and I understand that. But the winter nights in particular are very bleak when you're in a big house on your own. Pam's helped me to get rid of that feeling of desolation. I know how she makes me feel. I know what it is to have a little joy back in my life!' He heard himself breathing heavily, struggling to keep control of his words as he delivered them. Yet he was glad that at last he'd managed to say these things.

'It looks ridiculous, that's how it looks! I can tell you that.'

'At this moment, I don't much care how it looks to the world at large. I was just hoping that my eldest daughter would understand a little better how I feel about it. I see now that that was a vain hope.'

'And I'm just trying to get you to put things into some sort of perspective, Dad!' She shook her head, drummed her fingers on the arm of the easy chair in which she sat so stiffly upright. 'I don't know what Jemal is going to think about this.'

Geoffrey wanted to say that he didn't give a damn what his son-in-law thought about it, that it was none of the man's business. Instead, he controlled himself and said, 'If he's the man of the world he claims to be, perhaps he'll rejoice in the fact that a man of my age is getting a little more happiness out of life than he did at this time last year. A lot more happiness, if you want the truth.'

'Oh, we want the truth, Dad. Let's have the truth, however unpalatable it may be. It would have been nice to have it a little earlier, instead of being the last to hear about these goings on.'

'Surely you can see that we wanted to keep things fairly low-key until we knew this was heading somewhere. We had no idea how far it would go when it started. If it had just fizzled out, it would have been better for everyone that we hadn't made a song and dance about it.'

She wanted to scream at him that he should stop using this 'we', that the less she knew about this new woman the better, that it was an insult to the mother she had loved that he should even be thinking about other women, let alone consorting with one of them. But even in her fury, Carol was beginning to realize that she must somehow come to terms with this new situation. She paused for a moment, made herself speak more calmly as she said, 'How far has this gone, Dad?'

Geoffrey wondered if his daughter was going to ask if they were sleeping together. Would she ask how often, and demand the times and the places? It was like having their roles reversed, with her as the stern parent and him as the recalcitrant teenager.

'It's serious, Carol. That's why you need to know about it.'

'And how old is this woman?'

'Pam. She has a name. That name is Pamela Williams, if you want the formal details. And she's fifty-seven. She has her own family. She'll be telling them about this today, as I'm telling you and Louise, I expect.'

'At least she's not a bimbo, then. At least you're not making a complete fool of yourself in that way!'

He noticed with wry amusement that he must be getting really old, since even his children were now using out-of-date slang. He tried to lighten the exchange, sensing that both of them wanted that but did not know how to engineer it. 'I don't fancy young women. It's one of the few reassuring things about getting older.'

'But you fancied Pamela. Pam.'

He rushed in quickly to try to explain himself. 'Initially, I wanted companionship. I expect everyone says that, to disguise the stirrings of libido, but I think it was true for me. I was lonely, Carol, deeply lonely. It seemed at first like a desperate thing to advertise for company, but—'

'Female company.' The interruption had come before she could prevent it, and she immediately regretted it.

'Yes, all right, female company. I agonized for months before I put my details into DATING POINT, and then immediately regretted it. Now I'm obviously glad that I made the move.'

'Obviously.' Her lips set again for a moment in that thin line he hated to see. Then he could see in her features an effort which it was almost painful to watch. 'Do you want your grandchildren to know about this?'

'Yes, of course I do. It's not something I'm ashamed of.'

'No. That's certainly obvious.' Another bit of acid, when she had not intended it. She wanted now to apologize to him for her reception of this news, to tell him that she had been taken off guard, that she would come to terms with it, given time. But Carol had never found it easy to apologize and the words would not come to her now. 'Do you want me to tell them?'

'I think that would be best, don't you?' When she did not reply, Geoffrey made himself reach across the space between them and take her hand in his. It felt stiff and cool, even on this warm day. 'I'll tell them myself if I must, but you'll do it much better, Carol. I trust you to do it tactfully, once you've got used to the idea yourself. You actually do tact rather well, when you want to, don't you?'

Carol gave him a brief smile on that, wanting to respond, but not yet having the capacity to do it. 'I'll tell them. When I've digested the news myself, as you say. It's been rather a shock, Dad. I'm sorry . . . I know I'm a bitch at times.'

Geoffrey knew that it had cost her a lot to say that, and he had the sense to leave it there and get out of the house as fast as he could. When he started the car, the Jaguar engine roared raw and loud, as he put his foot too clumsily on the pedal. He realized that his hands were shaking as he watched them upon the steering wheel.

For the first time he could remember, he was glad that he lived thirty miles away from his eldest daughter and her children.

Chief Superintendent Thomas Bulstrode Tucker walked moodily across the thick carpet of his penthouse office and stared through the window at the wide Lancashire vista outside it. Normally he enjoyed the combination of industrial landscape and the beginnings of greenery where town met country. Quite often, he spent a few minutes of his day studying this view and congratulating himself. The office and the panorama it commanded was his visual evidence of how far he had progressed in the police service.

Today Tucker's brain barely registered what his eyes took in, because he was preparing himself for a confrontation. It was a confrontation which he knew he could win. He repeated to himself the comfortable reassurance that there is no way round rank, that ultimately it must always triumph in the British police service. Without rank there is no discipline, and the system depends upon discipline. Chief Superintendent Tucker repeated these mantras to himself more than most. When you were chronically inefficient, you had to fall back on them surprisingly often.

He was nervous because his confrontation was to be with Chief Inspector Peach, and Percy Peach had a habit of circumventing the realities of rank more often than any other officer Tucker had met in his long and surprisingly successful career.

He could hear the voice of his formidable wife Barbara ringing in his ears. 'For heavens sake, Tom, be firm with the man!' she always said impatiently. 'I can't see why you put up with his nonsense!' She couldn't see why because she didn't appreciate the extent to which Tucker depended on Peach for the results which had buoyed his career. Barbara didn't realize the full extent of her husband's ineffectiveness, which she tended to presume was confined to the home.

'Ah, Percy! Do sit down and make yourself at home.' Tucker waved a wide, hospitable arm towards one of the armchairs in front of his big desk, hesitated for a moment, and then took the other one himself.

Peach sat down very carefully on the edge of the seat,

keeping his back bolt upright. When Tommy Bloody Tucker used your forename and offered you an easy chair, there was trouble in store.

'A splendid opportunity has come up for you, Percy. It is an opportunity which will be available to only a very few senior officers. One for which you have been specially selected.'

'By you, sir, no doubt.' It was as well to know whom you were fighting: no use wasting your ammunition on the people in front of you, if the real enemy was at a further remove.

'By me, indeed, Percy. As you know, I always have your best interests at heart. It will need the chief constable's approval, no doubt, but I think you can be confident that my word carries considerable weight in that quarter.'

'Yes, sir. The chief constable is a man whose judgement I have learned to respect over the years. I have a good idea of just how much weight he will give to your pronouncements.'

Tucker looked at him keenly, but Peach's face had that glassy inscrutability which usually accompanied those insolences which his chief could not quite pin down. 'You'd better have a look at this, Percy. It's a confidential document, I need hardly say.'

Confidential, my arse, thought Percy sourly, as he glanced at the heading and skimmed the details beneath it. This matter had been an item of much gossip in the police canteen over the last three days. A group of very senior police officers were to spend a weekend in a prison in Nottingham. The idea was to allow pillars of the police service to appreciate exactly the conditions to which they were consigning their criminal opponents. As well as increasing understanding between criminals and those who had to operate the law against them, this temporary incarceration would improve relations between the police and the officers of the prison service, with whom they had so often to liaise. This exercise would be good for public relations all round, the document concluded.

Good, my arse, was Percy's succinct conclusion. It has to be said that that was often his conclusion where public relations were concerned. Whilst his brain worked furiously, he said, 'This promises to be an interesting experiment, sir.'

'Indeed it is, Peach.' Tucker leant forward and touched the side of his nose. 'It is also an opportunity for you to further your career, Percy. To do a bit of fraternizing with the right people.'

'My career is fine, sir. I don't wish to rise beyond my present rank and move away from the crime-face. I'm not very good at fraternizing, sir, not being one of the brotherhood of Masons like you.'

Tucker bristled, as he usually did when Peach mentioned the Freemasonry which was one of his favourite targets. Then he controlled himself: he needed this odious man's cooperation. 'We all need to fraternize, Percy. When it's with people of a higher rank, it can be very useful.'

'I'm happy arresting villains and seeing them put away, sir. I haven't got your overview.'

He managed to invest the word with a heavy irony, but irony wasn't Tucker's strong suit. The chief superintendent was too concerned to get himself off this particular hook: the chief constable had actually suggested that Tucker himself should spend a couple of nights in a prison cell. He stood up, returned to the chair on the other side of his massive desk, and said determinedly, 'I've been asked to make a decision on this, Peach, and my decision is that you should go.'

Percy noted the return to his surname and to the normal dispositions of the sides in this contest with some relief. He pretended to study the detail of the sheet about the weekend which Tucker had given him and said with an air of surprise, 'There'll be some big police guns at this. Some very big guns indeed. Are you sure that you can afford not to be there, sir?'

'Important people, you say?' With the prospect of creeping to the bigwigs, Tucker was immediately thrown into doubt, as Percy had anticipated that he would be.

'It's one of your strengths, that, sir. Everyone says so.'

'Peach, if you're trying to suggest that I would—'

'Fraternizing, sir. It's often said that you're the most fitting fraternizer in the force.' In his enthusiasm for alliteration, Percy had almost used another epithet entirely.

Tucker stared at him malevolently. But he was torn. There would be a lot of important people showing the police flag on this prison exercise. A chance for him to butter up those people. A chance to make it clear that he was a conscientious senior officer, supporting the latest initiatives. 'I suppose it's important for Brunton to be represented at Nottingham by a reliable senior officer.'

Percy read the runes of his chief's too-revealing face and knew that he had won. He said daringly, 'Of course, I appreciate you thinking of me for this, sir. But I'm not the consummate diplomat that you are. I'd be afraid of saying the wrong things to important people. Afraid of damaging the reputation of the CID section and thus of you, sir.'

'You'd be a loose cannon, Peach!' Tucker nodded firmly and jutted his chin in decision. 'You're entirely the wrong man to send off on what could be an important public-relations exercise for us. I don't know how I could ever have been persuaded to consider you for this privilege.'

'No, sir. I'm glad it's been sorted out to your satisfaction. I'll tell the boys and girls down in CID all about your selfless devotion to duty.'

Percy went downstairs with the smile of a man who had managed a difficult situation adroitly. Arsehole-creepers were always easily distracted.

Alone in his office, Tucker too smiled, lifted by the prospect of a weekend of saying the right things to important people. Then his face clouded: how was he going to explain to his Brünnhilde of a wife that he was going to be away for a whole weekend?

Five

G eoffrey Aspin liked this time of the day, when all the office staff at the factory had gone home and he had the place to himself. It was the time when he savoured his control of the place. When everything was quiet, he liked to roam at will and remind himself of what he had achieved. Walking round the little works on his own had become first a small pleasure and then a habit in the lonely, sometimes desperate, days after Jill's death.

He liked to wander round the various machines which did the printing, revelling in having the latest technology, marvelling at how compact, efficient and clean these machines were compared with the heavy printing presses on which he had begun work as a teenager in the printing room of the now defunct *Brunton Times*. The three men he now employed could do the work of twenty when he had started in the trade nearly forty years ago.

The two women who came in to clean could get around the floor of the small works in an hour. They were finishing now, talking cheerfully to each other as they stowed away their tools. Through the window of his office, he watched them getting into a car, and thought how much the conditions for that sort of work had improved since his mother had cleaned for the gentry of the town half a century ago when he was a boy. The minimum wage which some people had predicted would be such a disaster had helped to transform life for women like these.

It was good to remember your roots. It made you appreciate what you had done and where you stood now. And to acknowledge the luck which had after all never been far away, even in the darkest hours of the last three years.

Tonight, though, Geoffrey Aspin was waiting here alone

for reasons which were not merely philosophical. Two minutes after the cleaners' car had left, another small vehicle nosed its way into the deserted car park. The driver looked swiftly round him, as if checking that he was unobserved and not vulnerable to attack. He stood upright and glanced at the evening sky for a moment as he locked his car, yet still he carried a furtive air about him as he turned and hurried into the factory.

It was a bright evening in early spring. This visitor looked as if he would have preferred the cloak of darkness for his movements. It was still quite warm, but he wore a faded blue anorak and a shabby maroon baseball cap. Even on this evening, which seemed a herald of the summer, this man looked like a creature of the night who was reluctantly forced to operate by day.

He was brisk and efficient, not only in his movements but in the delivery of his report. He refused the armchair in Geoffrey Aspin's office and chose instead to sit upright on a chair he brought forward from the edge of the room. He made brief references to a notebook he produced from the pocket of his raincoat, but Geoffrey thought that he could have delivered his report without the benefit of these reminders, if that had been necessary.

Geoffrey was sitting at his desk. He made brief notes of times, dates and actions on the pad in front of him as the man spoke. His visitor noted this and said, 'I can submit a written report if you like. I have all the details under lock and key at home, but I think we agreed that I would not report to you in writing at this stage.'

Geoffrey smiled, trying to lighten the atmosphere of this bizarre exchange. 'We did indeed. I'm merely making a few reminders for the sake of my own failing memory. I can memorize them and eat the sheet of paper, if you think that's necessary for security.'

The thin figure in front of him gave a wan smile. Humour wasn't part of his brief. 'What you do with any information which I bring to you is of course up to you, Mr Aspin. For both our sakes, I trust that you will be very careful that it is kept away from any prying eyes.' He looked swiftly round the office and at the closed door which led to the clerical area which was so busy by day. Every one of these absent, anonymous people was a threat, his bearing said.

'Be assured, I shall be very careful. You don't build up a successful business by leaving confidential information lying about.' Geoffrey smiled wryly at his attempt to reassure this man whose services he was paying handsomely to hire. 'I can't say that what you have brought me is welcome, but it confirms my suspicions.'

'It's mostly circumstantial. But it's beginning to add up. I'm sure I shall have more concrete evidence for you in due course.' The man in the raincoat tried to deliver that statement with an air of regret. His was a strange occupation: your most efficient work was often greeted with dismay by those who paid you.

Geoffrey Aspin understood the reasons for the man's low-key delivery. 'You're confirming what I suspected. I'm not saying that I welcome it, but I need real evidence before I can proceed any further. I'm grateful for your efforts.'

'You're paying me well enough for them. Gratitude isn't necessary,' said the man gruffly. He didn't want emotions like gratitude, any more than he wanted anger or exultation. These things were better kept impersonal.

Geoffrey nodded. He reached into the top drawer of his desk, produced a chequebook, wrote and signed, then passed the cheque across without another word and with only the smallest of smiles.

The man looked at the amount, saw that it was for three thousand pounds, raised his eyebrows a little even as he pocketed it. 'There may be some change from this. It's entirely up to you to end our arrangement. When you think you have enough, let me know and I'll cease to operate immediately.' Recommendations in this game usually came by word of mouth. It was important for clients to know that you operated honestly, that you provided just as much information as they wanted and didn't rip them off.

'I understand that. I'll let you know when I think I have enough.'

Geoffrey Aspin watched the man drive out of the car park and sat down at his desk. After a moment, he buried his head in his hands. He felt like weeping, but his eyes remained obstinately dry. Knowledge is power: his father had repeated that to him many times, long, long ago.

This knowledge would give him power, of a kind. It would also bring him much pain.

On the outskirts of Clitheroe, ten miles away from where Geoffrey Aspin was meeting his mysterious employee, his daughters and their husbands were comparing notes on the unexpected crisis which their father's affair with Pamela Williams had presented to them.

'It may still come to nothing,' said Steve Hawksworth, Louise's husband. His voice carried no conviction. He was an accountant with a small firm in Brunton, a man who was better with figures than with people, a man who seemed destined to be an employee working for others rather than a man in control. When he did take independent action, it was often on impulse, and sometimes mistaken. That in itself had affected his self-confidence over the years.

'He's serious. He wouldn't have come over specially to tell me about it if he wasn't serious,' said Carol impatiently. 'We should be discussing what we are going to do about this, not dithering about whether it's serious.'

'I agree with that. That's why I called us together for this meeting.' Jemal Bilic, the husband of Geoffrey Aspin's elder child, was a striking contrast with Stephen Hawksworth in both appearance and attitude. He was by six years the elder of the two; he exuded confidence and was a formidable presence in any company. His father was Croatian and his mother Turkish. He had been born and reared in Turkey, but he had spent the last fourteen of his thirty-six years in the United Kingdom. With his large brown eyes, dark skin, a beard which was trimmed to little more than stubble and the thin moustache which ran in a thin line around his mouth to join it, he was very handsome. It was a sleek and dangerous beauty, which had captured the woman who was then Carol Aspin when she was on her way out of a failed engagement and at her most impressionable.

It was his sister-in-law who now spoke up in his support. Louise said, 'Jemal is right. When Dad spoke to me, he was trying to be sober and sensible, but his pleasure and excitement kept showing, as though he was a teenager who had just discovered love.' She raised a hand nervously to her short brown hair, though not a strand of her simple cut was out of place; she was nervous because she was about to voice a thought which she sensed wouldn't meet with the approval of the other three. 'There's a part of me says that we should be glad for Dad, that he deserves some pleasure out of life.'

Carol Bilic smiled indulgently: her little sister could be pardoned a certain naivety, but those with more experience of life must put her right on this. 'We're not denying his right to pleasure, Louise. But we have our own interests to consider. These affairs aren't conducted in a vacuum.'

Steve Hawksworth nodded. He was a naturally quiet man, but he was anxious to make some contribution to what now seemed to be becoming a council of war. 'What kind of affair is it? How much do we know about this woman? Has anyone met her?'

His wife glanced at her sister. 'No. He's kept her away from us, so far. He told me that he would introduce her to us, once we'd had time to digest the idea.'

Jemal Bilic frowned. 'The idea of what? He must be thinking of something long-term, by the way he's talking. That means we may be talking about him setting up house with a woman we know nothing about. I don't like unknowns, when we're trying to take serious decisions. I think I should set about finding more out about this Pamela Williams.'

They all accepted that he would be able to do that, though none of them had any idea about how he would do it. He was the dominant force in the room, with his dark good looks and his fierce brown eyes and the sheer force of his will. He spoke perfect English, with only the faintest of accents giving its precision an edge of menace. There was a pause before Louise Hawksworth said uncertainly, 'For all we know, this woman may be someone we'd quite like. Carol and I are naturally resentful, because we still think of our dead mother, but Mum's been gone for over three years now, and Dad might have twenty years or more to live.'

Louise realized that she was acting as a counterbalance to her forceful brother-in-law. She did not look at him, did not look at anyone, but stared down at the rich patterned carpet in the centre of the room.

Carol stared at her for a moment before she said quietly, 'There's something in what you say, Louise, of course there is. But there's a lot more in what Jemal says, as far as I'm concerned. Even if we only had Dad's interests to consider, I'd find this disturbing. He told me how lonely and desolate he'd been recently. That makes him vulnerable in my book. We may need to look after his interests for him, if he's not seeing straight. This woman none of us knows may be a gold-digger.'

Jemal hastened to support his wife. 'And there are times when it's right to consider our own interests as well. My father-in-law has been very successful in his business; I'm sure we're all glad of that, for his sake. But I suggest we're glad for our sakes too. We have children who are doing well at school, whom we shall probably have to see through university. And you – you have your own problems, Louise.' He stopped in embarrassment.

His sister-in-law gave him a wan smile. 'You mean that I have a Down's syndrome child as well as a normal one. You needn't be afraid of voicing that: I'm not ashamed of Michael's existence!'

Steve reached across and put his hand on the shoulder beside her flushed face. 'Jemal wasn't suggesting that, my love. He was just making the point that we have all made assumptions about your father. About financial support in various areas, if we want to speak bluntly.'

There was a silence as the idea they had all skirted was suddenly openly voiced. Jemal Bilic looked round at the three anxious faces and saw that they were acknowledging with varying degrees of reluctance that he was right. He said ominously, 'What I'm saying is that we shall have to keep a careful watch on how this situation develops.'

A bright June day. The long slope of Longridge Fell a study in the various shades of green marking the rich growth of the vegetation on its flanks. The higher mound of Pendle Hill sharp against the intense blue of a sky trumpeting the pleasures of the summer which stretched ahead. And Lucy

Blake looking round with a smile at all of this, then sniffing the clean morning air appreciatively as she threw her overnight bag into her blue Vectra car.

The postman came, and she handed the letters to her mother as she went back into the cottage. Lucy was anxious as usual to down her breakfast and be on her way to see what had turned up in the world of crime on her day off. Agnes Blake had been delighted by the promise of her daughter's wedding next spring – 'I knew that Percy would talk some sense into you!' she'd said – but Lucy didn't want her to pin down dates.

Her mother was diverted by the post. She disposed of the junk mail with a few sharp words of dismissal, but the other letter gave her pause for thought. 'It's from your Uncle Geoff,' she said.

'I haven't heard from the Aspins in years, apart from Christmas cards,' said Lucy. She had once been great friends with Louise Aspin: their birthdays were within a month of each other, and they had gone through the village primary school together and then on to the comprehensive in Brunton. Geoff wasn't a real uncle, but the habit of the time had been to call the parents of childhood friends uncle and aunt and the epithets had stuck, even when Geoff Aspin had moved his family away from the village and become a successful man in Brunton.

'I hear he's been making a fool of himself, your Uncle Geoff,' said Agnes darkly. 'Since your Aunty Jill died, he's been on his own. Men on their own lose their judgement, if you ask me.'

Lucy grinned. 'Making a fool of himself in what way?' she asked innocently. She could make a fair guess from the look of disapproval on her mother's face.

'Chasing after women. That's what I heard. Should have more sense at his age. Of course, there may be nothing in it.' Agnes Blake's face said that she'd be very disappointed if it turned out that there was indeed nothing in it.

'He was always very kind to me, even when I was a bolshy teenager,' said Lucy loyally. 'He was very attached to Aunty Jill and I'm sure he must have been devastated when she died. But he might live a long time yet, Mum. He's entitled to a little pleasure, surely.'

Agnes sniffed, a reaction she often exhibited when her child produced reasonable arguments. 'Sometimes men don't have the sense they're born with. Not where women are concerned, anyway.'

'I thought you said Percy Peach had a lot of sense when he made his choice.'

'I didn't say *all* men, our Lucy. Just some of them. And when they've reached a certain age, they can make themselves look much more foolish than youngsters.'

'I haven't seen Louise since a school reunion years ago,' said Lucy thoughtfully. 'I think she's got a couple of children now.' She sensed her mother was preparing to draw comparisons with her own spinster state and said hastily, 'One of them is handicapped, I heard. Down's syndrome, I think. I should have kept in touch, but there's always been things to do.'

The familiar melancholy refrain of lost friendships; the familiar lament for a closeness which it once seemed would never end.

Her mother was staring in puzzlement at the card she had drawn from the envelope. 'Well, it looks as though you're going to renew acquaintance with Louise. This is an invitation for both of us to a celebration of Geoff Aspin's sixtieth birthday. Posh do, by the looks of it. I shan't be able to go: I've already paid up for our Women's Institute outing on that day. But you'll be able to see your friend and catch up on things. I shall be interested to hear what her dad's been getting up to.'

'I shall report back in detail in due course, Mum. That's if the grapevine of the village mafia hasn't already informed you of all the facts.'

'Just you make sure you do that, our Lucy. I don't get a lot of excitement in my life.' Agnes brightened visibly. 'Though now that I've got a wedding to look forward to, at last, things might be different.'

Lucy took the stiff cardboard invitation card with its gold lettering from her mother. 'Very impressive. Uncle Geoff will have printed this himself, at his own works. And it will be nice to see Louise again. It looks as if it might be quite an exciting evening.'

Quite how exciting, she could never at that moment have anticipated.

Six

Agnes Blake was proved correct in at least one of her assumptions. The celebration of Geoffrey Aspin's sixtieth birthday turned out to be as she had forecast 'a posh do'.

Agnes held to her resolution not to go, but her daughter took the opportunity to buy a stunning dress, have her hair cut in a new style and present herself to be admired in the splendid setting of Marton Towers, the former stately home which was to house the great occasion. Many heads turned to look at the young woman with the striking dark-red hair and the lustrous deep-green eyes, which changed colour intriguingly as she moved into different lights. Lucy Blake told herself primly that it was not pleasant to be the centre of attraction. Yet in the bright sun of high summer she found it difficult to convince herself of that. After a week of hostility from the bad lads of Brunton, it felt good to attract so many admiring glances, as the noise of laughter and conversation rose and the crowd milled on the gravel in front of the old stone of the mansion's impressive frontage.

The girl she had known as Louise Aspin and now had to get used to thinking of as Louise Hawksworth was delighted to see her old friend. Lucy was shocked to see how the laughing, mischievous companion of her schooldays had changed and aged. Perhaps Louise sensed her thought, for she said generously how young and pretty the woman who was turning heads around them was looking.

'You're still a girl to them,' said Louise, the tilt of her head taking in the chattering crowd around them. 'Pity I can't say the same for me. Two children tend to hurry on the years, I'm afraid.'

'I understand the younger one is . . .'

'Handicapped, yes.' Louise Hawksworth came in on the

hesitation which was now so familiar to her. 'Michael is a Down's syndrome child. He's a little charmer most of the time, and I wouldn't be without him. But it changes your life, there's no denying that. There are no children here today: we decided it wasn't an occasion for them.' She looked at the lineless, lightly freckled face in front of her and tried not to be envious of Lucy Blake's appearance and career. 'I hear you're quite a high flier in the police service. CID, isn't it?'

Lucy cursed herself for the blush she should long since have grown out of. She grinned the grin which took Louise back to their days in the fourth form. 'I'm only a Detective Sergeant. But there are prospects of promotion, in the medium term. And in any case, I love the work.'

'And still a free woman, despite all the male attention of our youth. There are some eligible bachelors around here, who are showing every sign of interest. But I don't need to tell you that. You were always the one who could spot interest in a man from a mile away, even when we were seventeen.'

'Or a woman.'

They giggled together, remembering the part-time female General Studies teacher who had been brought in to teach them about the religions of the world and then shown a surprising and unwelcome interest in sixth-form female thighs.

Then Lucy said slightly self-consciously, 'I'm engaged, actually, Louise.'

'You're a dark horse, aren't you? Still playing things close to that delectable chest of yours. If you'd only let me know, he'd have had an invite for today.'

'I doubt whether he'd have come. Though come to think of it, he probably would. We had a murder case here only a few months ago. When the place was under different owner-ship. When Marton Towers was the private residence of a drug baron who is now safely under lock and key.' She looked up at the impressive elevation above her, then away towards the location of the former stable block. It was there that a charred body, which had been discovered after a mysterious fire, had turned out to be a murder victim.

'What an exciting life you do lead, Lucy Blake!' Louise

Hawksworth's tone was wistful as well as ironic. Then for a moment she was back in those old days, before the world closed in upon her, when every day seemed an occasion for laughter and Lucy Blake and she had kept no secrets from each other. 'So tell me about this mysterious lover of yours. He's in the job, obviously. That's what you call it, isn't it? And I expect he's tall, dark and handsome. The kind of man we promised ourselves in those green and salad days at the comprehensive.'

'He's not, actually. He's not exactly short, fat and ugly, but he's not got the appearance I'd have envisaged for either of us in the old days. He's nearly ten years older than me; he's also divorced, bald, and with the sort of neat black moustache which would once have turned me right off.'

'He must be bloody good between the sheets!'

'Louise Aspin, that is very coarse indeed. And coarseness is a thing I will not tolerate in my girls!' Lucy mimicked the high-pitched, outraged voice of a long-lost form teacher.

Louise giggled for a moment like the schoolgirl of those days, then said with a sudden seriousness, 'I haven't been that Louise Aspin for a long time now, Lucy. More's the pity, I think sometimes.'

Lucy took her arm, moved her a little to one side, sensing that they were about to be called indoors for the meal and separated. 'Come on, girl, this is no time for regrets or the remembrance of things past. This is a happy occasion! This is your father's day.'

For a moment, Louise was tempted to tell her old friend of the darkness which had come between herself and her father. But the crowd began to move beneath the high stone portico of the mansion and the moment passed. She watched her father ten yards ahead of her, shepherding his new woman towards the dining room and laughing happily with those near him, and tried not to think of the mother who had been dead for less than four years.

Pam Williams had always known that this would be a difficult day for her. She was being presented, not to the immediate family, most of whom she had now briefly met, but to a whole range of business and social acquaintances of Geoffrey Aspin. Many of these people had known him for many years. Most of them had also known Jill Aspin, the wife who was now dead, the wife who for so many years had been the happy supporter of the man who was the centre of this occasion. The wife whom all of them remembered with affection, the wife whom a tragic death had inevitably invested with a moral stature which was nearing sainthood.

Pam was aware as she moved among this smiling, happy, increasingly noisy throng that she was being assessed, being weighed as a possible replacement for the departed Jill and found wanting. She was aware that there was a kind of inescapable ritual involved here, that this was an ordeal which she had to endure, but that did not make it any easier for her. She told herself repeatedly that it was better to get all of this over in one day, that her life would be easier hereafter for this. She took care to say nothing controversial and went on nodding graciously. It was a little like being the queen, she thought, but without the million auxiliary perks which accompanied the progress of that resolutely smiling lady.

She was introduced to a succession of people who hid their curiosity behind a cheerful frontage. She gave up trying to remember names after the first few minutes. There would be other occasions, other meetings in different environments, when she would get the chance to exchange more meaningful words with those who really mattered among this noisy throng, she told herself. She was glad when the time came for the meal and she could pay attention to and converse with only her immediate neighbours.

Geoffrey Aspin, on the other hand, was feeling more and more at ease as the warm afternoon drew on. He was among friends, the nervous business of introducing Pam Williams to people had in his view gone well, and it was time to relax and enjoy the celebration of his sixtieth birthday. It was costing enough, so why not extract full pleasure from the day? He looked around: everyone seemed to be enjoying themselves. Geoffrey raised his glass of champagne to the company in general, downed it in two takes, and beamed his approval of the world.

It was probably at that point that he had his great idea.

He revolved it in his mind during the soup and fish courses.

The more he thought about it, the more it appealed to him. He was sure it would bring applause from the company at large, especially as most of them would have had at least three glasses of wine by then. Perhaps the more cautious faces of his immediate family, around him on the top table, should have warned him off the idea. But Geoffrey Aspin was looking over their heads towards the world beyond them. He gazed out to the friendly faces of his friends, stretching away into the distant recesses of the room, and saw also the sunlight streaming in from that anonymous and it now seemed to him benign world beyond the walls of Marton Towers.

Geoffrey had forgotten that the wine which he had thought would mellow any antipathy in the room to his announcement would affect him too. By the end of the meal, the central character in this little drama had lost any apprehension about the way his bold initiative would be received. He wanted to share his happiness with the world, to let a tiny part of his own wellbeing overflow into the glum lives of those around him.

In other words, Geoffrey Aspin was pleasantly tight.

He was not drunk by any means. Nor was he one of those tiresome men for whom drink is a prelude to aggression. He tended to see the best in people, to embrace the world as his friend, when he had had a few drinks. Thus he listened benignly and with gratitude to Steve Hawksworth's speech of congratulation on reaching his seventh decade in this teeming world.

It was a speech which was acceptable for the occasion but otherwise unremarkable. His son-in-law made a couple of innocent and rather feeble jokes about how frightened of Geoff the prominent industrialist he had been, when he came into his life as the wooer of his younger daughter. The audience, by now in benevolent mood, laughed happily and even produced a little sporadic applause. Steve, who had been inhibited by the sour demeanour of Jemal and Carol Bilic, gathered confidence from this. After being initially tentative, he grew quite fulsome in the latter stages of his address. Geoff Aspin was altogether a splendid fellow, who looked far too young to be sixty. But Steve wasn't going to argue about that, since they had all been provided with this splendid party to celebrate the milestone. General applause and bucolic 'here here's'. He was sure there would be many more happy occasions of this kind in the future and he looked forward to them eagerly.

Steve made no mention of the woman sitting with a modest smile at Geoff's side, because that is what the family had agreed and he was careful not to move outside that brief. He concluded by asking the company to rise and toast the achievements of their hero's first sixty years and his health and happiness in the next forty. The guests shuffled awkwardly to their feet, raised their glasses with a ragged chorus of 'To Geoff!' and then applauded with the enthusiasm of those not called upon to perform as they sank happily back into their seats.

Geoffrey Aspin had drunk another glass of wine as he smiled modestly at his son-in-law's compliments and waited a little nervously for the moment when he would respond. But he had always carried drink well, and he did so now as he rose to respond to his son-in-law's modest panegyric. He scarcely swayed at all, and there was no sign of a slurring in his speech.

He failed to recognize that alcohol and adrenalin can be a dangerous combination, but that can hardly be accounted a moral defect in a man.

He thanked Steve for his generous comments and everyone in the room for attending this celebration of what must indeed be a milestone in anyone's life. It was good to have your family around you at moments like this. He gazed fondly round the top table at his two daughters and their husbands and received rather stiff and self-conscious smiles in response – it is not easy to behave naturally when the public spotlight is turned suddenly and unexpectedly upon you. Only Steve Hawksworth, still full of relief at completing the ordeal of public speaking, beamed spontaneously. Geoffrey glanced at his notes and moved on. It was likewise delightful to have your close working colleagues of many years here to share this occasion. Geoffrey nodded at another table, and his business partner and senior staff nodded a more spontaneous acceptance than the family had managed.

After replying to Steve's anecdotes of apprehension with

a couple of stories of his own about his son-in-law, Geoffrey spent two minutes more in this conventional vein. Then he moved away from the carefully written notes in his hand.

'The vast majority of people here today will remember my wife Jill.' There were murmurs of assent, and then the big room fell unnaturally silent and people began to study the impressive oak panelling of its walls. This was serious stuff, when they had not expected it. It might be necessary to realign their responses. 'Jill and I were very close. Very close indeed, as most of you knew.' Geoffrey paused a little too long; there were shufflings of feet as slumped forms made themselves a little more upright, making noises which were suddenly louder in the otherwise silent room. Geoffrey was conscious of the change in atmosphere, but it prompted him only to move a little more quickly into his change of agenda.

'Jill's passing was a blow to all of us. But the greatest blow of all was to me. I don't mind telling you that both my work and my private life suffered for quite a long period after Jill's passing.' He looked round the room, but saw only people staring fixedly at the immaculate table linen in front of them: it wasn't safe to look at your neighbour when speakers embarked upon reminiscences of this sort. 'I don't mind telling you that I was a lonely man. A very lonely man indeed. Some of the evenings and the nights took an awful long time to pass.'

This was Britain, and men didn't reveal things like this. The absolute silence was telling him that, and warning him to move on quickly to other and lighter things. But Geoffrey Aspin, with the bit between his teeth and a proud purpose in view, was oblivious to such warnings, just as he was to the uneasy movement of caution as the helpless Pam Williams lifted an admonitory hand beside him. 'But one cannot grieve for ever, and as Steve was kind enough to say a few minutes ago, hopefully a lot of my life still lies before me. And a few months ago, a new presence came into that life. A presence which has both enlivened and enlarged it.' He was proud of that phrase, which he had scribbled on the back of his hand only ten minutes earlier.

A nervous murmur of approbation ran through the tables

furthest from his. Those around him stared up at him, striving to secure his attention, willing him to abandon what they now sensed was coming. Geoffrey stared over their heads towards those distant, less intimate faces, smiled the secure smile of the man with a pleasant surprise to deliver, and pursued his grand design.

'This is a happy occasion, as Steve has been good enough to remind us, a sentiment which you have just endorsed with your toast. It is an occasion which I now propose to make even happier. Many of you have been introduced to Pam Williams today. No doubt you have found her a winning lady, as I have.' He glanced affectionately down at the woman beside him, who was staring stonily at the full glass of wine in front of her. 'You do not know her well, as yet. But in the years to come I hope that you will have the opportunity to get to know her very well indeed. Ladies and gentleman, I ask you to rise once again to your feet and drink to the health of the future Mrs Aspin!'

He lifted his own glass as his voice rose exultantly on the final phrase and waved it over the heads of his listeners in a wide, triumphant, all-embracing arc. There were slightly drunken cheers, maudlin male shouts of congratulation, a round of applause which was just a little late in coming but which embraced most of the company beyond the top table. People shuffled to their feet and muttered 'The future Mrs Aspin' with varying degrees of clarity and embarrassment. Then there was a ragged, rather inebriated cheer for Geoff's news and the minor, pleasant sensation which it afforded to most of his listeners.

No one in his immediate vicinity applauded. There were various expressions upon the faces of those nearest to Geoffrey Aspin, but only Steve Hawksworth attempted approbation, and his attempts to clap were instantly stilled by molten looks from his wife and her sister.

Geoffrey remained on his feet for a moment, apparently unconscious of the reactions on his own table as he gazed out at the wider world beyond and savoured the effects of his surprise announcement. Then he subsided happily into his chair, smiling the inane smile of the man happily a little drunk, and refocused with difficulty on the face of Pam Williams next to him.

He was surprised to find that it was not filled with pleasure. Indeed, it was tight-lipped with anger, as he had never seen it before. Still he ignored the warning signs, as only a man overconfident with wine would have done. 'That's told 'em, love. No turning back now, eh?'

Pam Williams hissed rather than spoke her furious reaction. 'You should never have said that, Geoffrey Aspin. Believe me, you're going to regret it!'

Seven

Geoffrey Aspin's declaration of his marital intentions formed a natural climax to the day's activities.

Most of the people present thought that it was a premeditated move, that he and the family had known all about it in advance but had kept the secret so as to allow the day's central character to make an appropriately dramatic announcement. There were many references to dark horses and cunning old foxes as his friends shook his hand, thanked him for the party and said their farewells, though it did seem a little odd that the lady in question should not be at his side to receive their congratulations. A natural shyness, Geoffrey explained affably.

The atmosphere on the wide gravel forecourt outside Marton Towers was scarcely one to encourage suspicion, or indeed any emotion other than bonhomie. The late afternoon sunshine was warm still, gilding the old mansion with a serenity it had not always enjoyed during its chequered history. The gentle southerly breeze was welcome after the warmth of the panelled dining room, and people lingered a little, gazing down the half mile of the long, arrow-straight drive, which ran between the twin rectangular ornamental lakes towards the monument under the trees in the distance. Perhaps they were reluctant to abandon this glimpse of a life very different from the ones most of them were about to resume.

Lucy Blake wrung the hand of the man who had been so kind to her in her youth, aware as she offered her best wishes for his new life that Geoff Aspin in his excitement was only dimly conscious of who she was. She managed a brief word with her old friend Louise. They promised each other that it would not be so long before they met again, but Lucy saw that Louise Hawksworth was preoccupied with other things, and suspected for the first time that her father's declaration of his marital intentions had been a shock to her.

Lucy drove away with a feeling of sadness. At one time she and Louise had had no secrets from each other, and she would have pressed her friend about what was worrying her without any qualms. How natural, unthinking and uncomplicated are the friendships of adolescence, and how much more difficult such unthinking spontaneity becomes as life proceeds.

Such melancholy reflections were soon dispersed by the familiar delights of the Ribble Valley on a perfect late-June evening. Bathed in the setting sun, Pendle Hill looked unusually benign, like the flank of some huge primeval animal which had settled in the green pastures around it to sleep away the night. She drove slowly through the quiet countryside, enjoying glimpses of the River Hodder through the fresh green of the trees, then the derelict and picturesque stones of the ruin the locals called Cromwell's Bridge. This traditionally most Catholic part of the country had endured some stirring times in the past, with the old faith under fire and the primitive superstitions of the age bringing the Pendle witches to trial and death at Lancaster.

One of Lucy Blake's interests was local history, and she mused on these and other things as she enjoyed having the lush growth of the valley largely to herself early on this Saturday evening. She felt perfectly relaxed; she was not working until Monday morning. A lazy Sunday with a lie-in and the newspaper, and a mother who would very probably overrule her protests and spoil her with breakfast in bed, stretched invitingly before her. Then she might relax and enjoy a little sun in the privacy of Agnes Blake's neat cottage garden, with the long green ridge of Longridge Fell which she had known since childhood rising protectively above her. She loved her modern flat in the town, but she did miss the old stone houses of the village, the garden, and the illusion of an unchanging world around her.

Thoughts of her mother brought her back to more practical considerations. Agnes would want to know all about her day: about Louise, about Geoff Aspin and his new lady.

Particularly about Geoff Aspin and his new lady. Lucy addressed her thoughts to the account she would deliver.

The row of old stone cottages looked well as she eased the little blue Corsa into her mother's drive. In front of the house which Lucy Blake knew so intimately the roses were now in full flower and the Cambridge blue of lobelia fringed the neat oblong beds in the small front garden. Lucy remembered holding her father's hand and trying to pronounce the names of the summer bedding plants when she was a very small girl, in the years before she had gone to school and learned of the wider world beyond the boundaries of this cottage. She allowed herself a moment of sadness for those dear, almost forgotten days of innocence, then went up to the open front door and called cheerfully to her mother that she was here.

'How was the food?' asked Agnes Blake, as she brought in the teapot in its knitted cosy and relished the moment which always delighted her, when she sat down to discuss the latest events in her daughter's life.

Lucy enlarged on the delights of the five courses and the coffee and the impressive setting of Marton Towers, but she knew it was but an elaborate prologue to her impressions of the principals involved in this impressive setting. 'It was good to see Louise again,' she said presently. 'She's Louise Hawksworth now, of course. It's surprising how quickly the years pass. She was looking much older than I expected. I suppose she thought that too, when she saw me.'

'Some people just ignore the years,' said her mother darkly. 'Some people think they can behave like kids for ever.'

Lucy refused to rise to that. 'Louise's husband made the speech proposing the health of Geoff Aspin.'

Mrs Blake was not to be diverted. 'Your friend Louise has two children now, I believe.'

'You believe correctly. It was I who informed you of it.'

'Some people are busy getting on with life, whilst others are still wandering around waiting to get married.'

'I'm neither wandering around nor waiting to get married, Mum.'

Agnes Blake sniffed her dismissal of that view, a seemingly difficult feat which she achieved with practised aplomb.

'Most women of my age have several grandchildren. I have one daughter, who hasn't even bothered to get married.'

'That's in hand, as you know, Mum.' Lucy saw immediately that she had made a mistake: her mother would move immediately to the subject of dates. She said hastily, 'One of Louise's children has Down's syndrome. There were no children at the party, so I didn't see him, but I think he's quite badly handicapped. Louise is plainly very fond of him, but I think she has quite a hard life.'

Her mother looked at her sternly, as if she suspected a diversionary tactic, an attempt to dismiss her demand for grandchildren by the use of this poor child. She decided on inspection of her daughter's face that she was being too cynical. However, Agnes had no wish to discuss the possible pitfalls of pregnancy at this point. 'And how was my old friend Geoff Aspin?'

Lucy wondered whether with ten years between them the two had ever been close friends. But she remembered her mother's disapproval of the rumours she had heard about the entry of another woman into Geoff's life, and she was determined to make the most of this welcome diversion. 'He looked a lot older than the man who was so kind to me when Dad died and Louise and I were still teenagers. But that's only natural. Geoff Aspin was looking well. Very well indeed, in fact. He seemed genuinely happy.'

Another sniff which carried more import than a paragraph of words. 'And was this woman he's been consorting with there?'

'I like that phrase, Mum. "Consorting with." I'll remember that. Covers a multitude of unworthy speculations, that does.'

Agnes gave her daughter the look which had quelled all insolence when she was a child. 'Was this woman there?'

'Yes, she was there, Mum. Sitting happily at Geoff's side during the meal, as a matter of fact.'

'Bold as brass, then.' Agnes nodded, as if there were a grim satisfaction in having her worst fears confirmed.

'She seemed a very pleasant woman, actually, Mum. I think Geoff might in fact be quite lucky to have found her.' Lucy knew very little about Pam Williams, but she felt compelled to be her ally against this maternal disapproval.

The sniff this time was of unmitigated contempt. 'You know nothing about these things, our Lucy.' She paused whilst she waited for the argument which did not come. 'Good-looking, is she? Plenty of paint to cover the wrinkles, I expect.' Agnes nodded happily on the thought.

As far as Lucy knew, her mother had rejected all offers of close male companionship since her father's early death. She wondered for the first time whether that had caused Agnes any distress. 'It's not like you to be so uncharitable, Mum. The lady's called Pam. From what little I saw of her she seemed a charming woman. She's only a little younger than Geoff, I think. And certainly not the painted trollop you seem to have in mind.'

Agnes was silent for a moment. Then she said briskly, 'Aye, all right, then. But you'll not deny that men of Geoff Aspin's age have a habit of making fools of themselves, when they're left to their own devices.'

'I bow to your superior knowledge, there, Mum.'

Agnes flashed her a warning look, then broke into the grin she could no longer resist. 'So is it serious?'

'Very serious indeed, Mum. Geoff Aspin announced in his speech that he's planning to marry her. And good luck to them, I say!' she added defiantly.

Her mother did not argue as she had expected her to. Lucy realized with a little shock that she was quite disappointed about that. Instead, her mother said quietly, 'Jill's been dead for coming on for four years now. I suppose it might be time enough.'

'Geoff's a healthy man who's only just reached sixty. With any luck, he's got a lot of his life still ahead of him. And so has Pam Williams!' Lucy said with a belated feminist emphasis.

Agnes agreed a little reluctantly that it might be so. She was anxious for more details of Pam Williams' background, but her daughter was distressingly ignorant about this. 'You were with the man's daughter, and you didn't find out any more than this about the woman who's to become her step-mother? And you call yourself a detective?' Agnes Blake said with mock incredulity.

'We were talking about old times, Mum. We didn't have that long together. And I'm not sure Louise knows all that

much, anyway. I think her dad's announcement that he was
going to marry Pam might have come as a bit of a bombshell to her, actually.' She thought back to the glimpses she
had seen of the faces on the top table when Geoff announced
his intentions to his audience, and wondered for the first
time how many of them had known that he was going to do
this.

They discussed the rest of the Aspin family and the lives
they were now leading, but Lucy was a disappointingly sparse
informant for a mother hungry for news. Agnes managed to
elicit the fact that although Geoff Aspin was ten years younger
than her, he had four grandchildren already, and to comment
anew on her daughter's shortcomings in this field. Finally,
she reluctantly abandoned the story of the day at Marton
Towers and the Aspin family, telling her daughter, 'Well, I
expect you'll find a lot more about what's going on in the
next few months.'

'I don't really think I shall, Mum. Louise and I promised
each other we must meet up again soon, but we probably
won't. We both have busy lives, in our different ways. And
if I don't meet Louise, I'm hardly likely to learn much about
the rest of the family, am I?'

Lucy Blake was sometimes wrong about things, as her mother
was always happy to point out. This was one such instance.

At quarter to eight the next morning, Lucy was stretching
deliciously in bed, noting the morning sunlight on the flow-
ered curtains, and telling herself that there was no need to
hurry into the long summer day. Then she heard the phone
shrill, and her brow furrowed. It was early on a Sunday
morning for this disturbance of her mother's life. A moment
later her mother was in the room, handing her the portable
phone, telling her resentfully that it was the station at Brunton
asking for her.

The switchboard operator told her briefly that she was
being connected. Then Percy Peach's familiar voice was loud
in her ear. 'Sorry to spoil your weekend, girl, but I think
you'd better get that delicious arse of yours down here pronto.
There's been a murder. At Marton Towers, of all places.
Bloke by the name of Geoffrey Aspin.'

Eight

Chief Superintendent Thomas Bulstrode Tucker stood before DCI Peach in the peacock splendour of his golfing gear.

It was a pity that it was Sunday morning and the CID section at Brunton police station was so sparsely populated, for Peach considered that this vision deserved a much wider audience. Perhaps the whole of CID and the uniformed boys as well. Policemen, despite adverse publicity in some sections of the press of late, had a testing job. They deserved a little light relief at times – or even a lot of light relief, as seemed to be on offer here.

Tucker wore plus twos in a violent purple and green tartan to which no clan had ever laid claim. Beneath them, his mustard yellow socks were beautifully ribbed, leading the eye naturally downwards to two-tone tan and white shoes, which the old sweats had called 'co-respondent shoes' when Percy had been a young copper on the beat. The horizontal blue and white stripes of Tucker's rugby-style top emphasized an increasing tendency towards corpulence in the head of CID.

'Colourful shirt, sir,' said Peach cheerfully.

Tucker divined correctly that this was code for garish. 'They're very fashionable, these,' he said defensively.

'So I've been told,' said Percy with a nod. But not fashionable for long, if displayed on models like this, he thought. 'And brand new socks. Brunton Golf Club is in for a treat today, sir.'

Tucker looked at him suspiciously. 'How do you know that they're new?'

Peach had noted that the socks did not have the multiple pulled threads which represented the inevitable results of

Tommy Bloody Tucker's frequent visits to the brambles which fringed the fairways of his course. Straightforward detective work, if you had witnessed Tommy Bloody Tucker's attempts to play golf. Percy decided not to give the detail of his reasoning. 'I just played a hunch, sir.'

'Don't give me that Hollywood nonsense. We don't play hunches in Brunton CID. We assemble the facts and make proper deductions.'

Tucker was at his most pompous. Percy decided he looked more like a strutting turkey than a peacock, after all. 'Then I deduce that this is only a fleeting visit, sir. I have already deduced that you are on your way to golf.'

Tucker examined his lower limbs and blinked a couple of times, which seemed to Peach to imply that his chief still retained some deeply hidden aesthetic sense. 'You're wasting my valuable time, Peach. There is a serious crime to be dealt with, and as usual you are following diversions.'

'Yes, sir. Sorry, sir. It has yet to be confirmed by the pathologist, but my gut feeling is now supported by your vast experience: it seems that we have a murder on our patch.'

'Geoffrey Aspin, the message on my phone said.'

Peach's heart sank. He knew now why Tucker had made this unprecedented and gaudy Sunday morning appearance. 'Yes, sir. Prominent local businessman, I'm told. You knew him, sir?'

'Indeed I did. Geoff Aspin was a man without enemies.'

That was the kind of banality you expected from the family, even the public, but not from a chief superintendent. Unless it was Chief Superintendent Tommy Bloody Tucker.

Peach said quietly, 'It seems not, sir. Unless you think that having your head well-nigh removed with a piece of rope is some sort of accident.' He hadn't seen the corpse yet, but a degree of poetic licence was surely permissible when you were coping with T.B. Tucker.

'We'll need to solve this one quickly, Peach.'

Meaningless, as usual, like most of Tucker's attempts to galvanize his team. The man couldn't even muster a decent bollocking these days.

'That would certainly be a result, sir. Be taking direct charge of the investigation yourself, will you?'

Tucker thought he caught a slight and unnecessary emphasis on that word 'direct'. The head of CID said stiffly, 'I never interfere with my team, as you well know, Peach.'

'As I well know, indeed, sir. But no doubt in due course we shall have the benefits of your overview of the situation.'

'You will indeed.' In his relief at avoiding any direct contact with the crime-face, Tucker overlooked what he should have recognized as insolence from his DCI. He said with as much threat as he could muster, 'I shall be keeping a close watch on this, since I knew Geoff so well.'

'Yes, sir. Member of the Brotherhood, was he?'

'Mr Aspin was not a Freemason, as a matter of fact. Not that it would have made any difference at all to my feelings if he had been,' Tucker added hastily. His Freemasonry was such a frequent target for Peach's barbs that the head of Brunton CID had grown sensitive about it.

'I see, sir. Just a close personal friend of yours, was he?' Peach spoke as if it were inconceivable that there should be any such animal.

'I knew him through the golf club, if you must know.'

'I think I must, sir. All facts are vital, as you reminded me a couple of minutes ago.'

'We didn't play a lot together. Geoff Aspin was quite a good golfer, as a matter of fact.'

There might be some connection between those two facts, thought Peach. You could no doubt be rather a modest golfer and yet be rated 'quite good' in Tommy Bloody Tucker's assessment.

Peach leant forward towards Tucker's huge empty desk. 'This gives us an enormous advantage at the beginning of a murder investigation, sir.'

'What does?'

'Well, having a man with your background who was on intimate terms with the victim, sir. With the combination of that friendship and your grasp on the world of crime, I'm sure you'll be able to write down a list of suspects for us immediately. Perhaps even give us a prime suspect at the outset.' He rubbed his hands together enthusiastically. 'Whoever planned this crime reckoned without the formidable presence of Chief Superintendent Tucker!'

'I didn't know him all that well, you know.' Tucker was immediately and agreeably on the defensive.

'Come, sir, there's no need for modesty! Not with a fellow-professional who realizes just how much your insight will be worth.'

'I knew him a little at the golf club, that's all.' Tucker was decamping faster than school cadets before the SAS.

'But at least you'll be able to tell us all about his family. Sixty per cent of killings take place within the family, as you reminded me last week, sir.' Peach was delighted to fling Tucker's predilection for the obvious and insulting fact back into his face.

'I don't know the family. I was merely—'

'You weren't at this celebration of the victim's sixtieth birthday at Marton Towers? What a pity you had to refuse your invitation, sir! We might have had our detective master-mind at the scene of the crime. Or at least at the fore-scene, as you might say.'

Tucker ground his teeth, an activity he only seemed to engage in when Peach was around. 'I wasn't invited to Marton Towers. I wouldn't have expected it. I imagine this was a gathering of the immediate family to celebrate—'

'Over a hundred people there, I'm told, sir. Quite a large circle of friends, apparently. Pity you were overlooked, as it turns out.'

'Look, Peach. I knew the man as a good egg at the golf club, that's all. But he was a prominent local businessman and you need to find his killer quickly. Very quickly, if you're to avoid criticism from the local hacks.'

Peach repeated 'good egg' slowly, as if it were of great significance, and wrote it carefully at the top of the pad in front of him, noting for the hundredth time how Tucker's 'we' became 'you' as soon as difficulties threatened.

Then he reviewed once again his chief's garb of many colours, as though it was somehow important to him that he committed this picture to memory. 'Enjoy your golf, sir.'

The weekend in England has a deadening effect even upon essential services such as the police. Sergeant Jack Chadwick, one of the few policemen not to have been replaced by a

civilian as Scene of Crime Officer, was ready for action as
soon as he was apprised of the facts at eight o'clock: a body
discovered in suspicious circumstances at Marton Towers.
But on Sunday morning, it took him longer than usual to
assemble his SOCO team and to begin the detailed examination of the site.

Nevertheless, by the time that DCI Peach and DS Blake
arrived at ten thirty, things were well in hand. The pathologist had been and gone and the police van known within the
service as 'the meat wagon' was waiting to take the corpse
away. The site was screened off by high canvas walls to
protect it from the insatiable public curiosity which always
accompanies violent death. The official photographer had
almost finished his grisly work of recording pictures of the
corpse and the place in which it had died from every conceiv-
able angle.

Chadwick greeted his old friend Peach with some relief.
'The manager's been down to see me three times. And each
time he's told me they've got a silver wedding with over a
hundred guests planned for this afternoon; he's shit scared
they'll have to cancel and waste the food.'

'Will you be finished here by one?'

'We'll have all we can get by midday at the latest. I think
we're almost finished now.' He glanced towards the spot
where two of his team were crawling on hands and knees
across the gravel, picking up detritus, ninety-nine per cent
of which would almost certainly prove to be quite irrelevant to the case: cigarette ends; fibres of clothing; a broken
shoelace; a couple of hairs which might or might not be
human, which might or might not have come from the head
of the person who had attacked the man whose remains
still sat in the Jaguar which was at the centre of all this
attention.

Peach wandered across to a lady who had once been a
copper but was now a civilian part-timer. He looked down
at the dubious treasures she had gathered. 'Any good?'

'Probably not. Most of this stuff looks as if it's been here
for days rather than hours. It was a very still night, so hopefully nothing's blown away. I've picked up a couple of hairs
from right under the front passenger door of the car.' She

nodded down at the small plastic bag in which these fragile traces were already enclosed. 'Of course, forensic will probably tell you in due course that they come from the cadaver's head,' she said with professional pessimism.

Peach gave her a wry smile and went back to Chadwick. 'I suppose there's no doubt it's murder?'

Chadwick grinned the cheerful grin of a man about to slide the problem across to someone else. 'No doubt at all, me old mate. Someone put a cord round the poor bugger's neck and snuffed him out. Within about forty seconds, I'd say, without even the benefit of the post-mortem. You've got a nice juicy murder all right, Percy. With ninety-two suspects: that's the number of guests at yesterday's party, the manager tells me. Plus all the staff at Marton Towers, of course.' He beamed his satisfaction at the complexity of the CID life, which had been denied to him after he had been shot and badly wounded in a bank raid years ago.

For the first time Peach went and looked at the corpse itself. Lucy Blake wondered whether he had been saving the best or the worst until the last.

You didn't want anyone killed, of course, but she was used by now to the extra spurt of excitement produced by the most serious crime of all. After the inevitable and often depressing round of thieving, domestic conflict and thuggish drunken violence, murder was a challenge to which every CID pulse responded. It was high profile: there were satisfaction and kudos if you got it right and produced an answer, but plenty of professional and media brickbats if you failed.

Geoffrey Aspin lay where he had died, in the driving seat of his Jaguar Mark 8. His head was thrown back; the livid, blackening scar on his throat indicated exactly how he had died. The cord or cable which had killed him had cut deeply into his neck, so that only the ends of it must have been visible. Peach's remark to Tucker about the head being almost severed was an exaggeration, but not by very much. There had been determination, probably high passion, driving the hands of whoever had held the ends of this cord. The carotid artery had been smashed very quickly: Peach could see why Chadwick could be so certain that this man had died in seconds.

Lucy Blake said softly, as if it was necessary for someone to speak to move things on, 'It looks as if he was killed from behind.'

'It does, yes. And that suggests that this was probably premeditated. But not necessarily so. It could have been an argument that went wrong, an assailant who lost his temper and reached for the nearest implement.' The killer was always 'he' until events threw up other possibilities, an acknowledgement of how few women actually commit the ultimate crime. 'But it would have been odd if he'd found this implement so conveniently to hand.'

Lucy looked automatically through the open rear door of the car, where this sinister and as yet mysterious figure might have waited for his victim. The rear seats and the floor looked to CID eyes depressingly immaculate. But she knew that any fibres or hairs, even any dirt or dust from footwear, would have been meticulously removed and bagged by the SOCO team.

'OK, thanks, Jack. Let's have him away,' said Peach, and the waiting men from the anonymous grey van beside the crime scene moved in with the plastic body shell, anxious to remove the remains before advancing rigor mortis made the task any more complicated.

Peach watched the van drive away from the wide stone steps at the front of the mansion, then turned and went inside Marton Towers to the manager's office. He had been there before, when investigating another and very different murder, but the man who had occupied this office then had long since gone. The manager now was somewhere around Peach's age of thirty-nine, though with a full head of hair he no doubt looked much younger. He had the permanently worried look of the man who oversees receptions and catering, Percy decided. He took pity on him and gave him the good news first.

'The body's being taken away at this moment. I see no reason why you shouldn't go ahead with today's function.'

He thought for a moment that the man was going to spring forward and wring his hand in relief. But he controlled himself and said, 'That's good news. We'd have lost a lot of goodwill. And most of the fresh food would have been wasted, you see. The hygiene regulations don't allow—'

'We'll need to keep the site screened off until our forensic boys have been in and studied the car in situ. Very particular, these boffins are. But a murder site will just be one more of the attractions of Marton Towers.'

'Oh, I doubt that. It's a silver wedding you see, and the kind of people—'

'Trust me, there'll be a lot of interest. Give the public the slightest contact with a nice juicy murder and you can't keep them away. I'll make sure there's a uniformed copper on duty, so that you won't need to worry about what they're getting into.' He beamed generously at the anxious face.

'Well, our guests will be in here most of the time, so I don't expect—'

'Go off well, did it, yesterday's little bunfight?'

The manager swelled with professional indignation. 'It was rather more than a bunfight, Detective Chief Inspector. It was a five-course meal with genuine champagne and fine wines.'

Percy was tempted to ask whether you could have champagne that wasn't genuine. Instead, he said, 'Must have set someone back a quid or two, then.'

'Apart from the extra bottles of champagne and wine consumed on the day, it was all paid for in advance by Mr Aspin.' The manager felt that such splendid financial habits should be widely publicized.

'And there were ninety-odd people, I hear.'

'Ninety-two covers to be precise.'

Percy Peach sighed deeply at the prospect of whittling this number of suspects down to something manageable. 'Five or six thousand quid then.'

The manager bridled at this mention of actual sums of money, which he thought vulgar and un-British. He said stiffly, 'That would be a fairly accurate figure, yes.'

Percy whistled softly. 'And you think the day went off well?'

The manager frowned. 'I am concerned on these occasions with other things than the interchanges at the tables, such as the serving of food and the comfort and well-being of our guests. But yes, I'd say the day went well. Very well, as far as I could see. Everyone seemed very happy at the end of it.'

'And yet one of these ninety-two delighted punters bumped off the poor sod who had paid for it all.'

'That seems likely, yes.' The manager sought desperately for something which would avoid unwelcome publicity for Marton Towers. 'I suppose it could have been someone who came in from outside, someone who hadn't been involved in the day at all.'

'You should have been a detective, sir. Now tell me what happened at the end of this happy occasion.'

'Well, there were speeches. I was in the kitchen with our catering staff, so I didn't hear much of what was said. But I think they were fine. There was a lot of laughter. And then at the end of Mr Aspin's speech, there was a lot of applause as well. After that, things broke up pretty quickly. It was a beautiful afternoon – well, early evening, by then – and I expect people were delighted to get out into the fresh air.'

His face clouded over for no more than a second. But a second was enough for Peach, who was used to studying people's faces without embarrassment. 'There's something else, isn't there, sir?'

'It's probably nothing.'

'Indeed it is, sir. But it wouldn't be wise to hold anything back, in what seems sure to be a murder investigation.'

'No. Well, I heard some shouting, that's all. Some sort of argument. After most people had left the dining room and gone out on to the terrace.'

'A row, you mean. A fierce disagreement.'

'Yes, I suppose it was. I didn't see it.'

'And who was involved in this row?'

'I don't know. It was behind closed doors, somewhere in the cloakroom area, I think. I was still in the kitchens.'

'It must have been pretty loud, then, for you to hear it at all.'

'It was.' He was suddenly anxious to be involved, to maintain his contact with the gruesome glamour of a murder investigation, as innocent people with nothing to fear often are. 'I think one of the people involved might have been Mr Aspin.'

Peach tried not to show his excitement. 'And who was the other person?'

'I don't know, I'm afraid.'

'Couldn't you even make a guess about that? Even speculation might be useful to us, at this stage.'

'No, I'm afraid I couldn't.' He frowned, not wanting to let it go at that, and then said rather desperately, 'Except that I'm sure it was female.'

'There you are, sir! You've eliminated approximately half the people there at once. Any idea which female?'

'No. I couldn't even speculate about that. I hadn't heard any of the women in that room speak, so I couldn't identify the voice.'

'But there were only the two people involved, you think? Mr Aspin and some unknown woman?'

'Yes. At least I'm certain that I only heard two people. It was a private argument and nothing to do with me or my staff.' A sense of propriety belatedly reasserted itself.

'And did you see or hear anything else suspicious?'

'I'm afraid not. I was busy with other things. The time when our guests depart is a frenetically busy time for us. Especially when we have another function the next day, as in this case.' He looked anxiously at his watch.

Peach stood up. The manager stood with him in anticipation of a return to his tasks.

'The body wasn't found until this morning,' Peach said.

'By one of our domestic staff, yes. She was on her way in to—'

'Why do you think that was? We already know that he was killed last night, you see. Wouldn't you think that one of his family would have realized that he hadn't left the Towers along with everyone else last night?'

'Yes, I suppose I would. I'm afraid I haven't given the matter much thought.'

'No reason why you should, sir, is there? But *I* shall have to give that question quite a lot of thought, in the hours to come. Good morning to you.'

Peach went out and stood for a moment on the forecourt, which was at present deserted. He looked down the long, straight drive between the serene rectangular ponds, where the first vivid white and pink flowers of the water lilies gave promise of high summer to come. He believed what he had just heard, that most of the people at yesterday's function had thoroughly enjoyed their day here.

Yet at the end of that day, one of them had almost certainly brutally murdered the man who had set up that enjoyment for them.

There was nothing on either the television or radio morning news about the death.

That was good. It almost certainly meant that the body had not been discovered last night. The longer the interval between a killing and its discovery, the greater the chance that the killer would go undiscovered. The murderer was sure that idea was borne out by the statistics the papers loved to print when they had no hard news. It was surely common sense anyway.

As the Sunday morning dragged along and grew steadily hotter, the murderer tuned to Radio Lancashire and listened nervously to successive news bulletins. There was nothing. The news of rising temperatures in north-east Lancashire and of the aspirations of local cricket teams for the afternoon matches began to seem like a deliberate avoidance of the greater issue.

Then, on the one o'clock news bulletin, it came. The news-reader's tone seemed to rise a little with the excitement of it, as if she recognized that all the trivia of the news summaries during a dull morning had been but a preparation for this.

'*A body was discovered this morning in a car at the former stately home, Marton Towers, seven miles outside Brunton in the Ribble Valley. Police are treating the death as suspicious. The identity of the corpse has not been revealed, but it is understood to be that of a male in late middle age. This follows the murder of the estate gardener at Marton Towers, Mr Neil Cartwright, last year. Mr Cartwright's body was discovered after a fire in the stables: his killer was convicted in January and is now serving a life sentence. We understand that at this moment the police see no connection between the two crimes.*'

No connection indeed! They were padding it out, trying to make the old news supplement the new because they did not have enough details. That was good. It didn't necessarily mean that the police knew nothing because they hadn't given the radio people anything, but they hadn't even said that they were anxious to talk to anyone. They usually said that as soon as they could, just to let the public know that they weren't completely stupid and baffled.

It certainly looked as if they hadn't found anything useful yet. They'd have started from scratch this Sunday morning, pulling out all the stops to get a team together, to pursue a scent which had already gone cold. They had no witnesses to what had happened last night and they wouldn't find any. There'd been no one around. The police would have plenty of suspects, in due course – too many for their comfort. There was safety in numbers.

It was almost a relief to have the first report of the murder on local radio. It had seemed like a long wait through the morning. The killer left the room for the first time in hours and went outside. It was a cloudless day, with the sun at its highest and just enough light breeze from the west to ensure it was not excessively hot. The sound of children's voices, high, innocent, anonymous, drifted over the hedges.

The murderer felt first relieved and then exhilarated.

Nine

Pam Williams was trying hard to compose herself. Each time she thought she had done with them, the tears kept starting anew.

Her son tried not to look at the clock. Justin Williams had been called over from Leeds this morning: the policewoman had been insistent on the phone that Mrs Williams needed someone from the family close to her.

It was really most inconvenient. His own family needed him on a Sunday. He knew what to do with them, whereas he did not know what to do with this weeping woman who felt like a stranger. They hadn't been close over the last few years. He knew that she needed physical contact, an arm round her shoulders, a bear hug to assure her that the world would go on, that there were other people in it who cared for her. But Justin could not hug his mother naturally when he most needed to do so, could not offer that simple, instinctive contact which he should not even have had to think about.

He should have been able to deal with this easily enough. He was a doctor, used to dealing with death and those left behind to cope with it. But the usual emollient phrases, meaningless but consoling, wouldn't work with a mother who had become estranged from him. He felt a self-loathing which withered his every move, which made any words he uttered sound artificial, trite, useless. And all because of this man he had never seen. The Geoffrey Aspin whom he had in fact refused to meet, because that would have acknowledged that he was important to his mother. The man he had never wanted in his mother's life. The man who even in death was the disaster he had foreseen he would be in life.

'Are you sure you won't have anything to eat, Mum?' Justin

asked. 'You should have something, you know.' The words sounded like a parody in his ears, as if he was throwing back at his mother the things she had said to him during his childhood upsets.

She shook her head, not looking at him. 'I want to go away. To get out of this house and away from this town.'

He almost asked her where she wanted to go. Just in time, he stopped himself and said, 'You're welcome to come and stay with us, of course. For a few days, if you like.' It was lukewarm: he didn't want her, but if it had to be, why could he not sound enthusiastic about it? 'For as long as you like. You know that.'

She shook her head minimally, staring down at the carpet in front of her from the chair where she had sat for hours now. 'I still can't believe it's happened.' She wrung the wet handkerchief unconsciously between her fingers, the only parts of her which were mobile.

He said, trying to sound as if he regretted it, 'But you shouldn't really leave here at the moment, you know. Not in the immediate future, anyway.' He cursed himself for that last artificial phrase. Why, when words came so naturally to him in his work, would they not fly from his lips now, when they should have been easy?

She looked up at him, for the first time in at least an hour. 'Why's that?' The wide grey eyes in the tear-stained face had a childish wonderment, which he should have welcomed as a return to this world from the dark one which had atrophied her for the last few hours.

'I don't really know.' He knew very well, but he couldn't put it into words which would be acceptable. 'I – I just feel that perhaps you need to be somewhere around here, for the next few days. Haven't you a female friend in the area that you could stay with for a night or two?'

He saw horror dawning in her face as her brain came back to life and worked upon what he had said. 'You mean they'll want to talk to me about Geoff and how he died. You mean that they'll be thinking that I killed him, don't you?'

'No. No, I don't mean that, Mum.' For the first time, the diminutive sprang naturally to his lips. 'I just think they'll want to talk to you, that's all.' He said with increasing desperation,

'I don't know what happens in these things, do I? But I expect the police will want to talk to anyone who was close to Mr Aspin. And you were, I know.'

'I can't talk to them. Not now. Not until I've got my head together.' There was panic in her face. She looked twenty years older, vulnerable as he had never seen her before, like a frail pensioner threatened with violence. Justin felt a sudden, searing tenderness for her. He took both her hands in his, pulled her from the chair, and at last held her clumsily but naturally in his arms. 'All right. I won't let them speak to you. Not now. Not immediately. I'll stay with you here for the rest of the day. We'll work something out.'

He held her for a good ten seconds, feeling even more relief in this belated contact than she did. Then the doorbell rang, as if responding to a cue. Justin detached himself gently from his mother and went and opened the front door of the semi-detached house. This house and its furnishings were similar to many of the ones he entered as a doctor. It felt so normal, so conventional, in this most abnormal of situations.

A short, powerful man with a bald head and a very black moustache, immaculately dressed in a dark suit and tie even on this warm first day of July. And beside him, a young woman with striking dark red hair and a bright, intelligent, face, lightly freckled towards her temples. Quite a looker, his libido told Justin irrelevantly, when he least wanted it to speak to him.

The man flashed a warrant card with a stern, unsmiling photograph of himself, which told the reader that he was a Detective Chief Inspector Peach. 'And this is DS Blake,' he said. 'Is Mrs Williams here? I'm sorry to intrude at a time like this, but I'm afraid we need to speak with her.'

'She's here, but she isn't fit to speak to anyone at the moment. I'm her son. I'm also a doctor. She wouldn't be much use to you at the moment. She isn't coherent, because she's still in shock.'

He thought for a moment the man would argue. Then he said, 'When would it be convenient, Dr Williams? I'm afraid that from my point of view it's rather urgent, you see.'

'I do see, yes. If you'd like to call back late afternoon or early evening, I'll try to ensure that she's a little more composed. I won't give her a sedative until after she's spoken with you.'

The man with the moustache nodded. 'Thank you for your cooperation, sir. We'll come back later, as you suggest.'

Justin shut the door and went back down the hall. He was hoping that he had said they could come back today rather than tomorrow for his mother's sake rather than for more selfish reasons of his own. He had done that much for her at least, had kept the police at bay for a little while until she was better able to deal with their questions. It would be better for her to have the police business out of the way sooner rather than later, since it was surely inconceivable that his mother could have anything to do with this death.

He took a deep breath and went back into the sitting room wondering just what she had got herself into with this man Aspin.

'Of course I'll see you. It shouldn't take long, because there's nothing I can tell you.'

Jemal Bilic spoke dismissively: in his experience, the brisker you were with the police the better.

'Remains to be seen, that, sir. You'd be surprised what useful stuff people are able to give to us. It often happens when they think they're telling us nothing at all.' DCI Percy Peach was like a dog pricking up its ears at the sight of a juicy bone. The prospect of a contest always animated him. 'My experience is that the sons-in-law of deceased men are often sources of much valuable information, when there has been a violent death.'

Bilic was shocked by what sounded to him like a frontal attack. It seemed to him likely that Peach was bluffing, but the man looked very confident. Jemal had a very low opinion of police brainpower, but presumably you didn't become a detective chief inspector without a certain amount of ability.

He said sullenly, 'I didn't have a lot of dealings with Geoffrey Aspin. You'll get better information from my wife.'

'Which in due course we shall do, Mr Bilic.'

'I'll get her in now, if you wish. You can talk to the two of us together.'

'No thank you. We prefer to collect individual statements and impressions of what happened.'

'So that you can trick us into contradicting each other.'

Jemal thought the man would deny that, but Peach merely smiled tolerantly. 'We don't trick anyone. Sometimes people trick themselves, but they're usually people with something to hide. I don't suppose you've anything to hide, have you, Mr Bilic?'

'Of course I haven't.' The denial came a little too promptly; just for a moment, Jemal had thought that they'd been watching his movements over the last few weeks. But they couldn't have been doing that. This watchful man and the softer female presence at his side must surely only be concerned with last night's death. He must concentrate on that. 'I wasn't close to Mr Aspin. I've no idea who decided that he should be killed.'

'That's an odd choice of words, sir. Most people would say, "I've no idea who killed him". Are you suggesting that someone employed an agent to kill Mr Aspin? A contract killer, perhaps?'

'No. Nothing of the sort.' Jemal heard his accent becoming stronger with rage. He must control that. He forced a smile. 'English is not my native tongue. You must make allowances for me.'

'Your English is very good. I believe you are originally from Turkey?'

He felt a pang of fear that they should know so much. Was he under investigation? Or had they just done their homework on him before coming here today? 'Yes. How do you know that?'

Peach gave him one of his broadest smiles. 'I believe the official line is that we don't reveal our sources, sir. But you will understand that in a murder inquiry we talk to a lot of people.'

'I run a successful business. I provide employment.' He was being defensive, even though he knew he had intended to dismiss them with a swift arrogance from his house.

'I'm sure you do both of those things, sir. But that is not our concern today. What was your relationship with Mr Aspin?'

So here, after the preliminary fencing, the question he had anticipated was abruptly upon him. He searched his brain for the phrases he had planned during the morning. 'I told you, we weren't close. We got on OK. He's the grandfather of my children. He's my wife's father. We got on because we needed to. We weren't enemies, but we didn't talk to each other a lot.'

Peach wondered if there had been any racial prejudice in Geoffrey Aspin, whether he had resented this brown-skinned, dark-eyed, handsome, dangerous-looking man for carrying off his elder daughter. They had the perpetual problem of murder: the victim cannot speak for himself, cannot reveal his own thoughts on the people closest to him, cannot list the people he saw as friends and enemies. 'Tell us about yesterday's events, please.'

A shrug of those slim, muscular shoulders; a small smile which was wiped away as soon as it appeared. This at least he was prepared for. 'Geoffrey had organized the whole thing. It went off well enough, I think. I am not so keen on your English celebrations.' He pronounced the long word carefully, but a little of the contempt he had not meant to reveal came out on it. 'There was a good meal and speeches at the end of it.'

'How many people spoke?'

'Just two. Steve – that's Stephen Hawksworth, Geoffrey's other son-in-law – proposed Mr Aspin's health and congratulated him on reaching sixty. There were quite a few laughs and applause at the end. So it seemed fine. I have not much experience of these things.'

'And the second speaker was Mr Aspin himself.'

'Yes. He too got laughs. That seems to be the convention for these things.'

'Indeed it is. And Detective Sergeant Blake here agrees with you that the speeches seemed to go well. She was present, you see: she is a friend of Mrs Hawksworth.'

He glanced swiftly at the woman with the very British style of beauty who sat alongside and slightly behind Peach. He realized for the first time that she was preparing to make notes on what he had to say. He could not prevent his anger showing as he said, 'Why did you not tell me this? Why do you need me to tell you these things at all, when you had a policewoman at the event?'

Peach was at his most urbane. 'We shall be asking a lot of people how they saw yesterday's events, Mr Bilic. DS Blake saw them from afar. You were more intimately involved, as a member of the family on the top table. Different perspectives are always of interest, when one has to piece together events which ended with the brutal dispatch of the man at the centre of them.'

It sounded like a threat, and Percy was quite pleased about that. There was something feral and sinister about this Turkish man. He was already feeling hopeful that their killer might be sitting right in front of them. 'Tell us a little more about the content of Mr Aspin's speech, will you?'

Bilic glanced at Lucy Blake, cursing himself for not remembering her among yesterday's throng of guests. He must have been too preoccupied with his own concerns. He'd better tell it pretty straight, if this woman had been there listening. 'Geoffrey make jokes, the way I said.' Again he heard his accent becoming more guttural, was obscurely aware that he had made a mistake with the tense. 'Then he tells us at the end that he is going to marry this woman.'

'Mrs Williams?'

'Yes. The woman sitting beside him during the meal.'

'You didn't like that?'

The question came quietly from Peach's round, innocent face. Jemal almost flared out that of course he didn't like it. He was chafing in a situation that was controlled by others: he was used to directing his own conversations. He made himself pause and control his breathing. 'It was a shock, that's all. He hadn't told us that he was going to do it.'

'An unpleasant shock?'

'No. Well, I don't think my wife was happy about it. It didn't matter to me. But you'll need to speak to her about that.'

'Which we shall do, in due course. Do you think everyone was as surprised as you by this announcement?'

'I don't know. I think so. I expect the woman knew. She would, wouldn't she?'

'I don't know, Mr Bilic. We shall speak to her about it,

in due course. At the moment, we are concerned with your impressions. I understand that the party broke up very quickly after the speeches. Did you speak to Mr Aspin at that time?'

'No. Other people did. My wife did, I think.'

'Were there any arguments as a result of what Mr Aspin had said?'

'No. If they were, I did not hear. I talk to some people I do business with, before they drove away.'

You are washing your hands like Pilate of any involvement, thought Percy. But this watchful, restless man was a rather unlikely Pilate. 'Who do you think killed Mr Aspin?'

This was more sudden and direct than Jemal had expected. 'I don't know, do I? Perhaps some business associate of his.'

'Not a member of his family, you think?'

'No. I don't think that is likely.'

No, you wouldn't, Peach thought as they left the house.

'He must have known about this major row Aspin had with someone not long before he was killed,' he said to Lucy. 'Even if Bilic wasn't around at the time, which I doubt, his wife would have told him about it. I wonder why he's lying about that.'

Ten

The man who had met Geoffrey Aspin in secret at his printing works some weeks earlier was without the shabby anorak which he wore almost as a badge of office. He was on holiday. His wife had insisted upon it. Even private detectives had to take holidays, she had told him.

All through the winter she had said it. 'I know,' he had replied. 'You're right, I know you are.' And then he had gone on ignoring her. Spring came, and nothing changed. When they reached the beginning of June and still nothing had been done, his hitherto meek wife took the matter into her own hands. She walked into a travel agent, spent nearly an hour thumbing through the brochures they gave her, and then walked determinedly to the desk with her queries.

Twenty minutes later, she had booked a holiday in Italy for two. You can please yourself whether you come or not, she told her husband: I'll find someone else if you don't want to go. She didn't say whether this companion would be male or female, and her husband didn't enquire about the gender.

'This is not like you,' he said mildly.

'This is the twenty-first century,' his suddenly sparkly wife told him, 'in case you hadn't noticed. I'm behaving like a modern woman.' She was surprised how much satisfaction that gave her, surprised how much she enjoyed the look of an ill-treated spaniel upon her husband's face.

And so John Kirkby, ex-copper and now private detective, found himself on the first day of July staring out over the still blue waters of Lake Garda. It was a pleasant scene, and he was sure that when he'd unwound over another day or two he would quite enjoy it. Habit had made him speculate on the previous night about which couples at the adjoining tables were married, but his wife had put a swift embargo on such conjecture.

If he was honest, which in domestic matters he usually was, it was as good a time as any for a private detective to take a holiday. The lighter nights meant that there was less of the pursuing of co-respondents which formed the main body of his work. People preferred the winter months for their extramaritals; it was almost as if the cold encouraged them into new beds, whilst sixteen hours of darkness encouraged them to think they could keep such things secret from their spouses.

John Kirkby wasn't without work, far from it. But he had presented his latest reports to his clients and left the number of his mobile with four of them who might consider consultation necessary as things moved along. He was secretly rather disappointed that none of them had found it necessary to contact him in the two days he had so far spent in Italy.

His wife was taking advantage of the hairdressing facility offered by the hotel, amazed and delighted that in a totally un-English way it was available even on a Sunday morning. John Kirkby strolled along the promenade by the lake, watched the passing crowds of tourists, and tried not to wonder about their relationships with each other. He bought himself a coffee and watched the boats on the lake. They looked very attractive, but he had always distrusted water.

He picked up the English newspaper which the couple at the next table left behind them when they left, only to find that it was three days old and told him nothing he did not know: even the cricket scores were the ones he had already seen. He had walked conscientiously past the newspaper kiosk; his wife had forbidden English papers, not only on the grounds of their high cost abroad but because she and John were here to 'get away from it all'.

One of the people to whom he had confided his mobile number was Geoffrey Aspin, who had assured him that he would ring him on this Sunday morning, after he had digested the import of Kirkby's latest report. There had been no call from Aspin. John knew enough of the reliability of the public at large not to be disappointed by this omission. And yet he was a little surprised: he would have put Aspin down as a meticulous man, who would observe any arrangement he made. Well, he who paid the piper called the tune, John Kirkby told himself glumly.

He set off back towards the hotel, walking slowly to make the exercise fill as much time as he could.

True to his word, Peach returned to the house of Pamela Williams in the early evening.

Her son immediately said, 'My mother's coming over to Leeds with me for a day or two as soon as you've finished with her. I shall be out in the drive packing the car, if you want me.'

His mother still looked in shock. Her eyes were swollen with weeping. She had applied some make-up in preparation for the ordeal of this meeting, but it would have taken more than cosmetics to disguise the lines which seemed to have deepened so suddenly upon her face. Lucy Blake scarcely recognized her as the attractive, slightly diffident woman whom Geoffrey Aspin had been introducing to all his friends before the formal part of the proceedings at Marton Towers not much more than twenty-four hours earlier.

She took them into the front room of her semi-detached 1954 house. It was also her dining room; she sat herself on one side of the table and her two visitors on the other, as though they were about to conduct a formal meeting. Peach was ushering them through the opening politenesses when she cut through his words. 'You think I killed him, don't you? The wife or the mistress is always the first suspect.'

Peach smiled as though he were trying to settle a disturbed child. 'Do you read detective novels, Mrs Williams?'

'I do a little, yes. Well, quite a lot, actually. Why do you ask?'

He smiled, so gently that Lucy Blake at his side wondered anew how her DCI could be so different from the man she had seen in the day's earlier interview with Jemal Bilic. 'We always speak to people in your position as early in an investigation as we can, yes. That is because they are likely to know more about the deceased and his habits than any other person available to us. I know nothing about you as yet, but

I shall be surprised if we do not get a fuller and more balanced picture of Mr Aspin's likes and dislikes from you than from anyone else we see.'

She nodded slowly, as if trying to make herself accept a difficult idea against her better judgement. 'I suppose I have seen more of Geoff in the last few months than anyone else.'

'There you are, then. You can be very useful to us. We may depend quite a lot on what you can tell us, as we try to find who did this awful thing.'

Pam found to her surprise that she was pleased to hear this. Even in the midst of grief, it was good to be told that she could be useful. She remembered that Justin had told her to be careful with these people, not to take them at face value. She said cautiously, 'But you still think I might have killed Geoff, don't you?'

Lucy Blake said, 'We're here to get information, Mrs Williams. People who are innocent have nothing to fear from us.'

Pam looked at her properly for the first time. If she had had a daughter, she might have been about this age. She might even have had a bright, intelligent, sympathetic face like this one. She wondered inconsequentially what it would have been like if she'd had a daughter, instead of sons who seemed only to distance themselves from her as they got older. She managed her first small smile of the day as she said to DS Blake, 'I'm still a suspect, though, aren't I?'

'We don't like to consider people suspects unless they give us a reason to think of them like that. DCI Peach was quite right when he said that we are here to gather information. As much information as you can give us. That may enable us to eliminate some people – perhaps including you – from any suspicion at all. By far the best thing you can do is to be totally honest with us.'

'The family didn't like me.' She hadn't the energy left to be diplomatic. She came straight out with it, without any of the polite preliminaries.

She had expected this nice young woman to say that she was sure that it wasn't so, that Pam had probably been over-sensitive to some unguarded remarks. Instead, it was Peach who came back in at this point. He said encouragingly, 'This is the kind of thing we need to know, Mrs Williams. But perhaps we should begin a little earlier. How long had you known Mr Aspin?'

She noted his change of tense. When she'd spoken about being with Geoff during the last few months, she'd spoken about him as if he was still with them, but they hadn't corrected her. She supposed they must be used to such banalities from people in shock. 'Four and a half months ago.' She heard her own precision and wondered what they would make of it. Like a young girl smitten with her first boyfriend, she'd have said herself. 'I suppose you want to know how we met.'

They wouldn't have pressed her, but they realized she must think it was important. Blake said gently, 'We want every bit of information you can give us, Mrs Williams. You can leave it to us to decide what's important, when we've spoken to a lot of other people and have a fuller picture.'

'He advertised. I answered.' Pam was too shocked and too exhausted to feel the embarrassment she would normally have done. She wanted this out of the way at the beginning. The family were sure to tell them about it, to make out that the two of them had been desperate. Or probably, worse still, that Geoff had picked up a designing woman when he was lonely and at his most vulnerable.

'Mr Aspin advertised for a housekeeper?'

Pam Williams gave them a wan smile, in spite of herself. 'He put a little description of himself in DATING POINT.' She saw that this pretty woman who was still in her twenties and had no need of such devices was puzzled by the title. For a moment she was bitter about that lustrous chestnut hair and that naivety. Then she took pity on her and explained. 'It's a dating page in the newspaper which allows lonely people to get in touch with each other.'

'And you met through this?'

'Yes. On the sixteenth of February. In Starbucks coffee house in Brunton.' She glanced up, saw the woman recording the date and the place in her notes with a gold-cased ball-point pen, wondered what she made of such adolescent precision about the details. 'You meet somewhere neutral at first. You don't give away any details about yourself, in case you don't wish to go any further when you see what turns up.' She piled on the details, thinking bitchily that one day in the distant future this buxom young filly might have need of them.

Lucy gave Pam a smile which she hoped would encourage her to go on being so frank. 'And obviously on this occasion you both decided that you would like to proceed. Had you much experience of this sort of meeting at the time?'

'I had. Geoff hadn't.' She smiled at the thought of how innocent he had been at that first meeting, how she had needed to educate him in the rules of the elaborate rite of middle-aged encounters. Then her face twisted in pain as she realized anew that all of this was gone, that Geoff was gone, that she had to face the rest of her life without him. 'He didn't know anything about the pitfalls. I'd had one or two bad experiences before. I never advertised myself, but I responded to other people's entries. Geoff was the first person I met whom I felt I wanted to see more than a couple of times. We went to the theatre in Manchester for our first outing. Then later I gave him my address and we began to meet regularly.'

Blake was beset by a new sympathy for this woman left alone in the world, as she fought back the tears which threatened her anew. Blonde hair was the worst for grief, Lucy thought inconsequentially; it always seemed to become more easily dishevelled, and the fair colouring which went with it made it more difficult to disguise the ravages which anguish brought to a face. She reminded herself that Pam Williams was at present still a murder suspect, as she herself had reminded them at the outset.

DS Blake prompted encouragingly, 'Things obviously went well, because you were planning to get married.'

Pam glanced at her with a sudden fierceness, which was accentuated because her eyes, puffed with grief, were unnaturally narrowed. 'No. We hadn't got as far as that. I wanted to take it more slowly.'

Lucy Blake said gently, 'But he announced to everyone that you were getting married in his speech yesterday. I thought he must have discussed all that with you beforehand.'

Pam Williams shook her head with a surprising vigour.

'No. He hadn't done that. I wasn't pleased with him when he suddenly told all of you like that. I wanted more time to make sure that it was really the right thing to do. I wanted more time for the family to get used to me.'

It was Peach who took up that. 'The family didn't like the idea?'

'They didn't like me. They were suspicious of me. They found me threatening.'

She was plainly almost at the end of her resources. They could hear movements from her son, who was back in the hall beyond the closed door of this room. They couldn't prolong this much longer. Peach said quickly, 'One thing puzzles me, Mrs Williams. Mr Aspin's body wasn't discovered until this morning. That seems odd. I should have expected him to leave Marton Towers with you or one of his daughters, after yesterday's celebration was over.'

'He would have left with me. He should have left with me. But I was annoyed with him for what he had said about marriage in his speech. I flounced off and left him. You're telling me that he might be alive now if I hadn't, aren't you?'

Suddenly, she was sobbing uncontrollably, and Justin Williams was in the room, telling them that it must end here, that he wouldn't have her talking to them any more whilst she was in grief and in shock.

They apologized and took their leave, telling Mrs Williams that they would need to speak to her again in a few days, after they had spoken to other people involved. They left her weeping silently but uncontrollably, with her son's arm clasped awkwardly round her shoulders and her body held at an odd angle against his side.

Eleven

Superintendent Tucker was at his most officious. It was Monday morning and time to galvanize the troops.

'Have you made an arrest in the Geoffrey Aspin case yet, Peach?'

'No, sir. It's early days yet.'

'Negative attitude, Peach. Don't like that in my teams. A positive attitude is necessary for progress.'

'Yes, sir. DS Blake and I tried to remain positive whilst spending ten hours of our Sunday visiting the crime scene, setting up the investigation, and doing the first interviews. I hope the golf went well, sir.' Peach did not look at the chief's face; he chose to study intently a shallow but significant scratch across the back of Tucker's right hand; the man had obviously had an argument with the brambles. 'Driving still a little erratic, is it?'

'Never mind that. I hope you're not exploiting DS Blake because she is a woman.' Tucker, who had assigned Peach a female detective sergeant years earlier because he had been seeking to annoy him, was still blissfully unaware of the fact known to everyone else in his CID section, that the two were an item. 'There is no room for sexism in the modern police service, you know.'

'I do realize that, sir, yes. I seem to remember hearing that somewhere before, but thank you for the reminder.'

'So why haven't you got a killer yet? I told you yesterday that Mr Aspin was a prominent local businessman.'

'Yes, sir. Does that make his killer more obvious, or just give his murder a higher than normal priority?'

'Don't be insolent, Peach. I was merely reminding you that this is likely to become a high-profile case, with the reputation of Brunton CID on the line.' His chest barrelled a little behind his desk on that thought, a phenomenon which Peach stared at with some interest.

'Yes, sir. We've already seen the man's son-in-law. A man by the name of Jemal Bilic. A Turkish immigrant. Admits he had no great friendship with Mr Aspin.'

'Ah!' The Tucker prejudices, which Peach found fascinating to explore, surfaced in his voice. 'A likely candidate for the crime, wouldn't you say, Percy? Men of that background are always prone to violence.'

'Interesting you should say that, sir. Bilic struck DS Blake and me as a man capable of violence.'

'Well, there you are, then. First impressions can be very valuable, you know.'

'I see, sir. The snag is that Mr Bilic is himself a prominent local businessman. Probably a man of some influence in our community. But if you think we should pull him in and rough him up a little, I'm sure that your opinion will—'

'Peach, you must take no precipitate action! I've had occasion to warn you before about your tendency to jump to hasty conclusions.'

'I thought you said that first impressions could be very valuable, sir.' Peach was a picture of puzzlement.

'You really must learn to take a much wider view of the world. If this man Bilic is a local businessman, that in itself argues a certain respectability.'

Peach reflected that he had known several highly respectable killers in his time. He considered an excursion into crime among the Freemason fraternity, then decided that he must not waste too much time on this buffoon who was the figurehead of detection in the town. 'I shall of course keep you briefed on events as they develop, sir. No doubt we shall have need of your overview of things.'

'Yes, do that.' Tucker stirred uneasily behind the big desk. 'It is possible that I may not be around every day this week. I may need to take a day or two off as the weekend approaches.'

'Indeed, sir?'

Tucker had not intended to enlarge on his statement, but Peach's eyebrows, arching impossibly high towards the white dome of his bald head, were instruments which had broken stronger wills than his. 'You may have forgotten that I shall be away on duty this weekend.'

'No, I hadn't forgotten, sir. You're to be incarcerated in the nick at Nottingham, aren't you, sir?' His pleasure in the thought could scarcely have been more manifest if Tucker had been the Yorkshire Ripper.

'I shall be in the company of senior officers in the service. Many of them, indeed, will be more senior than myself.'

'You'll need to watch your back then, sir. Don't drop the soap in the showers is my advice! Ha ha!' Peach allowed himself a peal of artificial laughter, to show that he didn't consider the danger was serious.

Tucker glared at this misplaced and politically incorrect sally and decided it would be better not to react to it. 'I shall be representing Brunton in this experiment. Trying to raise our profile among important and influential people.'

Peach considered this novel idea. 'Wouldn't it raise it even more to solve a high-profile murder case, sir? I'm quite willing to surrender direct control of the investigation to you if you wish it, sir. My *amour propre* will not be wounded by such a move, sir.'

'Nonsense! I wouldn't hear of it. I shall demonstrate complete confidence in my team by leaving the matter in your capable hands, Percy.'

Peach sighed, noting with apprehension this second use of his forename. 'We shall do our best, sir. But without the pilot at the helm, who knows what will ensue?'

'I am planning to take a little leisure time to myself to compensate for being away at the weekend.'

'Mrs Tucker putting her foot down, is she, sir?' Peach divined correctly that the formidable Barbara Tucker, Brünnhilde in twin-set and pearls, had given a cold reception to the news that her spouse was to be absent at the weekend. For himself, Percy would have welcomed the absence of Thomas Bulstrode Tucker with an alleluia chorus of delight, but there was no pleasing some people.

'My wife has nothing to do with this. She is thoroughly behind me as always.'

'And as always you are well behind us, sir. We shall try

to muddle through without you. I shall offer the lads and lasses the picture of you slopping out in Nottingham as some sort of compensation.'

'Get about your business, Peach. I'm expecting rapid results, and a minimum of overtime hours for this investigation.'

'Your demands, as usual, sir, are modest and understanding. I shall relay to the team just how thoroughly I think you are behind us.'

Steve Hawksworth looked much less like a possible murderer than Jemal Bilic. He had a habitual diffident air about him and he was physically much less impressive than his brother-in-law. Where Bilic moved swiftly and gracefully, his lean frame carrying with it an air of menace, Hawksworth's thin limbs seemed less coordinated, more those of a man who sat at a desk for most of his day and didn't take exercise after it.

Like many another nervous person in the presence of Peach, he talked too much about trivialities, as if he felt silence itself might be a danger to him. 'Mr Robinson is away today. He kindly said that we could use his office for our meeting. We shall not be disturbed in here. It's much easier to talk to you at work than at home, as I said on the phone. The children might interrupt us there.'

He looked anxiously around the deserted room where the boss's secretary normally sat as he led them through it and into the office. Once there, he invited Peach to sit behind the antique mahogany desk. He himself sat in one of the two armchairs in the room, after settling Lucy Blake into the other one. When Peach brought the swivel chair out from behind the desk and positioned it opposite him, he looked aghast at this rearrangement of his superior's room, as if he feared that the absent Robinson might appear like a wrathful person from Porlock to disrupt the proceedings.

'Where do you want me to begin?' he said, again feeling the need to fill the silence which the DCI allowed to fall upon the room.

'I think you should give us your account of the latter part of Saturday's events. Take us up to the last time you saw

Mr Aspin. Then we shall no doubt have some questions for
you.' Peach made it sound as if the accountant were already
on trial and would need to be very careful with his words.

'I spoke at the end of the meal. It was I who proposed
the health of Geoff Aspin.'

DS Blake said, 'Yes. I heard you, because I was there, Mr
Hawksworth. I'm an old friend of your wife's from school
days. We were introduced to each other on Saturday afternoon, but you've forgotten that.'

'I do apologize. I was introduced to quite a few people
on Saturday. You're Louise's friend Lucy, aren't you? I
remember now. I'm afraid I was so nervous at the prospect
of speaking that I wasn't taking much in when we met.'

She smiled, wondering why she so often seemed to end
up playing soft-cop to Peach's hard-cop, when they had never
discussed any such tactic. 'So tell us how you saw things
evolve late on Saturday afternoon. I suggest you begin from
the end of your speech and the beginning of Geoffrey Aspin's
reply.'

Steve tried to concentrate on this gentler female face as
he strove to remember the phrases he had planned for this
moment; this friend of his wife's seemed altogether less
threatening, less sceptical, than that fierce male presence who
had positioned his chair to sit within four feet of him. 'Geoff
seemed pleased with what I'd said. But you've known him
longer than I have, DS Blake.'

'I hadn't seen him for ten years. I'd known him only as
my school friend's father when I was a rather immature
adolescent. You really knew him much better than I did at
the time of his death.' Lucy could sense Peach's annoyance
at the delay being occasioned by her own presence at
Saturday's meal.

'Well, Geoff seemed to be enjoying himself. I think he
wanted to surprise us and he certainly succeeded in doing
that. I don't think any of the family was prepared for his
announcement that he was going to marry the woman beside
him at the meal. I know for certain that Louise and I weren't.'

She wondered how significant it was that he hadn't even
used Pam Williams's name. She said, 'And do you think Mrs
Williams was prepared for it?'

'Oh, I should think so, wouldn't you? I think that lady must have known what was planned.' His voice took on an uncharacteristic waspishness when he spoke of the woman who had sat so quietly beside the man at the centre of the attention.

'I was a long way from the top table admittedly. But I got the impression that Pam Williams was surprised when Geoff said that he was going to marry her. However, you were sitting very near to these two people and apparently you recall things differently.'

'I was relieved to have my speech over. I'm afraid I was staring at the table linen and the glasses and not listening to the first part of Geoff's speech very closely. I don't recall looking at either his face or hers. But I'm sure she must have been aware of his intentions, even if she pretended to be surprised when he announced them.'

Blake nodded slowly. 'You would expect that, yes. I'm just saying that when Geoff said he was going to marry her she looked as surprised as the rest of us. Surprised and not particularly pleased, I'd have said. But that was just my impression from thirty yards away.'

Steve Hawksworth gave that thought his careful attention. Then he said slowly, 'Perhaps you're right. After all, you're trained in observation and I'm not.' He smiled awkwardly over this belated attempt at gallantry towards the woman he had at first failed to recognize. 'I'm just saying that I expect she knew what he was going to say, even if she chose to look surprised about it.'

Peach said a little impatiently, 'Well, we shall check your thoughts against those of other people. Tell us what happened after Mr Aspin had finished speaking.'

Steve nodded and took his time. He felt quite cool. There was no threat here: this was the kind of innocent detail he could relate competently enough. 'Well, there was a lot of noise over Geoff's announcement. There was shock, and then laughter, and then a lot of people wanted to shake his hand and congratulate him. I remember a lot of scraping of chairs, a lot of noise and confusion, and then things broke up pretty quickly.' He looked anxiously towards Lucy Blake for confirmation, but her head was down and she was making notes.

It was Peach who said, 'And no doubt the first people to congratulate him were those members of his immediate family who were sitting around him.'

Steve sensed a trap, as he was now prepared to do in everything this man asked. 'No. To be honest, we weren't pleased. I don't think you could say we were shocked, because obviously we knew that Geoff had been seeing Mrs Williams for a month or two. But we didn't know that it had got as serious as this. We weren't prepared for any announcement of his intentions on Saturday, or even in the immediate future. It certainly took Louise and me by surprise.'

Peach noted again that he was making a distinction from the others around that top table. Not a very close-knit family, this one. Another fact learned; another factor to bear in mind when he saw others. 'So what happened afterwards? You say you didn't add to the congratulations Mr Aspin was receiving from his friends. Did you in fact take up the matter with him?'

'I didn't. Neither did Louise.' The denials came promptly, perhaps a little too promptly. 'I would have chosen a less public occasion to discuss the matter with Geoff. So would my wife.'

'And what about your sister-in-law and her husband?'

'I can't speak for Carol and Jemal. I know they were dismayed and annoyed. They may have made their feelings known to Geoff.'

'But you don't know that they did.'

'No. There was a lot of confusion as things broke up, with the staff at the Towers moving in to clear the tables and almost a hundred people taking leave of Geoff, as well as congratulating him.'

'Tell us about the last time you saw Mr Aspin, please.'

He took a deep breath, determined to handle this carefully. 'I didn't so much see him as hear him, as a matter of fact. I was at the far end of the dining room for about ten minutes, I suppose, discussing with my wife what Geoff had said about remarrying and trying to come to terms with it. We'd come in separate cars, because Louise had stayed at home with the children until the last possible minute. She went out to her car whilst I went to thank the manager for the meal and all the other arrangements. By the time I was ready to leave myself, nearly everyone had gone. I didn't have a coat to collect – not many people did, because it was such a warm day. But I suddenly heard raised voices from the cloakrooms.'

'One of which was that of Mr Aspin.' Peach nodded affirmatively: it encouraged honesty in interviewees to let them know that you had other sources of information.

For a moment Steve Hawksworth looked disconcerted. 'Yes. I couldn't be absolutely sure about the other one. It was certainly female.'

'You say you couldn't be sure. That implies that you think you know who it was.'

'Yes. I think it was Pam Williams.'

'And what was the argument about? It was an argument, wasn't it?'

'Yes. It sounded a pretty fierce argument, in fact. But I'm afraid I couldn't tell you what it was about. I couldn't hear what was being said.'

'Not even the odd phrase? You say that emotions were running strong and voices were raised high.'

'Nothing at all, I'm afraid. The oak doors at Marton Towers are pretty thick, you know. And this one was firmly shut. In any case, I wasn't trying to listen to whatever was going on, because it was none of my business,' Hawksworth said primly.

'Pity you didn't have a little more natural curiosity, though.' Percy's sceptical smile said that he didn't believe this righteous figure would have suppressed his natural curiosity so completely. 'Especially now that we have a corpse on our hands. Obviously anyone having a quarrel with a murder victim very shortly before his death has to be of interest to us.'

'I suppose so, yes.' He looked anxiously towards the door, as if apprehensive that the fearsome Mr Robinson might wish to reclaim his office.

'What was your own relationship with the dead man, Mr Hawksworth?'

'We got on well.' He was aware that it sounded wooden. 'He was an understanding father-in-law. He'd been good to Louise and to me, over the years. He was a good grandfather to the children.'

There was something strained about this. They might find out more when they spoke to his wife. Though they'd hardly spoken about Geoff Aspin on Saturday, being more concerned with reminiscences of their turbulent youth, Lucy Blake thought now that Louise had been unnaturally guarded about her father and her present relationship with him.

Peach said bluntly, 'What were your own feelings about Mr Aspin's plans to marry Mrs Williams?'

'I hadn't really had time to consider all the implications before we got the shock news of his death.'

The answer had come out pat, and it was almost certainly false. Whatever the shock of Aspin's announcement over his final meal, the family had known there was a serious partnership developing. They must have been considering the implications for them of this new force in his life.

Peach allowed the silence to stretch, emphasizing the hollowness of what Hawksworth had said. For the first time, his interviewee did not feel compelled to break it. It was Peach who eventually said, 'Who benefits from this death, Mr Hawksworth?'

Steve was surprised at the curtness, even though by now he knew he should expect it from this man. 'I haven't even thought about that. I can't see that anyone will.'

'Someone must. Let me put it another way. Who would have been most affected if Mr Aspin had gone ahead and married Mrs Williams?'

'All of us. All of the family, I mean. None of us really wanted it to happen. But that doesn't mean we thought it would affect us in some material way.'

'Come, Mr Hawksworth. You're an accountant, and accountants are not in my experience naive. There are obvious financial implications in a second marriage like this. People with financial expectations would no doubt see a second Mrs Aspin as a threat to those.'

'I suppose so. But I'm sure none of us would have felt strongly enough to kill Geoff because of money.'

'Are you really? Our job makes us see the worst in human nature, I'm afraid. We tend to suspect people with financial motives, don't we, DS Blake?'

Blake allowed herself a thin smile. 'Someone did kill

Mr Aspin, Steve. Very probably someone in or around the family.'

'It could have been a business associate, I suppose. Someone quite outside the family.' Steve was pleased with himself for this late defiance.

Peach gave him a broad, totally unexpected smile. 'Indeed it could. Constructive thinking, Mr Hawksworth, and something we shall need to investigate. Go on thinking about this death, please, and see what else you can produce for us. Good day to you.'

He swept out of the boss's elegant office, leaving Steve Hawksworth feeling bludgeoned but relieved.

Twelve

Denis Oakley would have been considerably perturbed if he had heard Steve Hawksworth mention Geoffrey Aspin's business associates as possible killers or hirers of killers.

Oakley was the dead man's partner in the printing business which had made them both rich men. He had been the first man up to the top table at the end of Geoff's speech on that fateful Saturday, pumping his hand and congratulating him and Pam Williams on the marriage decision which had just been announced. It had been an instinctive response. It had also been the best way of concealing the turmoil which had beset his mind with this news.

Denis was a handsome man, a little shorter than Geoff, but with a plentiful head of hair, silvering impressively at his temples, a crinkly smile, humorous blue eyes, and the sort of profile which fascinated women. He had acquired ample evidence of this over the years; indeed, he was still collecting it. He was the sort of man who felt a continual need to test the fact that his ability to charm the other sex had not faded.

Denis had been married to his third wife for two years and was still paying generous marriage settlements to the first two. Three times he had declared to the world that he had found true love, whilst never mastering the elusive virtue of fidelity. Denis Oakley led himself and the women with whom he associated through a high-tariff emotional life.

Financially, he found himself perpetually walking a tight-rope, despite the success of the printing business founded and developed by himself and his long-time business partner.

He and Geoff Aspin had become close friends on their history degree course at Liverpool University, and once they had found that an arts degree gave you direct access to few careers beyond teaching, they set up in business together. They had chosen printing simply because Geoff had secured a student holiday job in a lithographic and printing works in Liverpool and thought he saw ways of making money from a modest local enterprise in that field.

It had all begun as something of a lark, but the harsh realities of commerce had quickly asserted themselves. Slightly to their own surprise, the two young men had proved themselves equal to these demands. In the early years, they had often worked twelve or fourteen hours a day to get their business off the ground. They were surprised as well as delighted to find how successful they were. What had begun as a modest enterprise in a single large, chaotic room behind a shop was from the outset a sturdy earner. Eventually it grew into one of the most successful businesses in Brunton, with nationwide clientele.

As the firm grew and flexed its wings, the two men who had been so close as twenty-one-year-olds moved steadily apart. Geoff was happy with his first wife Jill and his two daughters, so much so that Denis Oakley used to describe him as 'my tediously uxorious friend' to his succession of women friends. As the years advanced, Denis in contrast continued to play the female field with undiminished vigour and scant regard for bruising experiences, so that Geoff regarded him privately and tolerantly as 'my Labrador who escaped the op'.

In the first decade of the new century, the now affluent pair continued to work efficiently enough together, even though their social lives had long since diverged. They showed the sort of tolerance towards each other's lifestyles which derives from friendships made in the formative years of adolescence. But there was another, more concrete reason why the partnership survived; ergonomically, the two men's skills complemented each other.

Geoff Aspin was an excellent manager. He was continually conscious of the new skills he needed to bring in as the business grew. He was always ready to explore the new possibilities opened up by the revolutionary advances in printing over the last thirty years. He was also constantly aware of the needs and aspirations of his staff. Aspin and Oakley's company acquired the reputation of being a good place to work, which in turn ensured that the firm attracted talented and reliable staff.

Denis Oakley had proved to his own youthful surprise to be a natural salesman. Intensely aware of what the equipment in the factory could do and could not do, he had toured the country ceaselessly in search of orders. He was the chief agent in securing the contracts which gained the firm its first successes and then provided the profits to generate growth. It had been an exhilarating ride and Denis had enjoyed every minute of it. Sales had also fitted perfectly with the lifestyle he desired. His work demanded that he was constantly away from home, constantly meeting a succession of new people.

Whether or not modern sailors still have a girl in every port, the debonair and increasingly experienced Denis Oakley had women in most of the industrial centres of northern and midland England. Over the years, this was the source of much pleasure and much anguish both to them and to him.

On the morning after the revelation of Geoff Aspin's untimely death, the dead man's partner drove his big BMW through the drab industrial streets of Brunton to the new industrial estate, where the new Aspin and Oakley printing factory had been operating for the last two years. The staff there normally saw little of him, but today it was necessary to show the flag, rally the troops, and implement all the other energizing clichés which Denis had produced, as he had talked to his third wife over breakfast and nerved himself to the task.

The staff had never seen him look so solemn as when he came into the works in dark suit and tie and with head bowed. He accepted their commiserations on Aspin's death, then offered his own comfort and reassurance, particularly to the older employees, some of whom had known Geoff almost as long as he had. Denis was good with people, especially in passing encounters, and he knew it. Within an hour of his arrival, the staff knew that no one's job was at stake, that the business would be continued on the same lines as always, that any employee who wished to attend it would in due course be welcome at Geoffrey Aspin's funeral. Denis Oakley exuded confidence; those who came into contact with him found it both infectious and uplifting.

No one either on the shop floor or in the office divined that he was in fact extremely worried about his own future.

Denis encouraged all the senior office personnel to call him by his first name. It was modern industrial practice, he assured them expansively. If it had made the ways of the late and much respected Geoff Aspin seem slightly old-fashioned, that was certainly not his intention.

He was in Aspin's office when his former partner's PA put through the call to him. The bank manager expressed his condolences, probed a little about the circumstances of Aspin's death, received suitably conventional replies from Oakley. Then he moved on to more personal matters and began to ask searching questions. Denis's replies to his queries were delivered for the most part in uncharacteristic monosyllables.

At the end of the conversation, the bank manager's tone hardened to the one he used only rarely, when it was important that he should not be denied. 'I think you had better come in and see me, Mr Oakley. Bring any documents you think may be relevant. It had better be in the near future, please. I suggest some time later this week.'

Carol Bilic was very composed, for a daughter who had been informed of the death of her father only twenty-four hours earlier.

She was seven years older than her sister Louise. Lucy Blake, who had first met her as a mature twenty-two-year-old when she was herself a gawky schoolgirl of fifteen, had always found her intimidating. That hadn't mattered much, for during the next few years, when she and Louise had been very close, she had scarcely seen Carol, who had been determined to marry the darkly glamorous Jemal Bilic and leave the Aspin home. Now she thought for a moment that Carol was not even going to acknowledge any previous acquaintance. But, when Peach attempted to introduce her, Carol Bilic nodded and said curtly, 'DS Blake and I already know each other.'

Mrs Bilic was striking rather than beautiful, with very dark hair and eyes and a nose which was a little too large for perfection above a wide mouth. In her teenage years, Lucy had always thought of her as that favourite schoolgirl word 'sophisticated' and did so still. She was surprised to see the first crow's feet around Carol's eyes, and quickly divined that beneath the outward composure there was strain. Well, Lucy had seen enough of bereavement now to know that grief presented itself in many different ways.

If it was indeed grief that was responsible for this stress, she thought to herself bitchily.

Carol Bilic said, 'I understand that you have to ask these questions, but I shall be able to add nothing to what you already know.'

Peach nodded a few times, as if this opening scepticism was no more than he would have expected. Then he said suddenly, 'Why was your father left alone at the end of his party?'

Carol was shocked by the manner as well as the nature of the question. It was certainly not what she had expected as an opening. 'I don't know. I didn't realize that he had been, at the time.'

'It's an obvious question, isn't it? He was left at the mercy of whoever decided to kill him. You'd have expected other people to be with him, at the end of a day like that.'

'I suppose so.'

'Members of his immediate family in particular.'

'I suppose we all thought someone else would be with Dad. None of us was very pleased with what he'd just said in his speech.'

'Ah! I wasn't there, so you'll need to enlighten me. Was there any particular part of what Mr Aspin said which gave offence?'

She looked at him coldly. She wondered if this man was testing her, seeking to catch her out. 'He said he was going to marry that woman, didn't he? The two of them sprang it upon us in public, where they thought we'd not be able to do anything about it.'

'Perhaps someone did do something about it. Perhaps someone killed your father as a result of that sudden announcement. Do you think that is what happened?'

'I don't know, do I?' She heard her querulous tone, realized that she was losing her temper with this man and his quiet insolence. She looked straight at him and said slowly and emphatically, 'Let me make it clear that I've no idea why my father was killed. Nor have I any notion who might have killed him.'

Peach nodded slowly again, irritating her with the idea that she had said exactly what he expected her to say. 'How would you describe your own relationship with your father, Mrs Bilic?'

'We were affectionate towards each other, as you might expect a father and his eldest daughter to be.'

Peach gave her the smallest and most mirthless of his many smiles. 'That is hardly an answer, is it?'

'All right, we weren't as close as we used to be. Is that what you wanted to hear?'

'I want to hear the truth, Mrs Bilic.' He knew he was annoying her and was happy to do so. People who lost control revealed far more than those who remained calm.

She knew what he was doing as well as he did, but still she felt the anger welling within her. She could play the bereaved daughter and fall back on the sympathy that would bring, but that wasn't her way.

'Louise was always Dad's favourite.' She glanced at Lucy Blake with a flash of resentment. 'You should know that, from the old days. I don't think Dad ever really reconciled himself to my marrying Jemal. He opposed it at the time. He appeared to come to terms with it and they were civil enough with each other, but I don't believe Dad ever really accepted the situation.'

Carol wondered for a moment what her husband had said when he met this man who was so good at getting under your skin. Jemal wasn't good with people like this, wasn't used to coping with opposition. Well, Jemal would have to look after himself.

'Dad and I got on. He was a good grandfather to my two children. We didn't see as much of him as we'd have liked to in the last few years. And scarcely at all in the last three months, since he took up with this woman.'

'You obviously don't like Mrs Williams.'

It was her turn for a smile which had not an iota of humour. 'You divine things correctly, Chief Inspector.'

'And yet by your own account you scarcely knew her.'

'I knew enough. I knew she was after Dad's money.'

'How did you know that, Mrs Bilic?'

'It's obvious, isn't it? An older man, lured into a second marriage at sixty. A woman coming from nowhere and lining up a marriage within a couple of months. Don't be naive.'

'I hope I am not that, Mrs Bilic. It is not a good quality for a CID officer. Do you think that Mrs Williams was aware that your father was going to announce his wedding plans in his speech on Saturday?' asked Peach.

'I'm sure she was. Whatever she pretended then, whatever she tells you now, I can't believe that she didn't know all about it. I'm sure that she was delighted to hear the news being thrown into our faces.'

'Give us a detailed account of your own movements at the end of Saturday afternoon, please.'

He was telling her that she was a suspect for her own father's murder. That was no more than she had expected, but she still felt the blood pulsing in her temple at the thought. 'There was a lot of confusion at the end of the speeches. A crowd of people from the other tables gathered round Dad. They were shaking his hand and congratulating him; him and that woman together.' Carol still couldn't bring herself to call Pam Williams by her name; she knew that she was presenting herself in a bad light by this little shaft of spite, but she couldn't help it.

'Did these people include any of his immediate family?'

'No. None of us was pleased and we weren't going to pretend that we were. They were mostly his friends and business acquaintances.' People who knew nothing about the real situation and its implications, she found herself wanting to say. 'I remember Denis Oakley, Dad's business partner of many years, pushing his way through the crowd to him.'

'Did you speak to your father or to Mrs Williams?'

'No. It wasn't the moment for that. It was too public.'

Lucy Blake said gently, 'We need an account of your movements, Carol.'

Carol Bilic shot a swift, unguarded, molten look at the woman with her gold pen poised over her notebook, then composed her face into something more neutral. This was important and needed her full concentration. 'I watched the melee going on around Dad and the Williams woman for a couple of minutes. Then I looked for Jemal. I wanted to compare notes about what Dad had said, discuss what we were going to do about it.'

'And what did you decide?'

'Nothing. I didn't find my husband. I wandered about the cloakrooms, trying not to get too involved with all the people who wanted to speak to me, wanted to thank me for the day. But I couldn't find my husband. When I went out to the car park, I found that he'd gone.'

They might need to investigate this marriage if a prime suspect didn't emerge quickly. At the moment, they needed a clear account of the actions of the dead man's eldest daughter in the hours surrounding his death. Lucy prompted in her most neutral professional voice. 'That must have been inconvenient, to say the least.'

'It wasn't a problem. There were several friends going near to my house. I watched Dad for a few more minutes, decided I wasn't going to get near to him, and accepted a lift with one of them.' She looked at the rich chestnut hair bent over the notebook and said peevishly, 'I can give you her name and address, if you like.'

Lucy enjoyed giving her a bland smile. 'Please do.' She recorded the details unhurriedly and then said, 'So how long after the end of the speeches did you leave Marton Towers?'

'Twenty minutes, I should think. Perhaps twenty-five. After I'd heard Dad and his new woman having a shouting match with each other.' She hadn't wanted to introduce this herself, but she didn't want to let it go by.

It didn't produce the reaction she had hoped for. Peach merely continued studying her and the Blake woman did not even look up from her notes as she said, 'And what was this dispute about?'

'I don't know, do I? I didn't want any involvement in their sordid affair or their petty disputes.' She sensed they weren't going to believe that, but she delivered it vehemently and followed it with, 'My friends were waiting for me and I found I was anxious to be away from the place.'

Peach said abruptly, 'Who do you think killed your father, Mrs Bilic?'

'I don't know. If I have any useful thoughts on the matter, I'll be in touch. Don't hold your breath.'

Rather to her surprise, they left it at that. However, she had a feeling, which grew swiftly into a certainty, that they would be back.

Thirteen

Louise Hawksworth was much more affected by her father's death than her elder sister.

She had to hold herself together during the days, for the sake of her children, but during the short hours of darkness, she found herself unable to sleep and wracked by frequent, unpredictable bouts of weeping. For some reason, her husband seemed unable to comfort her.

Steve had always been a tower of strength in times of stress. She remembered that awful moment when they had been told that they were going to parent a child with Down's syndrome. As the doctor had taken them through the long-term implications of that simple fact, Steve had put his arm round her shoulders, pulled her to him, and convinced her by his loving strength that they were going to deal with this.

Yet through the Sunday which followed her father's death, he had been curiously distanced from her, so much so that in the evening she had tasked him with seeming cold. 'I'm sorry, love. I took the children out, got them out of your way for a while, didn't I? I suppose I thought that was the best way of dealing with your dad's death, to leave you some time to yourself for private grieving.'

It had made sense, she supposed. But now, a day later, he had come home from work and was still treating her as cautiously as if she were a stranger drawn into a tragedy by accident. Perhaps she needed to make more of an effort herself. While in the adjacent room the children were watching television as if nothing had happened, Louise raised a bleary smile and said, 'It was good of you to look after the children yesterday, while I was still trying to come to terms with Dad's death. I'm being selfish, as usual.'

'You're never selfish. But I have my own grief to deal

with too, you know. I was very fond of your dad. He'd been good to me over the years. He was planning to be good to me again, until . . .' His voice tailed awkwardly away. He should not have said so much. Now that he had, he did not know how to go on.

'Until bloody Pam Williams turned up, you mean, don't you?' The little flash of pique was a relief to her, after the long lethargy of her grief.

'I suppose so, yes. But this isn't the time to talk about that. I liked your dad a lot, as I said.'

She wondered why men found it so difficult to use the word 'love'. She nodded at Steve and said, 'You'd grown quite close over the years, hadn't you?'

'Yes. And I'd just been making the speech about all his virtues when he was . . . struck down.'

'Murdered, you mean. Let's have the proper word. "Struck down" sounds to me like natural causes.'

He glanced at her. 'You'd have suffered too. It would have affected your life if he'd gone ahead and married this Williams woman.'

'I suppose so. It's not something I want to think about at the moment.'

A pause. Then he said unexpectedly, 'You and he were never as close after the birth of Michael, were you?'

She looked at him sharply. 'I suppose not. But we'd got over all that. He was good to both of our children.' It sounded very lame and muted.

It had been a stilted conversation, not their usual spontaneous exchange. They continued in the same vein throughout that Monday evening, after the children had gone to bed. Almost as though they had been made strangers by this death, she thought.

At about ten o'clock, he said, 'The police will want to speak to you tomorrow, I should think. I'm surprised they weren't round here today. They don't seem to know much yet. They were all right with me. I don't think they'll give you any trouble, if you play it straight.'

She looked up at him from the magazine she had been unsuccessfully trying to read, struck by the nervous staccato manner of his speech. 'Why should I have any trouble?'

'No reason. You're just not used to being questioned by the police, are you? And you're still upset. They'll be regarding everyone as a suspect until they get things clearer. I just think you should be careful about what you say.'

Louise gave him a hard look, but he seemed determined not to catch her eye. She was too weary with shock and lack of sleep to argue with him.

She took two paracetemol tablets to try to get some sleep, but they did not work. She awoke after an hour or two of bizarre dreaming to find Steve lying with his back to her, on the other edge of the bed. She wanted his arm round her, his body firmly against the back of hers, as it usually was when she was upset about anything.

When you are wide awake at three o'clock in the morning, things in your life get wildly out of proportion and the mind plays strange tricks. Louise Hawksworth was suddenly seized by the notion that her husband had suspicions that the woman who shared his bed might have killed her own father.

Jemal Bilic looked at the two men with distaste. You needed to use men like this; they were no more than the tools of the trade. He knew that. But that didn't mean that you had to like it.

He said, 'You'll need to lie low, for the next week or two. I don't want you around.'

The slighter of the two was the man who did the thinking and the forward planning. 'We'll need to be in touch, Mr Bilic. There's another delivery due on Thursday. We'll need—'

'I know what you need. But you know the people who take delivery. Liaise with them, not with me. The machinery's in place, so just use it. I'll get in touch with you, when I think it's safe to do so. Safe for you, and for me.' They needed to be reminded that their own futures were at stake as well as his. The trade was lucrative for all of them, but there was no such thing as unthinking loyalty with men like this. The best you could hope for was to convince them that you had a common interest, that you survived or fell together.

The second man was more thickset, with an olive skin, an old scar on the back of his wrist, and a clipped black beard.

He said, 'We need you, boss. We need your direction.' He glanced sideways at the man beside him, aware that he was saying that he didn't really trust his judgement, wondering what the reaction to that would be.

Bilic said harshly, 'Look, I'm telling you what's going to happen, not discussing it. My father-in-law was killed on Saturday night. The police have already been sniffing around. They're going to come back. They won't leave us alone until they have an arrest.'

The squat man made a mistaken attempt at humour. 'Saw him off yourself, did you, boss?'

The mirth died in his throat. Bilic seized the front of the thug's collar almost before he had finished the question, his steely grip stopping the breath in the throat of even this powerful man. 'Don't even think that, let alone say it! One more crack like that and you'll be back in the gutter where I found you! Understood?'

'Understood, boss. I didn't mean no 'arm, 'onest!' The heavy man raised his powerful forearms, then thought better of laying his hands upon this dangerous, unpredictable employer.

Jemal Bilic held the throat of the coarse shirt for seconds more before he released him, twisting his grip so that the man was struggling to breathe, fastening his own dark pupils on the suddenly alarmed eyes beneath them, enjoying the feel of raw physical power in his fingers. He relaxed his grip slowly, as if reluctant to let the rough fabric slip from his grasp. He looked at the other man, the man who would need to control the mouth as well as the limbs of this oaf. 'Aspin's death had no connection with what we do. But it's brought the law sniffing around, as I said. We need to be careful. That means all of us.'

The bearded man made the right noises, assured Bilic that he knew what the score was, that he wouldn't be in touch with the man who controlled things until he knew that it was safe to contact him again. Jemal realized that this man had picked up some of his own anxiety, which was a bad thing. Nervous hirelings tended to panic when you withdrew direct control.

He gave them a few words of reassurance, reminded them

how rewarding this trade was for all of them, how worthwhile it was for them to be cautious for a while. He dismissed
them, then stood frowning at the door through which they
had disappeared

That was one of the disadvantages of what he did. You
needed scum like that to operate this racket.

Louise Hawksworth received the expected phone call at nine
o'clock. It was in the comforting, apologetic tones of her
old friend Lucy Blake. 'We need to speak to you, I'm afraid.
I know you must still be very upset, but we can't really put
it off any longer.'

'You've already spoken to Steve.' Louise didn't know why
she said that.

'We have indeed. And to lots of other people as well. But
we need to speak to everyone in the family. It's routine procedure, as you probably realize. I'm afraid we need to see you
today. When would be convenient?'

'This morning. As soon as you like. Daisy's at school and
Michael's at the care centre. We won't be disturbed.' She
rang off before Lucy could go into the clichés of sympathy.
She needed to prepare for this.

When they came, there were two of them, which she
somehow expected. But neither of them was Lucy Blake.
She hadn't anticipated that; she felt a thrill of fear as she
saw the two men on her doorstep.

The smaller of the two, who seemed full of a bouncy
energy beneath his surface politeness, said that he was
Detective Chief Inspector Peach, the man in charge of this
investigation. The young black man beside him was tall and
lean, with a neatly trimmed beard. The DCI introduced him
as Detective Constable Northcott. Perhaps Peach had seen
the apprehension in her face, for he explained that it was not
appropriate for Detective Sergeant Lucy Blake to be involved
in this interview, because of her previous close friendship
with Louise.

They took her through the routine stuff about Saturday's
gathering, about Steve's speech proposing the health of her
father, about what her dad had said in his reply.

Then Peach said, 'Other people were apparently unprepared

for Mr Aspin's announcement that he intended to marry Mrs Williams. Did it come as a surprise to you?'

'Yes, it did. I suppose we – the family, that is – realized that the affair was getting serious. I don't think anyone thought it had moved as far as marriage. I would have expected Dad to discuss it with us beforehand, rather than just announce it like that to the world at large.'

She wondered how much of her resentment had come out as she said that. You couldn't watch yourself from the edge of the room, couldn't even hear clearly exactly how you were speaking. Peach looked hard at her for a moment and then said, 'Do you like Mrs Williams?'

She had not prepared herself for anything as blunt as this. Yet she knew now that she should have expected it, from policemen. She glanced at the impassive, unrevealing features of the tall man beside Peach, who was watching her and making the odd note. But mainly watching her, it seemed.

Louise said carefully, 'I hardly knew her. Dad kept her to himself. None of us has really seen much of her.'

'And yet you all seem to dislike her quite fiercely.'

She was going to spring into a denial, but she stopped just in time. They'd talked to a lot of other people as both DCI Peach and Lucy Blake had already reminded her. There was no knowing what the others had said.

She forced a wintry smile and said, 'I suppose we resented her presence, rather than disliked her personally. She'd come unexpectedly into Dad's life, when we'd rather anticipated that he wouldn't get himself into any serious partnership again. We'd really no right to think that things would be that way, but I suppose we all knew how close he'd been to Mum and thought that he wouldn't want another wife.' She looked at the two unresponsive male faces and said a little desperately, 'You'd expect daughters who'd been very close to their mother to resent someone coming into her place, wouldn't you?'

Peach answered her little smile with a broader one of his own. 'We learn to expect nothing in CID work, Mrs Hawksworth. We have to establish the situation by talking to people. Lots of people, with many different viewpoints.' He made that sound like a warning.

'I suppose so. Pam Williams seemed like a money-grabbing harpy to us, but you can hardly expect us to be unbiased, can you?'

He left her nervous question hanging in the air for a moment. Then he picked up her adjective and mused upon it. '"Money-grabbing", you say. That made her a financial as well as an emotional threat to you, didn't it? And policemen are sordid creatures – they have to be interested in money. It's part of the job, you see. Your father was a rich man.'

'Yes. He'd worked hard and long for that.'

'I'm sure he had. And you and others saw Mrs Williams arriving unexpectedly on the scene and taking your father's money away from you. I see that.'

She was suddenly full of rage. Rage at this blunt, round-faced bald man, who wrapped up nothing and seemed to enjoy insulting her; rage at herself for inviting this line of questioning by her own thoughtless phrase. She flushed and said, 'I think we all had plans of different sorts. Plans we thought might be disrupted by a second wife for Dad.'

'Have you any evidence that Mrs Williams was planning to spend your father's money on her own schemes?'

'No. It wasn't like that. There was nothing as definite as that. But we all know of cases where a woman has come along and taken a rich older man for a ride. I expect you come across them yourself in your work.' She waited for a reaction, but Peach's hitherto mobile features became suddenly still.

The man at his side spoke for the first time, his voice deep but unexpectedly soft from so uncompromising a face. 'It is the opinion of your friend DS Blake that you were closer than anyone to your father. Would you agree with that?' he asked.

She hadn't expected this. Lucy didn't know what had gone on in the last few years. Couldn't know, if she'd told them this.

Louise Hawksworth spoke carefully. 'I suppose you could say that. I'm not saying my dad didn't like Carol, mind. But they say dads always favour the baby of their family, don't they? He and I were always very close when I was growing up.'

'But not so close recently.' Peach was back in, sensing a hint of weakness here. He made it sound like a statement rather than a question.

Louise wondered furiously what Steve had said to him. If only the fool hadn't been so distant with her on Sunday and Monday, she'd have known exactly what he'd told them.

She tried to sound as confident as she could. 'When you move away from home and start a family, you have your own life to lead. We probably weren't as close as we were when I was young and we were living under the same roof, but close enough. As close as most fathers and daughters, I'd say.'

Peach was sure that there was something here, but it was too sensitive an area for him to probe any further with a bereaved daughter. He said quietly, 'Who do you think killed your father, Mrs Hawksworth? You must have given it some thought in the two and a half days since it happened.'

Louise felt an absurd urge to tell him that her husband thought she might have done this unthinkable thing, to laugh in his face at the absurdity of the idea. She must be nearer than she'd thought to hysteria. She said, with a flash of resentment, 'I don't know, do I? I'm just as baffled as you seem to be!'

Peach gave no sign of annoyance. He glanced at the man beside him and said, 'Is there anything else you wish to ask Mrs Hawksworth at this stage, DC Northcott?'

Again that soft voice came unexpectedly from the forbidding constable. 'We need an account of your movements at the conclusion of Saturday's celebration, Mrs Hawksworth.'

They wanted to know what she was doing at the time of the killing. She was a murder suspect after all, a woman who might have killed the father to whom she had just claimed to be very close. Patricide, that was the word; pedantry seized her when she least expected it. 'I tried to get to Dad, but there was a big crowd around him. To be honest, I wanted to give him a piece of my mind about what he'd just said about him and Mrs Williams. But I saw there was no chance of getting near him or having a private word. I wandered about a little, hoping to talk to Carol, my elder sister, to see what she thought about it.'

'Did you speak to her?'

'No. I couldn't find her. So I went out to my car and drove home. I wanted to get back to the children. They were in good hands, but I'd been away for over four hours, and Michael tends to get agitated if I'm away for too long. It's not easy to make him understand things like time.' For a moment, her face was full of a tenderness they had not seen in it before.

Northcott made a note and nodded. 'Your husband didn't go with you?'

'No. Steve had his own car. I'd left as late as possible because of the children.'

'So what time did he arrive home?'

'About an hour after me, I think. Probably about eight o'clock. I can't be certain. We didn't know such things were important at the time.' For a moment, her face crumpled towards tears, but she recovered and turned it into an apologetic smile.

'Did he say what he'd been doing?'

She couldn't believe it. They were treating her mild, unassertive Steve as a murder suspect. It must be just the routine they went through, as Lucy Blake had told her. 'I think he'd been waiting to speak to Dad, but he hadn't managed it either. Oh, and he said he'd talked to the catering manager at Marton Towers. Thanked him for an excellent meal and good organization, that sort of thing.'

'Did either of you go out again during the evening?'

'No, I don't think so. The children were up later than usual. They were overexcited and took a bit of calming down. It took me quite some time to get them into bed and give them a story. After that, there wasn't much time left before we went to bed ourselves. It had been a tiring day.'

He made a few notes and then Peach told her that she must get in touch with the number on the card he gave her if anything which might have a bearing on this crime occurred to her. Anything she said would be treated in confidence, but she shouldn't hesitate to convey any thoughts she had, however minor or unlikely their connection with the death might seem.

And then they were gone. She watched them move swiftly down the drive and into their car. Only when it had turned the corner and disappeared from view did she fall to wondering whether it would have been technically possible for Steve to kill her father.

It was a preposterous line of thought, of course, but those two had encouraged her to think of even the most unlikely scenarios.

John Kirkby had now spent three days beside the vivid blue waters of Lake Garda. They had been the days of unwinding which the private detective had promised himself, the necessary prelude to the proper enjoyment of the remaining days of his holiday. The unwinding hadn't really happened. He wasn't really a holiday person, he concluded glumly.

His wife seemed to be enjoying herself, so that was good. He painted a dutiful smile upon his face whenever she was around, which was most of the time. If he felt that his proper metier was the grimy back streets of northern towns, his proper climate the grey drizzle of Lancashire and Yorkshire, he kept such thoughts to himself when Kate was around. He strove to find good things in the bright Italian landscape, but he noticed that his approbation consisted mainly of agreement with his wife's enthusiastic commentary.

He found the brilliant clear light the most alien thing of all. This was an artist's light, their tour representative informed them enthusiastically, particularly appreciated by the painters of the nineteenth and twentieth centuries, available in England only in places like St Ives in Cornwall. John felt unnaturally exposed in it. In so far as he appreciated art at all, John Kirkby was a Dutch interiors man, relishing the subtle tones of those men who had suggested darker secrets beneath the modest surface comforts they portrayed.

Today was Tuesday and Kate had booked them a half-day cruise upon the lake, with a stop at a village on the far side. Once away from the shore, the light seemed to John even more brilliant, as the sun sparkled upon waters which were ruffled by the gentlest and warmest of breezes. John nodded his approval of his wife's eulogies about lake and mountains, even contriving to point out with some enthusiasm the contrasting effect of the one patch of shadow on the hillside with the wisps of white cloud slowly dissipating above it.

Having done his duty, Kirkby left his wife with a cappuccino and retired to the shaded side of the vessel. Mustn't get
too much sun, he explained. He listened to the desultory
conversation of his fellow trippers on the boat and found
that it was not illuminating. He gazed over the azure waters,
shut out the meaningless chatter from his ears, and wondered
what the weather was like in Brunton.

When they toured the narrow streets of the tourist village,
John found a brief animation in preventing his wife from
purchasing the trinkets which the salesmen and their women
pushed at them so insistently. Kate admitted that these things
were mostly rubbish, but maintained nevertheless that she
was towing along a husband without a soul. When he questioned the logic of this reasoning, she told him with an air
of secret knowledge that he was not a woman.

They lunched on pasta and some Italian minced concoction
which John had never heard of. He found it unexpectedly
palatable, even tasty, and was slightly and secretly disappointed. It went rather well with the Chianti, and Kate saw to
it that her husband had more than his share of that.

John Kirkby quite enjoyed the sail back to their resort.
The sun was much lower in the sky by now. The lake was
a deeper blue and the hills beyond it were bathed in a gentle,
old masters' light, which was much more to his taste than
the noonday dazzle. He could see their hotel as they moved
nearer to the land; in another hour, he would be donning the
jacket and tie he still insisted upon for dinner.

The boat emptied rapidly when they berthed. After hours
of enforced inactivity, the crowd of trippers melted quickly
and noisily away to their evening concerns. Kirkby did not
join in this hasty debarkation. He waited until even his wife
had joined the stragglers at the end of the queue before he
moved from his seat. He was always interested in detritus.
What people left behind them could be more revealing than
they ever realized.

There was a lot of rubbish left behind: the passengers on
the boat trip had been mainly British. Kirkby shot a swift
glance at his wife's unconscious back, then selected an
English copy of *The Times*, which had been discarded on a
saloon bench by its departing owner. He rolled it tightly,

but it was impossible to conceal it from the disapproving Kate.

'Thought you might want to read the accounts of the finals at Wimbledon,' he said optimistically. 'And I can check on what's happening in the cricket.' He slapped the paper energetically against his thigh.

It was in the privacy of the en suite bathroom that he discovered why Geoffrey Aspin had not phoned him as promised. A single paragraph in the home news section told him that the body of this 'prominent industrialist' had been discovered after a celebration of his sixtieth birthday in a local stately home. Foul play was suspected and a police hunt was under way.

John Kirkby was a man not easily shocked. But he was stunned for a moment by this. Then he thought of the implications for himself. His first thought was that he might never be paid in full for the commission Aspin had given him. Then other and wider considerations took over. He was an ex-copper and old habits die hard. He knew what he had to do.

He decided not to tell his wife. Kate would not welcome evidence that his thoughts lay still at home. Moreover, he felt a genuine desire not to spoil a holiday she deserved and was obviously enjoying.

He waited until his wife was in bed and reading her detective novel before he looked up from his own book and said, 'I don't feel at all sleepy tonight, love.' He walked across to the window and drew aside the thin cotton curtains. 'It's a beautiful warm night. I think I might just go out for a breath of air and see the stars over the mountains.'

Kate yawned. 'If you'd said that an hour ago, I'd probably have come with you.' But she was glad that at last he seemed to want to get the full value from his holiday. 'Don't be too long. I'll get on with my book.'

Kirkby moved out of the shadow of the hotel, down to where he could hear the water lapping gently against the shore of the lake. This is where he would get the best signal. He looked at his watch. There was an hour difference in time: it would still be only nine thirty in Britain. He pictured the police station, quiet on a Tuesday evening, with only a skeleton staff. With a murder inquiry in train, he would still get their attention. He checked the number on the pad of his mobile phone, then tapped in the international code and the number.

'My name is John Kirkby. I run a private detective agency in Brunton.'

Some of the people at Brunton nick knew him. This one didn't. He said, with the air of a man repeating words he had spoken many times, 'Unless you have evidence of a crime being committed or urgent information, sir, you should contact the station in the morning. We have only a skeleton staff here at the moment, so unless you require urgent police assistance—'

'It's about the murder inquiry. The Geoffrey Aspin case. I was working for Mr Aspin at the time of his death.'

There was a pause. He could almost hear the cogs turning in the trained machine which was the brain of the desk sergeant. Then the voice said rather breathily, 'Detective Chief Inspector Peach is handling this investigation. What is it you have to report?'

John Kirkby was too fly a bird for this. There might be profit, or at the very least kudos, in this for him. There might even be a lucrative story for him to sell to the press if he played his cards right. 'I am at present on holiday in Italy. My own work for Mr Aspin may or may not be connected with this case. Please inform DCI Peach that I shall contact him as soon as I return to the UK. I shall be home by the weekend. Goodnight, Sergeant.'

Fourteen

Denis Oakley decided to see his CID visitors at the factory. He was not getting on well with his third wife and there was no knowing quite what she would say if they questioned him about his recent difficulties. The works of the new industrial estate would provide a more neutral environment for what he hoped would be no more than a routine exchange.

He set up his dead partner's room for the meeting, and marvelled again at how different Geoff had been from him. The attraction of opposites was a dubious concept in marriage, as far as Geoff was concerned, but it certainly seemed to have worked for them in business. Geoff had provided consistency, as well as the reassurance for the staff who worked here, whilst his own more maverick temperament had been ideal for the variety of situations he had met in the wider world outside.

This room retained something of the personality of the man who had used it. Behind an antique mahogany desk there was a matching round-backed chair; Denis would have had a lighter modern wood. Pictures of the Lake District and Scottish sea lochs adorned the walls; Denis would have had more colourful and less representational art. But it was an appropriate place to meet the police, he decided. They would surely be impressed by the way Geoff's office exuded success and old-fashioned values.

He was pleased to find that the plain-clothes chief inspector who was conducting the case was accompanied by a young and attractive woman in a dark green sweater and trousers. Plainly the police service had improved since he and Geoff had spent a night with them as drunken students forty years ago. The woman had remarkable dark-red hair;

she was introduced to him as DS Blake and Denis gave her his practised introductory smile. He congratulated himself upon his decision to conduct this exchange here: it might have rather cramped his style if that touchy wife of his had seen him exercising his charms.

As Peach took him through the early part of Saturday afternoon, he answered easily enough, amplifying his account a couple of times as he smiled at the woman making notes. Then the DCI said, 'I understand you were the first man to make contact with Mr Aspin at the conclusion of his speech.'

'One of the first, anyway. I was happy that my old friend was taking the plunge into matrimony again. I didn't think the old stick-in-the-mud had it in him. I think that's what I said to him as I shook his hand. Words to that effect, anyway.' He grinned deprecatingly at Lucy Blake, who raised her eyebrows minimally and then made a note. Peach had taught her lots of things over the last three years; the use of the eyebrows was one of the most unlikely of them.

'When was the last time you saw Mr Aspin?'

'That was virtually the moment we've just been talking about. I joshed him a little, gave a chaste kiss of congratulation to his future wife, and left him to it. He had a lot of people around him at the time and I'd said my piece.'

'Did you see any of his family talking to him after the speeches were over?'

'Do you know, I don't think I did? Curious that, isn't it? I expect they'd offered their congratulations beforehand.'

'Do you, indeed? Have you any reason for that opinion?'

He couldn't understand why this man Peach should seem so hostile to him. Perhaps he was like that with everyone; perhaps it was a CID technique. 'No, I haven't actually. I haven't really thought about it until this moment.'

'Really. That seems a little odd. Especially as you've no doubt been thinking about who killed your partner. Any ideas, Mr Oakley?'

'I've thought about it, as you suggest. I haven't come up with any answers, or I'd have been in touch with you. You have the advantage of having a large team of officers to help you.'

'And you have the advantage of previous knowledge of

the deceased over many years. Knowledge of his friends and his enemies, of the exact state of his business, of who might gain from Mr Aspin's death. Areas where we were in total ignorance when we began this investigation on Sunday.'

Denis didn't like the implication that they were not so ignorant now. He tried to sound calm and objective as he said, 'I suppose what you say is true. I – I can only think that it will be someone in his family who turns out to have done this. They were the people who were going to be most immediately affected by Geoff's plans, weren't they?'

'They are patently the people who seem most threatened by a second marriage for Mr Aspin, yes. How will this death affect your business, Mr Oakley?'

He was shaken by this sudden switch, when he had been expecting the opportunity to enlarge upon the family's motives. He smiled the practised, open smile he had developed for customers who threatened him with a switch to another printing company. Don't look threatened. Don't allow them even to suspect that this matter is of great importance to you. You're used to being out there in the world on your own; you're even used to fighting battles with little more than your wits as weapons. And in the field of commerce, you know far more than policemen moving out of their depth do. Take a deep breath and baffle them with science.

'It will be business as usual. I assured the staff of that at the earliest opportunity. No one's job is at risk. Aspin and Oakley's is a long-established firm. No one should pretend that the loss of a man of Geoff's talents and vast experience isn't a blow, but it is one which can and will be handled. It's early days yet, and I shall be speaking to senior staff later this week. My own thoughts are that I should continue as Sales Manager, doing exactly the work I have done over the last few years, whilst we appoint a works manager here to fill the void left by—'

'What are the personal implications of this death for you, Mr Oakley?'

Peach cut through the verbiage more incisively than any hostile client Denis had dealt with. He found himself struggling with decisions about his facial expression, when he should have been thinking furiously about his reply. He removed the smile: that was no longer appropriate, when talking about the death of his friend. But he did not want to look worried and send out totally the wrong message. He tried to look grave but untroubled, and found that combination very difficult. 'It will mean more work, I suppose. That is inevitable, at least until a new manager is securely in place. I shall have to take more executive decisions: I was used to discussing everything with Geoff and it will seem strange to—'

'What are the financial implications for you, Mr Oakley?'

Now he had to look puzzled rather than apprehensive. One part of his brain told him that they couldn't know anything about his difficulties, another that the huge team of officers assembled for a murder inquiry would be delving into the backgrounds of the people who had been closest to the victim. 'I can't see any immediate effects. We shall have to make sure that the business continues to run effectively, as I've already indicated, but—'

'Mr Aspin was a man with a long-established local reputation. Financial institutions often have their confidence shaken by the death of a prominent figure. It may be regrettable and unfair for those who have to continue running the business, but one sees it happen, even with major stock market companies.'

Denis wondered who had put this objectionable and aggressive man up to such thoughts. He forced a smile and said, 'Aspin and Oakley's is not in that league, you know. We don't have a stock market price to consider. Geoff was a great man to have beside you, but hardly a—'

'You never became a limited company, did you, Mr Oakley?'

They'd done some research. The problem was that he didn't know exactly how much. He parried the blow. 'We never thought it necessary. We are essentially a small local business which has become more successful than we ever imagined it would be when we set out.'

'And as that sort of business, you are more vulnerable. It is more likely that you will be adversely affected financially by the death of your partner. Is that the case here?'

'No. The effects of Geoff's passing are personal and administrative. I see no severe financial implications for me.'

He watched the woman he had tried to charm making notes, wondered exactly how she was recording his replies. As if she sensed his scrutiny, she looked up suddenly and said with the same sort of false brightness he had earlier essayed himself, 'So who do you think killed your friend, Mr Oakley?'

He smiled at her, bathing her in charm, automatically trying to establish some sort of relationship. 'I've really no idea, you know. As I said, I'd have to put my money on one of the family, if you pressed me. I expect you think the same. But I've no notion which one. I'll leave that to you.'

She looked at him steadily for a moment, as if making an assessment of his reliability, then gave him a curt nod.

Peach asked him a few more questions about his where-abouts on Saturday evening. He was glad for once that he hadn't spent the night in a strange bed. Then they were on their way, with a final warning that they might need to speak to him again when they knew more. He hoped that was no more than routine.

He rang the bank manager as soon as they were safely off the premises. 'I'll come in for that meeting you requested tomorrow, if you can fit me in,' he said as lightly as he could. It was always good to take the initiative in these things, even when you knew you had no choice. They fixed a time of nine thirty. Then he said as casually as he could, 'I've just had the police here, talking about poor Geoff's death. They haven't spoken to you, have they?'

There seemed to him quite a pause before the calm voice on the other end of the phone said, 'No. No one has approached me yet.'

Denis Oakley tried for the rest of the day to forget the little word at the end of that sentence.

'The full post-mortem report's in.' Detective Constable Brendan Murphy bustled in with the printout from the computer on which he was collating the accruing evidence in the Aspin case.

'I don't expect it will tell us anything we don't already know.' Lucy Blake spoke with professional pessimism: never expect too much from the forensic people, then you won't be disappointed. She summoned Peach on the internal phone and he came swiftly into the section of the CID area which they had set aside for this juicy local crime.

Lucy Blake was almost right: most of the information in the twelve-hundred-word report was what they already knew or would have expected. The deceased had been in excellent health for a man of sixty years, with no sign of major illness anywhere in the organs of his body. Death had come swiftly and almost certainly unexpectedly, because there were only minimal traces of a struggle.

There was a little skin tissue under the corpse's nails, but it was his own skin. In the guarded words of scientists who knew that their words might eventually be quoted and dissected by clever lawyers in court, this was commensurate with the victim having lifted his hands to his own throat in an attempt to dislodge the ligature which was ending his life.

Even hardened police officers paused for a moment on that, picturing the scene disguised by the formal wording of the report: a man surprised from behind, perhaps by a killer he knew but never even saw, struggling desperately but hopelessly as a crowded and previously happy day ended in brief agony and then the oblivion of death.

The instrument of that death was almost certainly some sort of steel-cored cable, probably plastic rather than fabric coated, since there were no fibres evident around the striations on the neck. The nature of the fatal wound, with the cord biting deeply into the front of the neck and crushing the carotid artery, suggested that the victim had been taken from behind, or possibly from the side, with the assailant twisting and tightening the cord at the back of the neck to garrotte the victim. His or her victim, the report indicated: due to the manner of this death and the element of surprise, no great strength had been needed. This killing could have been committed by a woman, or even a child of ten years and upwards, the report stated impersonally and unhelpfully.

The one helpful and revealing piece of information came towards the end of the report, in the section about stomach contents. It provided the answer to one of the mysteries within a mystery which had been puzzling Peach and his team: how had someone contrived to kill Aspin in the blazing sunlight of early evening, at the time of the year when the days were at their longest, without being seen by anyone?

Because they are always conscious of the possibility of cross-examination in a crown court, pathologists are notoriously cautious about times of death. In this case the report went against the trend. Because they knew exactly what Geoffrey Aspin had eaten for his last meal and at precisely what time, it was possible to deduce more than usual from the digestive stages the food had reached in this corpse.

That enabled them to place the time of this death with some confidence at between ten p.m. and midnight on the night of Saturday, the thirtieth of June. It seemed that the victim had been lured back to Marton Towers and dispatched in a deserted car park under cover of darkness.

Fifteen

Pam Williams looked and felt much more composed than when she had been required to confront the CID on the day after Geoffrey Aspin's death.

As she ushered them into the same room in the semi-detached house where she had seen them three days earlier, DS Lucy Blake tried a little of the social interchange which DCI Peach rarely chose to use. 'I hope we didn't cut short your stay with your son in Leeds.'

Pam gave the woman a small smile from beneath her now neatly coiffured blonde hair. 'I came home on Monday night. A day with Justin and his wife was long enough. They meant well and treated me with careful kindness.' She stopped for a minute, weighing that phrase and finding it apposite. 'I came away whilst they could still resist telling me that they'd always known my association with Geoff Aspin would end in tears.'

'They didn't approve of your relationship with Mr Aspin?'

She sighed, trying not to resent the youth and looks of this woman who had the kind of career she would have loved for herself. 'No one seems to have approved of it. Not those closest to us, anyway. The response from friends of our own age was generally, "Good on yer, go for it. You've both got a long time to live yet, so make the most of it." Our families, on the other hand, seemed to think we should retire into quasi-monastic seclusion. But they're of a different generation. You can't expect the young to see things the way you do.' She looked directly and accusingly at this girl with the dark red hair and the aquamarine eyes, as if she was accusing her of joining the conspiracy of youth against her.

They stared at each other for a second or two. Then Blake said quietly, 'I expect your children had their own agendas

and saw your plan to marry Mr Aspin as a threat to them.
I'm not saying they're right, of course, just that—'

'I had no plan to marry Geoff.'

'Everyone we've spoken to seems to think that—'

'They can think what they like. I'm telling you the facts.
I had made no plan to marry Geoff. I was as surprised as
anyone else when he blithely stood up and announced that
we were to be wed.'

Still she looked directly at Blake, as if the younger woman's
very presence here was a challenge to her. But it was Percy
Peach who said harshly, 'So what exactly was the nature of
your association with our murder victim, Mrs Williams? If
you didn't intend to marry him, what was going to happen?'

She looked at the stern round face with its moustache and
eyebrows which seemed even blacker beneath the shining bald
head. She wondered why she felt less threatened and less
angered by this forbidding figure than by the woman with the
looks and the notebook. 'I'm sorry. I'm giving you the wrong
impression. I said that I had no plan to marry Geoff. That
doesn't mean that I was against the idea altogether. It's just
that Geoff was making all the running, pushing things along.
Pushing them along too fast for me. I wanted time for our
families – well, in particular, his family, if I'm honest about
it – to come to terms with the new situation. Perhaps I wanted
a little longer for me to get used to it, too.'

'So you weren't against marrying Mr Aspin. Indeed, you
saw it as a logical development for the two of you.'

'Yes, I'm sure I did. But I didn't see the timetable as he
did. Or apparently did. I hadn't even an inkling that he was
going to stand up on Saturday and announce that we were
getting married. It's my view that he didn't even know that
he was going to say it himself when he stood up to speak.
I think he was carried away by the excitement of the occasion and lost his normal balance.'

Peach mused for a moment on this version of Saturday's
events, not troubling to disguise his train of thought from
her. This was a very different version from what others had
given them, but those others had been proceeding from sup-
position, not knowledge. The only man who could give them
the definitive version of these events was a corpse in cold

storage at the morgue. 'You had a serious disagreement with Mr Aspin in the cloakroom after most people had left Marton Towers.'

She gave him a wry smile. 'We had a blazing row, if that's what you mean by "a serious disagreement".'

'And what was that about?'

'About what he'd just said. I was furious with him. I told him that he'd just treated me as if I was some nineteenth-century woman who wasn't entitled to have opinions and a will of her own. That he seemed to assume that I was a pathetic, desperate female who was supposed to be grateful for his announcement and fall upon her knees in gratitude.'

'Had he not even discussed marriage with you?'

'I suppose you could say there was an assumption on both our parts that it would happen in due course. We both knew that it was going to be a serious partnership, so marriage was the logical outcome for us. We're not from the generation that just shacks up together and sees what will happen.' She shot an involuntary, hostile glance at Lucy Blake.

Peach regarded her steadily. 'What you're saying is that you objected to the timing of the announcement?'

'I wouldn't have thought the timing wise anyway. Geoff knew his daughters and their husbands were against it. He should have given himself time to win them round, or at least to allow them to reconcile themselves to the idea that it was going to happen. I objected mostly to a public announcement when he had not even discussed the idea with me.'

'Have you met the family?'

'I've only seen Geoff's elder daughter Carol very briefly, and her husband not at all. We spent an hour or two with the younger daughter, Louise, and her husband, Steve. They were guarded and cautious with me, but I can understand that. They seemed reasonable people. I think Geoff could have won them round, if he'd taken his time and used a bit of tact.'

'How much do you think they know about your past, Mrs Williams?'

Pam felt her mind reeling as Peach put the question without even showing embarrassment. This man had been watching her whilst she'd allowed herself to be irritated by his junior colleague: now he was preparing to dissect her life in the years before Geoff. She said as calmly as she could, 'So you've been prying into my private affairs.'

Peach gave her a smile which was not apologetic. 'In a murder inquiry, we gather all the information we can about those closest to the deceased. You could say that it is our duty to do just that. Unless it provides evidence for a subsequent court case, the information remains confidential.'

Who had told them this? And how much did they know? Surely it couldn't have been Justin or his wife? Probably neighbours, she decided: she could think of several who enjoyed a gossip, especially if they had a titbit of scandal to retail. She said cautiously, 'I presume that you're alluding to a legacy I received five years ago.'

Peach would have made an excellent poker player, she thought. His face did not flicker. After a second he said, 'We cannot force you to make disclosures: you are merely voluntarily helping us with our inquiries. Nevertheless, my advice would be to give us the details of this.'

'I have no objection to that. It is obviously already common knowledge. I would rather you got the true facts from me than relied on some third or fourth hand version of it.' Pam forced herself to shut out her conjectures on who had revealed this and concentrate on what she was saying to this calm interrogator. For the first time, she felt fear: she must pick her way carefully through this and not make any mistakes. 'About seven years ago, a female friend of mine died of cancer. She and her husband weren't really close friends of ours – they were twenty-five years older than us – but we'd visited them and they'd visited us whilst I was still with my husband. After my marriage broke up and I was divorced, they kept in touch with me. I was grateful for that: you may not realize it, but most couples just drop you when you become a singleton.' For some reason she could not fathom, she darted another baleful glance at the woman with the unlined face and the remarkable blue-green eyes who was making notes on this.

But it was Peach who responded. 'And after your female friend died, you continued to visit her husband. Mr Arthur Smailes.'

Somehow it seemed more damning when he quoted the full name at her. 'Yes. Arthur was in his seventies and his own health wasn't good. He'd been very close to his wife and he wasn't good at managing on his own. A lot of men of that age aren't.' It will come to you, you cocky young sod, she wanted to say to this bouncy chief inspector. It will come to you much sooner than you think. 'I used to go round to Arthur's house to make sure he was feeding himself properly. When I found he was struggling, I began to take food round for him fairly regularly. That was all there was to it, friendship. I dare say we were both pretty lonely, but Arthur Smailes was old and failing, though a nice enough man. Perhaps I should state to you formally that there was never any question of marriage between us.' Pam allowed herself a small, sad smile at such a preposterous idea.

'But you got to know him very well, nevertheless.'

'I'd have said quite well. I don't suppose that matters to you. I kept an eye on him, because his children lived over a hundred miles away. I got home helps and whatever else I could secure from the social services for him. When he eventually had to go into the council home, I used to visit him when I could. That meant about once a fortnight, I'd say.'

'Did you discuss his will arrangements with him?'

Pam Williams fought to control her anger. They had to ask such things, she supposed, whatever their questions imputed. 'I did not. The legacy was a complete surprise to me.'

Peach wondered whether that was so. But it wasn't their job to go into the detail of this. Whether or not Pam Williams had brought undue influence to bear on the old man, as his children had claimed at the time, had been decided years ago and was irrelevant now. There was no point in raking over ashes which had long been cold. Indeed, as far as Percy was concerned, the whole business was little more than a softening-up process to make the woman more responsive to questioning in this case. 'A legacy of fifteen thousand. Enough to set one of his daughters on the warpath,' he mused.

'The daughter who had visited him once in twenty-four months. I'd done more for Arthur than any of his children in those last years when he was lonely and ill. If he wanted me to have that money, he was entitled to leave it to me. His body was failing, but he was of perfectly sound mind.'

A hard woman, perhaps. Yet there was sense in what she said, if the facts were as she reported them. She was a woman on her own at the time and entitled to look after herself. What this matter did suggest was that she would have been alive to the fact that Aspin was a rich man, and perhaps out to further her interests as the family suspected.

'So you kept the legacy from Mr Smailes. Did Geoffrey Aspin know about that?' Peach asked.

Pam Williams flicked the fingers of her right hand quickly over her temple, as if at a stray tress of hair. But her blonde hair had remained perfectly in place: the gesture was merely a release of the tension she felt. She wanted to tell this pair to go hang themselves, to get out of her life and stay out of it. But she could not do that. She controlled her voice, and spoke neutrally, even dully.

'I'm not a rich woman, Mr Peach. I was anxious to get out of an unhappy marriage and that made me foolish: I accepted a settlement which was derisory just to see the last of a man I wanted out of my life. I was glad of my unexpected legacy, grateful for Arthur Smailes's thoughtfulness. And yes, Geoff did know about it. I told him only about a month ago, when I reckoned that we had a future together.'

'Mr Aspin was a rich man. He could have removed all financial worries for you.'

'He was planning to do just that. Surely the fact that I objected to a public proclamation of his plans to marry me shows that I was not a mercenary woman, driven on by financial greed.' She glared at Blake and said, 'You were there on Saturday. If you call yourself a detective, you should have seen that I was upset by what Geoff said in his speech.'

For once, Peach was conciliatory. This woman had been closest to the victim in the days before his death; it was important to keep her talking. 'Forgive me, but we have so far only your word that you were put out by his announcement that he planned to marry you. Other people believe that you knew what he was going to say. Other people also heard an argument between the two of you afterwards; no one has admitted to hearing what the argument was about. Money is the motive for a lot of serious crime, so you must forgive this line of questioning.'

She looked fiercely at the younger woman, who had said nothing to corroborate her story, and then back at Peach. 'I'm not a teenager. There was love between me and Geoff, but not a teenage, closed-eyes love. Of course I knew he was a rich man. Of course I knew that I'd be rid of the lonely life of genteel poverty in old age which I admit I'd sometimes feared. As a matter of fact, Geoff had already agreed to clear the mortgage on this house for me.'

'That was done before last Saturday's celebration?' Peach was thinking about what the family would have made of this; plainly they would have seen it as the writing on the wall, with any designs they had on Aspin's fortune needing rapid revision.

'Geoff insisted on signing the papers last week. I have them here in my bureau. There didn't seem any need for hurry in presenting them at the time.' Her voice faltered on that last phrase and she thought for a moment she was losing control. Then she said quietly, 'I have no idea whether what he signed last week now has any legal standing.'

Peach nodded slowly. 'My guess is that if it clearly predates his death, it would stand, but I'm no lawyer, so you must check it out yourself. Thank you for being so cooperative with us, Mrs Williams. Have you had any further thoughts on who might have killed Mr Aspin?'

She shook her head mutely, suddenly unable to speak and at the end of her resources. Then, as they were going, she gasped out a question about Geoff's funeral, and the woman she resented explained gently that the body wouldn't be released for some time yet, that when they had made an arrest, the defence lawyers would be entitled to demand a second, independent post-mortem.

They were out of her house and on the path when she called after them, 'It won't be up to me to make the arrangements, will it? I won't be down as his next of kin, you see.'

It was Peach who came back and said gruffly that he was sure that whoever made the funeral arrangements would want her to be there, that they would no doubt accept by that time that she had been close to Geoffrey Aspin in life and should therefore be near to him as the last rites of that life were concluded.

As the CID pair drove away, Lucy Blake looked back at the front door of the house, which was already closed. 'That woman doesn't like me and I'm not sure how much I like her. But I certainly felt sorry for her. For what it's worth, she was right about what I saw at Marton Towers on Saturday. She did seem upset by Aspin's declaration that he was going to marry her.'

Peach waited for her to overtake a cyclist who was wobbling perilously close to the gutter, then hastened to preserve his professional cynicism. 'It would have been politic for her to do so . . . if she was merely pretending that it hadn't been agreed beforehand, as the family think she was.'

'You got more out of her than we'd any right to expect about that previous legacy.' She glanced in her rear-view mirror at the train of vehicles which always builds up behind a police car within the thirty limit. 'You were kind to her at the end about the funeral.'

He shrugged his wide shoulders in the passenger seat. 'Costs us nothing, does it? But she's left us with a problem, of course. We still don't know for certain what that blazing row she and Aspin conducted in the cloakroom was about. Suppose he'd said if that was her attitude to marriage, he was going to withdraw his offer to clear off her mortgage?'

Wednesday night. A brilliant purple sky over the coast twenty miles to the west, where the sun had set hours earlier at the end of a perfect day of high summer. Midnight was the best time of all, on a day when there had been not a cloud in the sky and the temperature had climbed towards eighty.

Even the grimy old Lancashire cotton town was invested with a certain glamour on an evening like this. People always spoke of Lowry when they thought of art in contexts like this, but it was half a century and more since Lowry. At ten o'clock on such a July evening, Brunton now had a different kind of charm. Most of the mills had long since closed; the few which remained were manned by a workforce very different from Lowry's gaunt matchstick people.

In the twenty-first century, there were new and taller

buildings and different industries. Where once the town had boasted a hundred tall mill chimneys, the two or three which remained were now dwarfed by tower blocks. As the lights came on and darkness disguised the few remaining narrow streets of terraced houses, the skyline of the town could have been that of any one of a thousand towns and cities round the world.

The children were long since in bed, deep in the innocent sleep which they could enjoy. The world left to the darker designs of their elders. The murderer of Geoffrey Aspin looked down at the silhouette of the town for five minutes and then got back into the car.

The killer had always liked this road, which ran along the ridge above the recently restored Victorian public park; liked the height of it and the way you could survey the town from up here. Somehow, it gave you a feeling of power, to see the whole town set out below you. The murderer mused through quiet minutes on what the scene showed and what it concealed, and then drove thoughtfully away.

Five days now since the death of Geoffrey Aspin. The police had bustled about and caused a lot of disturbance, but they didn't seem to have made much progress. They'd caused a stir with their house-to-house inquiries, but they hadn't learned anything that was going to help them. They'd know when Aspin had died by now, for sure, but that wasn't going to help them much.

Aspin's killer drove carefully until out of the town; it would be the ultimate irony to be pulled in by the traffic police for a speeding offence, when you were baffling their CID colleagues over a much bigger crime.

Alone with your own thoughts, that was always a happy place to be. You needed silence and isolation to get your ideas in order, to make your estimates of the enemy's progress, and to plan your next moves. You grew more alone, when you'd done something like this, because you couldn't talk about it, even to those closest to you. That didn't matter. It was good having a big secret like this: you felt you could do almost anything.

It did not seem as dark once you moved away from the lights of the town. Without any conscious attempt to go there, the garrotter of Geoffrey Aspin found the long, low mound of Pendle Hill rising high above the car, black and sinister beneath the bright stars of a sky darkening towards navy. This was the country of the Pendle witches. On a night like this, with the darkness dropping in and a thin sliver of moon yet to rise, you could picture dark deeds, and imagine Satanic forces quietly watching from the folds of the hill.

The murderer parked the car on the side of the hill, where the summit towered above and made men and women and their concerns seem petty and unimportant. In daylight you could see Blackpool Tower from here, but now all that was visible over the flatness of the distant Fylde coast were the last indigo streaks of the day that had gone.

Ten, twenty, thirty minutes passed without a single car disturbing the silence. The murderer slid down the window of the car: it was pleasant to feel the cool night air upon your face after the heat of the day; it seemed to help you to think. You were more than ever a loner, once you had committed murder. It set you apart from other men and women. You against the world. You with a feeling of power which you'd never had before.

It was good to feel that you were winning against the odds. Five days now. A high proportion of murders that weren't solved within a week remained unsolved. It would be good to add to those statistics.

Sixteen

Jemal Bilic was on his own patch, but he was restless.

Peach found that very interesting. He looked round the sparsely furnished office and found it curiously spartan. In his experience, businessmen who had made it wanted to surround themselves with the trappings of success to impress visitors. This room had a 'Director' sign on its door, but it was unexpectedly shabby. The walls were without pictures or any form of ornamentation, which only served to emphasize that the place needed decorating. There was only a single chair behind the cheap desk. Percy considered the contrast with Chief Superintendent Thomas Bulstrode Tucker's opulent desk and penthouse office and permitted himself a private smile.

'We don't need expensive premises. That's one of the advantages of this business,' Bilic explained as he dragged in two chairs to accommodate his visitors. The Northgate Employment Agency supplied temporary replacements for office staff. 'We have a lot of clerical workers on our books. A lot of married women who only want part-time or occasional work; we even have one or two housefathers. They don't need to come in here once they've registered with us. Neither do our clients, the people who employ them. It's the lack of overheads which enables us to make good profits in a business like this.'

The only other person they had seen as they came into the place was a middle-aged woman in the outer office whom Bilic had introduced as both his personal assistant and the person who took incoming phone calls. Perhaps business hotted up as the day proceeded: they had not heard the phone ring since they had come into the place ten minutes ago.

'It's a quiet time, this, for us,' said Jemal Bilic, as if he had followed Peach's thoughts.

Percy looked out to where the police Mondeo was parked beside Bilic's sleek new Mercedes, then glanced at his watch: it was a minute past nine o'clock on Thursday morning. Just the time when office managers who found themselves under-staffed because of sickness or other factors would be phoning in for temps, thought Peach. Interesting, again.

Jemal was almost relieved when his visitors turned to the business which had brought them here. Peach introduced the man who sat watchfully beside him as Detective Constable Clyde Northcott and Jemal took the opportunity to appraise him. A tall, lean man, with a hard expression. A man whose eyes had not left his quarry from the moment he entered the room. The kind of man he might have employed himself, when he needed muscle to enforce his wishes. Not the man to have against you in a fight. A hard bastard, this.

Bilic would have been surprised to know that that was exactly the phrase Percy Peach used to describe the man he had recruited three years ago into the police service and two years later into his CID team.

Jemal decided that he would rather deal with this man than with the woman officer who had accompanied Peach when he had been interviewed at home on Sunday. He was not used to women in authority; her watchful, note-taking presence had unnerved him more than he would have expected, disturbing his concentration upon the matter in hand.

Concentration was certainly what he needed here. These people couldn't pin anything on him, if he concentrated hard and gave them nothing. Jemal Bilic was used to dictating situations, rather than leaving the initiative in the hands of others. These men were probably not among those policemen who could be bought: though such creatures existed every-where, there were not many of them nowadays in England. Jemal knew that he would have to accept that he was not the man in charge here and behave accordingly. However unnaturally it came to him, he must let others call the shots. He folded his arms and determined to remain still.

Peach said, 'The team has talked to a lot of people since I spoke to you on Sunday. Quite a few things have become clearer.'

But you don't know who killed Aspin, thought Jemal. So that's all right. Do a little careful fencing and don't give anything away.

Jemal said, 'I'm sure that you've found the family anxious to give you all the help they can.'

'Some have been more helpful than others. Mr Bilic, please give us an account of your movements on Saturday evening.'

Jemal had been expecting this, waiting for it from the moment they had arrived here. 'The children were away from home. Stopping over with some friends of theirs. We'd made that arrangement because we didn't know quite when we would be back from Marton Towers. My wife thought the family celebration of Geoffrey's sixtieth birthday might go on, after other people had left. Or perhaps we might all have adjourned to someone's home. What he said in his speech about marrying that woman ended all that.' He wondered if it sounded too glib, too much like the prepared statement which it was. It wasn't always easy, using a language which wasn't your own. Even though he was by now fluent in it, the English tongue seemed to have more nuances than could ever be mastered.

'You told us on Sunday that you did not leave the Towers with your wife. What time did you get home?'

Jemal tried to look at Peach and ignore the other officer who was watching his every move and making notes on what he said. 'I think I was home by about half past seven. I couldn't be precise.'

'Did you go out again during the evening?'

If that bloody wife of his had only agreed to co-operate, he could have lied about this. But there was no knowing what Carol was going to say, or even what she had already said. 'I did go out for a short time. I had to see a business associate. A client of ours.'

'Even though you had made no arrangements for that evening, because you thought the family party might be going on?' Peach gave him the smile of innocent enquiry which anyone at Brunton nick would have told Bilic was his most ominous expression of all.

Jemal found his fingers twitching, but he kept his hands resolutely upon his folded arms. He had an answer ready for this; he might even enjoy the man's discomfort. 'I believe I told you on Sunday that in the turmoil after my father-in-law's speech I spoke to business acquaintances. I arranged then to meet one of them later in the evening at his house.'

Northcott looked up from his notes and said, 'We'll need the name of this person.' It was almost as though he didn't believe the man, Percy Peach noted with approval.

Jemal gave the note-taker a name and address, apparently unruffled. He knew the man would bear out what he'd said: he'd already arranged that. Then he said, 'We met for half an hour or so. Not more – it was probably from about nine forty-five to ten fifteen, though I couldn't be absolutely sure about that.' A mirthless smile crossed his dark features at this combination of precision and declared uncertainty. 'I must have been back home by ten thirty or thereabouts.'

Peach nodded, as if the man had spoken as he expected. 'You told us a little on Sunday about your relationship with your father-in-law. You said that you weren't close, that you got on because you needed to, because Mr Aspin was your wife's father and the grandfather of your children, that you didn't talk to each other a lot.'

Jemal shrugged his shoulders heavily and then nodded a surly acceptance; any movement was a relief from the tension he felt. This man Peach seemed to remember what he had said very exactly; it was another reminder that he must proceed with caution. 'He was different kind of businessman from me. I not understand some of your British ways.'

Peach noted how although the man spoke very good English, his accent seemed to thicken and his syntax to degenerate when he was under pressure. 'And what do you think Mr Aspin thought of you, Mr Bilic?'

Another, even more elaborate shrug of those slim but powerful shoulders. There was something feral about this man; Peach felt that at any moment he might abandon self-restraint and erupt into violent physical action. But the control held as Bilic said guardedly, 'I don't think he liked me very much, Aspin. We were from different backgrounds. I like to do things quickly, he like to take his time.'

Peach nodded. 'Did he like what you do? Did he approve of the way you make your money?'

The man started forward, almost out of his chair, then forced himself back into it. He snarled, 'It wasn't Aspin's place to approve or to disapprove.' Then, hearing his own voice, he pressed his shoulders hard against the back of his chair and said more quietly, 'There is nothing to find fault with in the way I make my money. Providing staff for offices is legitimate business.'

'Indeed it is. Though perhaps not a very lucrative one, in your case.'

'How you mean? How can you—?'

'Mr Bilic, I have not heard a phone ring in this place since we set foot in here half an hour ago.'

'I told you, it's a slack time. Business comes in fits and starts.' He was pleased to be able to produce that very English phrase.

'Maybe.' Peach looked round the shabby room which had so few signs of regular use. 'This place doesn't look as though it supports the style in which you live your life.'

Jemal fought down the panic which threatened for a moment to overwhelm him. He was a natural bully and like most bullies he panicked when exposed. How much did they know? 'I have other sources of income. Private sources.' Most British people shut up as soon as you talked about money, as if it embarrassed them to pry into your personal circumstances.

Policemen did not. Peach said, 'Very private, I'm sure. Would you care to enlarge upon exactly where your real money comes from, Mr Bilic?'

They couldn't know. They'd have marched in here and arrested him, if they'd had the evidence. But it was a good thing he'd told his team to lie low for a while, whilst this lot were sniffing about like pigs after truffles. 'I have some private money of my own. Family money, Mr Peach. The details of that will remain private. The rest comes from this agency. This has nothing to do with you. You told me that you were coming here to investigate the murder of my father-in-law.'

'Indeed we did. And that is exactly what we are doing. So I repeat the question I asked you a few minutes ago. Did Geoffrey Aspin approve of the way you made your money?'

'I assume he did. He saw his eldest daughter and his grand-children being well provided for.' He shrugged again, attempting to be dismissive. 'This has nothing to do with his death.'

'I hope it hasn't, Mr Bilic. But I need to be convinced. If Mr Aspin was inquiring into areas where you didn't want him to go, it would provide a murder motive, you see. A motive for a man who has just told me that he was out of his house at the time when Mr Aspin was killed. Good day to you.'

As they left the director's room and nodded affably to the woman working in the outer office, the phone rang be-latedly behind them and was answered by Jemal Bilic. They had no means of knowing whether the call had to do with the employment agency or something more obscure and sinister.

Whilst Peach and Northcott were concluding their business with Jemal Bilic, Denis Oakley was giving the bank manager his polished, professional smile. The manager answered in kind: even in the world of finance, where everything is care-fully priced, courtesy costs nothing.

Denis glanced at his watch. 'I don't wish to be rude, Mr Baker, but you will understand that with the death of my partner this is a very busy time for Aspin and Oakley's. I'm having to take on a lot of functions which are quite strange to me, until we can make a new appointment.'

'I appreciate that. This needn't take long, if you can provide us with the answers we need.' The bank manager knew it was always safest to retreat behind the professional 'we' when you had tricky ground to negotiate.

'The firm is in a healthy state, as you must know. Geoffrey's death is a setback, of course, but I'm hopeful that the profits for the year will be very little affected. We have a healthy order book, and in due course—'

'The bank is not worried about the firm's health. It is your personal overdraft which concerns us, Mr Oakley.'

'My own finances are very much tied up with the firm. Inseparable, in fact.'

'That was not the view of Mr Aspin, I'm afraid. He told me specifically a fortnight ago not to honour any cheques presented by you on behalf of the firm without his specific authority. No doubt he informed you of his views. That is why I asked to see you after his unexpected demise.'

'We have always been partners. Either of us is able to sign cheques.'

'Company cheques, yes. Not cheques for personal benefit.'

'It's impossible to distinguish between the two.'

'Mr Aspin plainly thought that it *was* possible. He was disturbed by some of the cheques which you have written and some of the banking transactions you have conducted over the last year. Knowing Mr Aspin as I did for many years, I should be surprised if he had not spoken to you about the matter.'

Of course he had, repeatedly and latterly at length. Denis Oakley had always treated bank managers and accountants as dutiful dullards over the years, men who were no doubt necessary, but lacking in the cavalier touch which made life interesting. Now it seemed that this calm, grey-haired, immaculately dressed man was to be his Nemesis. Except that with Geoff gone, he could surely be overruled. Denis forced out a little burst of the confidence he used for customers, even though he knew that this man possessed knowledge they could never have. 'It's a cash-flow problem, that's all.'

'Mr Aspin didn't think so.'

'Geoff was a cautious man.'

Now it was the bank manager who allowed himself a smile. 'Prudence is a virtue which we approve of in the fiscal world. It is one of our duties to protect people against themselves, to prevent them from overreaching themselves.'

'Aspin and Oakley's wouldn't be where it is today if I hadn't taken a few entrepreneurial chances, especially in the early days.'

'That is something on which I couldn't possibly comment, Mr Oakley.'

Yes, and you look decidedly smug about that, Denis thought. He said imperiously, 'I may need to write a few large company cheques over the next month or two. I shan't have Geoff standing beside me any more, and there will be decisions to be taken.'

The manager gave him a small smile, which combined acquiescence with regret. 'The company is in a healthy state, as you point out, with considerable assets. There is no question of us failing to honour your cheques. It was, however, my duty to have this discussion with you. To record that your late partner had certain . . . certain reservations over your lifestyle.'

It was difficult to smile over the mention of a friend and partner who had so recently died. Denis Oakley managed it. He said indulgently, 'Geoff was a bit of an old woman, at times, you know. Perhaps that is one of the reasons why we worked so well together. Mr Baker, this has been a useful meeting and I shall take note of what you have said. Now I feel that I should get back to the works and to the sordid world of industry, and carry on safeguarding the pay-cheques of my workforce.'

The manager stood up behind his desk. He did not proffer his hand, as he sometimes did at the end of difficult one-to-one meetings. 'I am glad to have cleared the air and made clear to you the reservations of your late partner. Perhaps I should point out that at the end of the financial year the auditors will be reviewing all of your expenditure and all of the firm's outlay.'

That was a long way ahead, as they both knew. Things could be put right by then; they always had been in the past. Like most serial philanderers, Denis Oakley was an incurable optimist. He was on his way out of this inner sanctum when he had a disturbing thought and turned back to the man who was following him to the door.

'I take it that what has passed between us this morning will be treated in strictest confidence. It wouldn't help us in a difficult situation if employees knew you had been discussing matters of company credit with me.'

The manager was at his most benign. He gave no hint of any personal satisfaction as he said, 'The business is in a healthy financial state. No one who works for it needs to know any more than that. Banking wouldn't work if we didn't maintain our unwritten rules of discretion.' He smiled benignly over this truism on which they were agreed. 'The only people who are able to override such rules are police officers investigating serious crimes.'

Seventeen

S teve Hawksworth took the tax returns of the two clients
through to the head of the firm when the man's PA said
that he was free.

Alan Robinson was twenty-five years older than Steve and
he enjoyed the trappings of success. An antique silver desk
set, with solid silver setting and cut glass inkwells that would
never again hold ink stood on the tooled leather of his desk.
The man sported a waistcoat across his ample stomach,
though the watch chain which his father had favoured had
now been reluctantly abandoned.

Steve decided in that moment that he would wear a modern,
lightweight, two-piece suit, when he owned his own firm.
No one wore waistcoats nowadays. He would work in shirt
sleeves whenever it suited him, setting an example of industry
to his staff, and only put his jacket on for important clients.
It irked him to have to bring everything he did to this man
to sign, just so that the amiable buffoon could pretend that
he kept his practised hand on everything they did here. It
irked him to know that he was sharper and more efficient
than this man who kept the cigars ready to offer to high-
level visitors in the top drawer of his desk. There would be
no smoking anywhere in Steve's efficient ship, once he was
captain of his fate.

That dubious brother-in-law of his thought accountants
were people with no imagination and no business capacity.
He'd show Jemal Bilic what he could do once he had his
independence and his own firm. He'd make money, honest
money. He'd give Louise an easier life: get her more help
with the children, get the best schooling for Daisy, who was
a bright girl, and the best possible treatment for little Michael.
Down's syndrome didn't mean the end of the world: at the

parents' circle they'd met people who were far worse off than them and still very cheerful. But what no one said, what no one could afford to say, was that it was easier if you had money.

There must be money coming to them, now that poor old Geoff had gone. What you had to do was put that money to good use, which meant building something for the future with it. The best investment of all was in yourself, if you had the ability. He'd talked about it often enough, with Louise: now the time was coming to implement those plans, to show his wife that he was not just a dreamer. He was ready to do that.

Steve went back to his office and looked at his next assignment. It was the annual tax return of a BT executive with a second home in Cornwall and rents coming in from there. Routine stuff; boring stuff. But he'd do it, and do it well. They thought because he wasn't an extrovert that he was a dull man, but he had more imagination than any of the other five who worked here. He'd show them that, when his chance came.

Steve Hawksworth found that he was pleased, even exultant, when that friend of his wife, Lucy Blake, rang to say that the CID would like to speak with him again, now that they had talked to a lot of other people about Geoff Aspin's death. He was even disappointed that it couldn't be until the next morning. It was the next minor event in the story, the next small but necessary step in his career. The next stage towards independence and success.

Once all this excitement surrounding Geoff Aspin's death was out of the way, they could all move forward.

Carol Bilic took Peach and Blake into the big sitting room where the cleaner had just finished her work and indicated where she wanted them to sit. The late afternoon sun didn't come into this room, but she made sure that she was not facing the light from the window. She gestured towards the chairs she had set out for them and said aggressively, 'I hope you're near to making an arrest for Dad's murder. It has been five days now.' She sat down unhurriedly in her favourite armchair and ran a hand over her dark hair.

So she was going to carry the fight to them. Peach smiled encouragingly at her: he liked a challenge. It would mean he didn't have to handle a grieving daughter with sympathy and tact. This woman hadn't seemed devastated by her father's death on Monday and she now seemed completely recovered.

'The post-mortem examination has told us fairly accurately when your father died.'

'That's a different thing from knowing who killed him.'

'It is indeed. You told us that you came back here with friends after Saturday's celebration at Marton Towers. What time did you get here?'

'They dropped me off at about seven. Am I to presume that I am still suspected of killing my own father?'

'And what time did your husband get home?' Peach spoke as if he had not heard her question.

She mustn't lose her temper: that was no doubt what this pair wanted. 'A little while after me. About half past seven, I should think.' Jemal could damn well look after himself. If he chose to freeze her out of his affairs, she wasn't going to go out of her way to look out for him. She looked at the bent head of Lucy Blake as she made notes and remembered that chestnut hair from years ago, when the teenage girl had giggled with Louise over books and records. For some reason it annoyed her intensely that the hair should still be so lustrous. 'We were in for the rest of the evening, so if Dad was killed any time after that, you can rule us out. Or don't you accept testimony from husband and wife?'

Peach gave her his annoyingly superior smile. 'Not testimony yet, Mrs Bilic – and I hope it never becomes that. Testimony is evidence given in court under oath. What you're doing now is voluntarily helping the police with their inquiries, as all good citizens do.'

'I stand corrected. Or rather sit.'

Her attempt to lighten things fell very flat, even though Peach's smile widened. 'You're saying that neither of you went out again that night?'

'I am. So if Dad was killed later in the evening, you can't pin it on either of us.'

'Interesting on two counts, that is. First, you seem to

assume that your father was killed not immediately after the junket at Marton Towers but much later. You're correct, as a matter of fact. But it's interesting to suspicious coppers like us that you should seem to know that, when there's been no press release about it as yet.'

She decided not to react to this: defending herself might seem like weakness. 'You said interesting to you on two counts. What was the second?'

'Your account of the evening differs from that of your husband.' Peach was suddenly businesslike and unsmiling.

She was shaken now; her dark eyes flashed from one to the other of the contrasting faces opposite her. She found both of them observing her keenly and both of them unrevealing. Blast Jemal! What yarns had he been spinning to them, and what danger had he brought upon her? 'All I said was that we did not go out for the rest of the evening.'

'Is there anyone who can corroborate that? Other than your husband, that is: I've already said that his account differs from yours.'

She thought furiously. 'No. The children were away for the night. A stopover with friends of the same ages; sometimes they come here.' It seemed suddenly necessary to her to enlarge upon innocent facts.

'Mr Bilic told us that he went out again during the evening.'

'I don't recall that. I must have forgotten about it.'

'Do you now remember his excursion?'

She was tight-lipped, her dark blue eyes striking in a face which was now very pale. 'If he says he went out, then he did.'

'Do you know when he went out and when he returned?'

'No. I'm sure he can give you the times.'

'He has already done so. We would like to be able to corroborate them.'

'I'm afraid I can't do that.' She took a long breath, forming a resolution, gathering her resources to implement it. 'Mr Peach, if you are going to continue to regard us as murder suspects, there are things you need to know. My marriage is not all it might be.' Her face wrinkled into a little moue of self-contempt at this anodyne phrase. 'To put it bluntly, it is coming apart. I shall shortly be arranging a separation, and in due course I shall proceed to formal divorce.'

It felt strange to be making this first announcement of her intentions to these hard-faced policemen, who knew nothing of the battles of the last few years. She hadn't even told the children yet, though they must long ago have picked up that all was not well between her and the dangerous man who was their father. She found it disturbing to frame this momentous thing for the first time in words. By way of an ironic, self-deprecating postscript, she added, 'Dad would have been pleased to hear me saying this: he never liked Jemal.'

Carol expected Peach to say that he was sorry to hear this, to express the conventional sympathy with which people cover their embarrassment over insights into the intimate lives of others.

Instead, he nodded curtly and then asked, 'Are you saying that this is a reason why your report of what happened last Saturday evening differs from that of your husband?'

'I am. This is a big house. When the children are around, we maintain the semblance of a partnership, or we did until very recently. When they are not, we pursue our own concerns, usually in different rooms. The children were not here on Saturday.'

Lucy Blake looked up from her notes. 'You're now telling us that your husband might have left the house, after all, without your knowledge?'

'Jemal comes and goes as he pleases, at any hour of the day or night. He may well have gone out for a time on Saturday night. If he did, I was not aware of it.'

Blake forced herself to press this woman who had so intimidated her in the days when she had gone to the Aspins' house as a teenager. 'I'm sorry to hear about your marriage, Carol. You must feel very bitter. That bitterness wouldn't extend to undermining Jemal's alibi for the time of a murder, would it?'

Carol paused, gathering her thoughts for a haughty dismissal of the woman whose position here still seemed to her that of an upstart. 'That is a contemptible suggestion, Detective Sergeant Blake.' She managed to deliver both rank and surname with a ring of mockery. 'I am merely giving you the facts of the matter. It shouldn't need stating, but I am as anxious as anyone to see the person who killed my father brought to justice.'

Peach studied the bristling antagonism between the two women with interest, then turned his attention to Carol Bilic alone. 'Did you go out yourself on Saturday night, Mrs Bilic?'

'What are you implying?'

He sighed. 'It is obvious, I should have thought. DS Blake has just suggested that your father was murdered at around the time when it seems you now admit that your husband was out of the house. We therefore need to know where you were yourself at that time.'

She ground her teeth together silently, fighting for control, knowing that a descent into screaming and anger would suit the purposes of this brazen man. 'I was here throughout Saturday evening. Your suggestion that I might have gone out and killed my own father is not only insolent but preposterous!'

He nodded once again, giving her the infuriating impression that she had said exactly what he would have expected. 'What are the financial implications of your divorce plans, Mrs Bilic?'

'I've no idea. That is an impertinent question, which can have no possible bearing on your investigation.'

'On the contrary, it is a highly relevant question. If you had financial expectations of your father, that would interest us. You have told us previously that he never approved of your marriage. He might therefore have offered you every support in ending it.'

She wanted to tell him that Jemal was a rich man, that there wouldn't be difficulties. But she knew that he would fight her every inch of the way, that she would have to wring every penny out of him. Perhaps this man Peach, who seemed to have discovered so many things about this dysfunctional family, was already aware of that; she knew that he'd spoken to Jemal this morning. She gave him a tight-lipped, 'I'm sure Dad would have helped me.'

'And how would your plans have been affected if he had married Mrs Williams?'

'I don't know, do I?'

'I suspect you have a shrewd suspicion, Mrs Bilic. Shrewd suspicions are what the CID deal in, so they always interest us.' He gave her his blandest smile.

'You're saying that I was relying on Dad's money to finance my break-up with Jemal. That my plans were rudely interrupted by the arrival on the scene of the Williams woman, who would have vetoed it.'

Peach shrugged; he enjoyed a good shrug, particularly when he could see interviewees becoming more and more incensed with him. 'Since you plainly dislike Mrs Williams intensely, you could scarcely have expected her to be sympathetic to your plans.'

It was all going to come out, whether she liked it or not, if they questioned everyone as thoroughly as this. Carol had a sudden desire that they should have a plain, unvarnished account from herself, rather than a highly coloured version from Louise or Steve or Jemal, who would each put a different perspective on this. 'All right. The bloody Williams woman was a complication, I admit. I'll get money from Jemal in the end, assuming that he's still here and in a position to pay it. But I know I'll have to fight him for every penny of it. I want my children to have the best education available. And, as far as I'm concerned, that means paying for it.'

She paused automatically, then realized that she was waiting stupidly for them to argue with her. Instead, Peach said, 'And you were relying on your father to finance this?'

'Yes. Maybe. As I've said, I'll get money from Jemal in due course. But I want a decent house for myself and the best schooling for my children now. Dad would have seen to that. I'd have got the house because he'd have been only too glad to see me finished with Jemal Bilic and he wouldn't have wanted me under my husband's roof whilst I was pressing ahead with divorce. I'd have got the education for my children paid for because he cared for them and would have gone along with my wishes.'

It was Blake who ended the pause which followed this. She looked up from her notes and said tersely, 'No doubt the money from your father's estate will now enable you to fulfil these plans.'

With the perversity which is the most baffling part of human nature, Carol Bilic was less offended by this blunt challenge than she would have been by more conciliatory words. It was as if the confrontation marked for her the translation of this female she remembered as a pretty, vapid teenager into a mature woman, who could fight her on equal terms. 'I imagine that will be so, yes. Dad has made no will in the last few months; I have already checked that with the family solicitor.'

Carol found this forthright, even rather shocking, honesty a relief after the evasions she had planned. Directness was her style, the mode she was easiest with. As far as it was possible for her, she would employ it.

Blake too was happier with open contest rather than the previous unwarranted and largely unspoken hostility she had endured. 'Let us be quite clear about this: is there anyone who can confirm for us that you were alone in this house for the whole of Saturday evening? Even an incoming phone call would be useful, if you could give us the name of the caller.'

Carol gave her a tiny, unexpected smile, as if acknowledging the new relationship between them. 'I can't do that. There were no calls. I tried to ring my sister somewhere around ten, but there was no answer. You're saying you suspect me of killing my own father. That I wanted to be rid of him before he could change the terms of his will, before his new woman could work on his views about financial support for me. Well, I didn't kill him, but I can follow your reasoning. You know better than anyone that I was never as close to Dad as his precious Louise!'

Blake gave her a small, acerbic, answering smile. 'What I'm saying is that anything which could eliminate you from this inquiry would be useful to you and to us. The same advice I shall offer to anyone else who is closely involved in it.'

Peach had watched the exchange between the two women with professional interest and unprofessional pleasure. With one of these unexpected switches which were part of his technique, he now said quietly, 'How does your husband make his money, Mrs Bilic?'

Her head spun for a moment as she tried to take in this

new line of questioning and the implications of it for her. 'He runs a successful employment agency. It specializes in providing temporary replacements for people on maternity and sickness leave.'

'So we have been told. I do not think the bulk of his income comes from that source.'

'Then you must take up the matter with him. I know nothing about Jemal's work and he does not encourage me to ask questions. I cannot see that this is relevant to your investigation.'

'You have just told me that Mr Bilic was out of the house at a time when your father may have died. At the moment, we are interested in everything about him.' Peach, having been told about the antipathy between husband and wife, instinctively pursued it for whatever advantage it might afford him.

'You must ask him, then. I've told you, I didn't even know he'd left the house.'

'It's a pity he did, isn't it? Otherwise the two of you could have vouched for each other at the vital time.'

'In which case, you'd probably have said there was a conspiracy between us!'

He didn't react to that. It was true that alibis given by husbands to wives and wives to husbands were always suspected by the police, but they were always devilishly difficult to break down. These two did not seem like a couple who would look after each other. They had plainly failed to agree a version of what had happened on Saturday evening with each other.

And each of them seemed to have the ruthlessness and nerve required to plan and execute this murder.

'I've been waiting to see you for two hours, DCI Peach,' said Chief Superintendent Thomas Bulstrode Tucker petulantly.

'I've been out and about, sir. Pursuing a murder inquiry.'

Tucker looked at his watch. 'I should have been home by now. I'm away for the weekend, you know. Occupied with this important new experiment of prison experience for senior police personnel.' He tried to sound impressive and succeeded only in being plaintive: he couldn't rid his mind of the thought of another bout of Barbara Tucker's formidable resentment about his absence as soon as he reached the suburbs.

'Yes, sir. Locked up in stir for the weekend. Still, first time for several years, I imagine.'

'I am not in the mood for your pathetic attempts at humour, thank you, Peach. Give me your report and get on your way. I shall not be here tomorrow. I have things to do.'

You mean Brünnhilde Barbara has insisted on your being around before you're incarcerated for the weekend, Peach thought. So you're missing from here as usual when the heat is on in a murder inquiry. Good: we're much better off without you.

'We shall miss your oversight, sir. But you have every right to savour the bosom of your family before disappearing to a celibate cell and prison rations for the weekend. Even long-term criminals get their conjugals, nowadays.' He stared at the wall above Tucker's head, dreamily preoccupied with a vision of his chief's head disappearing into the formidable Wagnerian bosom of his wife.

'That's quite enough of this flippancy! Give me your assessment of the case as it stands and allow me to be on my way.'

'Considerable progress has been made, sir.'

As a man who prided himself on his PR statements, Tucker knew what that phrase in the police argot signified. 'You mean you haven't a bloody clue who did it.'

'You put things succinctly, sir, with your usual talent for words. In fact, it's not quite as bad as that. Almost a hundred people who were at Marton Towers for last Saturday's cele-bration of Aspin's sixtieth birthday have spoken to the twenty-five members of the murder team. We also now know the time of the death pretty accurately. As a result of these things, I am now pretty sure that this killing was conducted by someone very close to the deceased: either a member of his family or a business associate – obviously I wouldn't want that view included in any press release.'

'So you haven't a prime suspect for this,' said Tucker querulously.

Percy marvelled anew at his chief's capacity to encourage people working hard and long to enhance his own reputation.

'I wouldn't say a prime suspect sir, no. Some seem more likely than others, to me, but I'm keeping an open mind, as you always encourage us to do.'

Tucker looked at him suspiciously and immediately demonstrated how open his own mind was. 'You said there was a foreigner involved when last we spoke.'

'Yes, sir. Jemal Bilic, son-in-law of Geoffrey Aspin. Turkish. About to split up with his wife, sir, whether he likes it or not. Dubious character. I don't believe his considerable affluence is based on the employment agency he runs. I believe that business is merely a front.'

'A villain, Peach, you mark my word.'

'Yes, sir, I shall do that.' As he had just told the man that Bilic was a villain, to have his opinion returned to him did not constitute a startling revelation. 'One of the problems is that he is being investigated by another branch of the police service, Customs and Immigration. I know that murder takes precedence, but I don't want to prejudice their case if I can avoid it.'

'I don't want any repercussions from senior officers elsewhere, Peach.'

Of course you don't, you cowardly sod. If someone of senior rank complains to you, your support for us will slide away as fast as shit off a wet shovel. 'I shall be mindful of the need for diplomacy, as always, sir.'

Tucker's sceptical stare lost its effect because Peach's eyes were again trained not upon him but on the wall behind him. 'It sounds to me as if you should get in there and arrest this villain.'

'I see, sir. There is the problem of evidence, though. We certainly wouldn't get the Crown Prosecution Service to bring a murder case against him, on what we know at present. Of course, if you are prepared to stick your neck out and—'

'I shan't do that, Peach. Not at the moment. I shall defer to the judgement of the man on the ground, as always.'

'Yes, sir. As always.' Now he did look at Tucker: he always enjoyed the spectacle of a chief superintendent scrambling for the lifeboats. 'It may yet be that Bilic is a villain without being a murderer, sir. We haven't found a clear motive for him, as yet.'

'Well, get out there and find one, Peach,' said Tucker churl-ishly, demonstrating once again his open-minded stance.

'One may very well emerge in due course,' said Percy magisterially. 'There's also his wife, Carol. We already have a motive for her.'

'The man's own daughter? Seems much less likely than a foreigner who is already under investigation for other crimes.'

This time Percy had to agree with Tucker's prejudice. But he held in his mind the picture of the dark-haired, erect Carol Bilic, resolute as Lady Macbeth in the pursuit of her own ends.

'She's agreed that she felt threatened by the arrival of a new woman in her father's life. Financially threatened, at a time when her marriage was breaking up: she was looking for financial support from her father for herself and her children.'

'Women are unpredictable, you know.'

Percy remained silent for a moment in the face of this latest startling insight from the head of Brunton CID. Then he said, 'There's another daughter, too: the younger one, Louise. Her father's favourite, by all accounts. She's seven years younger than her sister. She has a daughter aged six and a son aged four. The boy is a Down's syndrome child. I think she was looking for financial support from her father with the children. She too may have felt threatened by Mr Aspin's sudden announcement that he planned to marry a woman who had only been in his life for three months.'

'Don't assume that just because this woman was his favourite that she couldn't have killed him. Women can be very devious, Peach, very devious indeed.' Tucker nodded his head with satisfaction at this Delphic proclamation.

'Your experience of life is an asset to us as always, sir. Her husband, Steve Hawksworth, is an accountant, sir.' He waited for a lordly pronouncement on the profession, but Tucker was this time silent, intimidated by the mysteries of mathematics. 'Hawksworth made the speech proposing his father-in-law's health on Saturday. He claims that he liked Aspin, and seems generally to have got on well with the deceased. No motive thus far, other than the one I mentioned for his wife. We're seeing him again in the morning.'

'Don't charge in there and put his back up, Peach. He's a professional man, remember.'

'Yes, sir. I seem to remember that it was an accountant we nailed on four serious fraud charges three years ago.'

'An exception, Peach. I'm trying to warn you that—'

'Mason, too, that chap, wasn't he, sir? That devious bugger was a major figure in my research into the high incidence of crime amongst Freemasons.' Peach smiled in fond recollection. In fact, the man was the sole basis of the supposed research about crime among the Fraternity with which Peach loved to taunt Tommy Bloody Tucker, but his chief had never quite worked that out.

'Be careful, that's all I'm saying. You have far stronger suspects in my view.'

'Yes, sir. A foreigner and the two women I mentioned. I'm glad you're keeping an open mind: we rely heavily upon your overview.'

Tucker's glare again lost its force when he could not catch the eye of his tormentor. 'Is that it, then? Can I at last get home?'

Now Peach did look at him and allowed himself the luxury of a small smile, which grew slowly and impressively into a huge beam. 'There's at least one more leading suspect, sir. Another businessman, I'm afraid.'

Tucker sighed a long, eloquent, hopeless sigh. 'You'd better tell me about him. Briefly.'

Peach addressed himself conscientiously to this last word of instruction. 'Partner of the deceased, sir. Man who built the business up with Geoffrey Aspin over thirty-odd years.'

'He doesn't sound a likely candidate.'

'No, he doesn't, sir. They were at university together. Started the business not long after graduating, I believe.'

'And a very successful business they developed. Aspin and Oakley's provides valuable local employment, you know. It really doesn't seem likely that a professional man like Oakley would—'

'Detective Constable Murphy has been out to the firm's bank this afternoon. He's brought back valuable information. From the manager. Another professional man, sir.'

Tucker had a familiar dilemma: he wanted to check this

man's insolence, yet needed him desperately to conduct an investigation he should have been directing himself. He contented himself with an explosive, 'Well?'

'He has financial difficulties, sir. He's on his third wife, with rumours that his third divorce isn't far away. He pays a fortune in alimony and yet allegedly continues to put it about around most of the northern counties. A lifestyle which honest working coppers like you and me can only dream of, sir.' He looked heavenwards and commenced his dream.

'It's an affluent firm,' said Tucker. 'Can't he pay his way from that?'

Percy reluctantly abandoned the beguiling Rubenesque images he had conjured on to Tucker's ceiling. 'There is some confusion about that, sir. The bank manager has pointed out to him the distinction between company outlay and personal expenditure. It seems that Mr Aspin was worried about just this at the time of his death, and was determined to put a stop to his partner's excesses. Mr Oakley is hoping that he will have greater autonomy with his long-standing partner out of the way. The manager thinks with regret that he probably will. Whether Oakley took steps to ensure his partner's permanent absence remains to be established.'

Tucker drummed his fingers impatiently upon his desk. 'You're telling me that you still have five suspects for this.'

'Six suspects, sir. It's possible that Mrs Pamela Williams, the woman Mr Aspin was planning to marry, enticed him back to Marton Towers that evening and killed him herself.'

Tucker had been half out of his big leather chair. He sank back into it slowly and hopelessly. 'And why would this woman want to kill him? Surely she had everything to gain from marrying him?'

'They had a blazing row after Saturday's beanfeast at Marton Towers, sir. Seems Mrs Williams wasn't at all happy that Aspin should trumpet to the world at large that they were to be married, sir.' He looked at Tucker's uncomprehending face and added by way of explanation, 'Modern women like to be independent, sir. She says that he hadn't agreed any wedding plans with her at the time.'

Tucker shook his head over the intricacies of the modern female psyche. 'So why should she want to kill him?'

'He'd signed papers to clear off the mortgage on her present house, sir. A sum of over a hundred thousand pounds, it seems. She has the papers, sir, signed by Geoffrey Aspin and dated five days before his decease. They'll probably have legal standing. But it seemed to us possible that in the light of their fierce agreement early on Saturday evening, Mr Aspin might have been planning to rescind his decision to clear her mortgage.'

Tommy Bloody Tucker showed a little belated and unexpected excitement at this latest suggestion of female duplicity. 'She could have done this, you know!' He leaned forward confidentially. 'Women are unpredictable creatures.'

'Thank you, sir. We shall bear that in mind.'

'Well, get on with it, then. I expect real progress, if not an arrest, by the time I see you again on Monday.'

'We shall do our best as always, sir, even without the skipper at the helm. Enjoy slopping out with the big boys over the weekend, sir.'

There was more than one way of taking the piss, Percy reflected as he went back down the stairs.

Eighteen

'You can do it, Michael! There! We knew you could, didn't we?'

The four-year-old tottered along uncertainly behind the truck of wooden bricks, held his balance precariously, and arrived delightedly in his father's arms at the other side of the room. 'Did it, Da!' he said delightedly.

That was one of the most delightful things about Down's syndrome children, Steve Hawksworth assured himself for the hundredth time. They were always happy. They had the unselfconscious delight of a two-year-old whenever they achieved things. And whereas walking across a room without falling was routine for a normal child like Daisy, it was a major achievement for four-year-old Michael. And kids like Michael never manipulated you, never began to play one adult against another for their own ends, as other children learned to do at a surprisingly young age.

'Let's build a tower with your bricks now,' he said to Michael. He knelt on the floor beside his son, watching the small hands moving the wooden blocks slowly, clumsily, carefully out of the truck and on to the carpet. This was the time he liked best, when Daisy had gone to school and he could give Michael his full attention, without having to attend to Daisy's bright but often dismissive commentary upon their efforts. His big sister was good with Michael in short bursts, but she became impatient with him too quickly, being unable to understand why he was not moving beyond the playthings of a toddler.

It was understandable, of course: Daisy was only six, after all. But Steve liked these moments when he could give his undivided attention to his son. They were precious because they were rare. Usually he would have been at work at this hour, but today he had arranged to be late because of his second meeting with the CID.

He was so lost in his innocent enjoyment and in conjuring from his son the few words which the boy could manage that he did not hear the bell. Louise was standing in the doorway, announcing that his visitors had arrived, before he realized that they were here. He scrambled awkwardly to his feet and said, 'We'll go into the kitchen, if you don't mind. We won't be disturbed there.' He led them across the hall and into a spacious kitchen, with units which still served their purpose but were probably twenty years old. 'Thank you for coming to the house. I don't think Mr Robinson would have been overjoyed to end the working week as he began it with a second CID visit to his offices!'

Steve Hawksworth had been hoping to see his wife's friend, Lucy Blake, alongside this bouncy, energetic DCI Peach. Instead, he found a lithe, tall, black man, who sat down on one of the kitchen chairs and sized Steve up without any sign of embarrassment. DCI Peach introduced this man as Detective Constable Clyde Northcott and he gave Steve the briefest of nods. This must be the man Louise had found so intimidating when they had come here on Tuesday. They must be deliberately keeping Lucy Blake away from them; he wondered if that was just police routine, or whether it was a decision by this man Peach.

'We'll keep this as brief as possible. No doubt you will be anxious to get to the office,' said Peach briskly.

'That would be helpful. I've thought about this sad business further, as you asked me to do on Monday, but I'm afraid I haven't come up with any thoughts which might be useful to you.'

'That's a pity. Still, I can bring you up to date with developments; we'll see if that prompts any inspiration. I'm afraid it's looking more and more likely that someone close to Mr Aspin killed him.'

'A business associate, perhaps. People in business make enemies: it's inevitable. Even someone as pleasant and caring as Geoff Aspin must have made himself a few enemies.'

'Yes. I believe you suggested as much last time we spoke to you. And as I promised, we have not neglected that thought.

We have made detailed inquiries into the workings of Aspin and Oakley's.'

'And have you come up with anything useful?'

'That will have to remain strictly confidential, for the moment at least.' Peach gave him his most knowing smile. 'It is entirely natural that your instinct should be to distract us away from the family and towards other candidates for this crime, Mr Hawksworth. However, it is correspondingly appropriate for us to investigate Mr Aspin's family: I'm sure you see that.'

'I suppose so.'

Steve found that he felt very cool. That was reassuring. He assessed the position. They surely couldn't be considering Louise for this, could they? They might be thinking about him, but he was certain he couldn't be high on their list. More likely that man who had never let the rest of the family into his private world: Jemal Bilic. He was surely a man capable of killing, and these professionals must by now be aware of that. Even Carol Bilic, who so effortlessly and unthinkingly patronized him and Louise, might be on their list: she had never seemed to him to be very close to her dad, and she was ruthless in pursuit of anything she wanted.

Peach studied him as if he divined the thought patterns behind that thin, anxious but composed face. 'Where were you on Saturday evening, Mr Hawksworth?'

'Well, I waited at the Towers until almost everyone had left, as I think I told you.'

'You did indeed. And the rest of the evening?'

This was clearly the important part of the interview, the bit where he must keep calm. Steve said unhurriedly, 'I drove back here alone and helped Louise with the children. It was a bit hectic, because they'd been playing with the friends who looked after them during the afternoon and they were rather overexcited and overtired. It was well past their normal bedtime when we got them down.'

'I see. So you helped to put them to bed, read stories, that sort of thing.' Peach drew on his slim knowledge of family life.

Steve wondered what Louise had told them. They hadn't talked to each other much since the shock of her father's

death. That was understandable, but regrettable, he now realized. He'd better be careful not to contradict anything she'd
said, if he didn't want to excite suspicion. 'I was tired,
although I'd been sitting down for most of the day. Making
a speech is more draining than you'd think when you're not
used to it.' He gave an apologetic giggle, which died too
quickly. 'I bathed Daisy and got her into her pyjamas. Then,
as far as I remember, I came down again and left Louise to
get them into bed and do the stories. It takes a long time,
especially when Michael gets overexcited; that makes him
less co-operative. He's a good lad really, but you need
patience: he doesn't understand it when you try to hurry
him.'

There was a pause whilst Northcott made a note. In the
silence, they could hear the Down's syndrome boy banging
away on some sort of musical toy, with faint, encouraging
talk from his mother.

Peach, smiling his appreciation of the domestic scene
Hawksworth had painted, said almost casually, 'And how
long was it before this process was complete and you and
your wife were together again?'

He should definitely have agreed something on this with
Louise; they needed each other, to take themselves safely
out of this. 'I couldn't really be precise. I felt at the time
that it was perhaps a bit longer than I expected. I should
think it was about an hour, but obviously I didn't time it.
I'm rather going on the fact that it didn't seem to be long
before we had a cup of tea and went to bed ourselves.' He
glanced at Northcott. 'I'm sorry to be so vague.'

Peach shrugged. 'Only natural, sir, isn't it? Innocent people
didn't know these timings were going to be important, did
they? Did you go out again on Saturday night?'

How abruptly the questions came! Just when the ques-
tioner hoped you'd be relaxing, Steve supposed. He said
equally brusquely, 'That's when it happened, isn't it? Geoff
was killed later on Saturday night, not immediately after the
party at Marton Towers.'

'We believe he was, sir, yes. And if you were safely
tucked up at home, it would take you out of the equation,
wouldn't it?'

Steve smiled blandly back, showing the man that the question didn't worry him. 'I suppose it would. And I'm happy to tell you that I didn't go out again that night.' He gave Peach a smile which was not triumphant but which showed a little relief: that was surely only natural.

'From what you say, you can confirm that your wife also did not go out again during the evening.'

'I certainly can. Unless she shinned down the drainpipe and was away like the wind whilst I thought she was telling Daisy her story. Hardly Louise's style, though, that!' He laughed at his ridiculous conjecture and found for the first time that they seemed to share his amusement.

'How much do you know about Mrs Williams?'

Another startling switch. He would have expected them to question him about Jemal and Carol, or perhaps to follow up his suggestion about business associates of his father-in-law. They seemed at any rate to be accepting that he and Louise were in the clear. 'I know that she'd had a previous legacy in dubious circumstances. I don't mean to suggest that she killed anyone to obtain it. Just that she – well, cultivated an old man and made sure that he left money to her. That's only what I've heard. When you work in the town and advise people about their monetary affairs, you tend to pick up things like that.'

'Rumours, you mean.'

He smiled deprecatingly. 'A little more than rumour in this case, Chief Inspector. I think the facts of the legacy are clearly established: it's only what Mrs Williams did to secure it which is a matter of conjecture.' He knew he was sounding petty, but he had no compunction about implicating the Williams woman in shady dealings. After all, she'd prompted all this. If she hadn't come upon the scene, Geoff Aspin would have been alive and well at this moment.

Percy said, 'No doubt you would have informed Mr Aspin of this, if he had remained alive. Or had you already done so?'

'No, I had not. And yes, we probably would have told Geoff, if someone hadn't murdered him. I imagine Louise and I would have discussed the matter with Carol and her husband, and then told Geoff. He clearly had a right to know everything possible about the woman he intended to make his second wife.'

And you'd have put it in the worst possible light, you prim sod, thought Percy. Or more likely got Carol Bilic to do it: she'd have been even more delighted to put the boot into Pam Williams.

'You were right about the participants in the argument you heard in the cloakroom at Marton Towers,' Peach informed him. 'Mr Aspin and Mrs Williams were having a blazing row.'

Steve wondered why they should be so interested in the Williams woman. 'What was the disagreement about?'

'Mrs Williams says she was taking him to task about his proclamation that he was going to wed her. She says that they hadn't discussed it and that it was far too early to be making public announcements.'

'I can't believe that is true. Can you?'

Peach gave him a small, rueful smile. 'We have no reason to disbelieve it, Mr Hawksworth.'

'Except that it runs in the face of the facts. However, it doesn't make the Williams woman a murderer, does it?'

'No, it certainly doesn't. The facts you are so fond of would argue that it was very much in her favour to keep him alive.' He was certainly not going to tell Hawksworth about that other interesting fact, the papers which Aspin had signed to clear Pam Williams' mortgage. But he decided to offer him another opportunity to indulge his taste for gossip. 'How healthy is the state of your sister-in-law's marriage, Mr Hawksworth?'

'Carol? Oh, you'd need to ask her about that. Perhaps you already have, for all I know. You may have gathered from our little exchanges and from what he has told you that there is no love lost between me and Jemal Bilic. He's a chancer, in my view, and he associates himself with some pretty dubious people. Personally, I think Carol would be well rid of him, but that's her decision, isn't it?' A delicious idea took possession of him and he leaned forward and said daringly, 'You haven't got Bilic in the frame for this, have you? I'd say he'd be well capable of it, but I'm hardly an unbiased witness, I suppose.'

'And why would he have done it? He was probably no more pleased than you by the advent of Mrs Williams, but he doesn't seem short of funds, does he?'

Steve felt the skin on the back of his neck prickling with resentment. Did they mean that the possible withdrawal of Geoff Aspin's financial support was more important to him than to bloody Jemal? That he was less able to provide for his wife and family without outside support than that crook?

Steve said huffily, 'I have no reason to think that Bilic killed his father-in-law. I should have told you at the outset if I had. You appeared to be asking me for my impressions, and my impression is that Jemal Bilic is a dangerous man.'

Peach agreed with him there, but he hadn't as yet come up with any real motive. He stood up and said, 'Thank you for your help, Mr Hawksworth.'

'That's all right. I'll come out with you and get off to work. I'm afraid I've not really been able to offer you much.'

'Oh, you may find that you've been far more helpful than you think, when we fit this into the pattern of other people's statements,' said Peach gnomically.

Steve Hawksworth was still trying to work out the implications of this as he arrived at work twenty minutes later.

Jemal Bilic's eyes flashed with annoyance. He was used to his orders being obeyed without question, but in his home that had long since ceased to happen. He said harshly to his wife, 'You should have talked to me before the police came here to see you. We should have discussed what you were going to say. We need to agree things, if we're to get through this.'

'It's a little late for co-operation. You should have thought of that earlier. Much earlier.' Carol's drawn white face twisted with contempt.

'We don't have a choice in this. We need to defend ourselves. They'll pin this murder on to one of us, unless we work together.'

It was the first time she could remember seeing fear in that dark, acquiline face. She noticed it with a mixture of apprehension and exultation. She realized now how much she hated her arrogant husband, how much she would like to see him brought down by this or any other offence. 'I want a divorce.'

'Do you? Well, you won't get one. I've more important things to deal with than a whining wife at the moment.'

'I'll get one, whether you like it or not. You don't have a choice!'

He wanted to leap across the room and fling the back of his hand against her complacent face; to shake her, to tell her to get her priorities right and deal with this before she screamed on about her damned divorce. He knew that he should be bargaining with her, telling her that she might just get what she wanted if she went along with his wishes in this. But that wasn't his way. Jemal Bilic wondered now what he'd ever seen in this defiant woman, whether it had just been a challenge to him to carry her off in the face of her rich father's opposition. 'We're in danger. Both of us are in danger!'

'You might be! I'm not. The police don't believe that a daughter would kill her own father.' Even as she said it, she knew it wasn't true, but she delivered it with all the confidence and contempt she could muster. Then she said more quietly, 'Where did you go to on Saturday night?'

'To see a business colleague.' He did not want to make any concessions to this haughty woman who now seemed like a stranger, but he forced himself to say, 'I did not kill your father.'

She was too far gone in hate to discuss anything now. Her voice was full of bile as she snapped, 'You'll need to convince the police of that, not me.'

Denis Oakley was not afraid of work. He wanted to show that to the staff at the factory. He had been working in shirt sleeves for most of the day, clearing out old files and creating one or two new ones for important customers. The fact that he had also been able to remove one or two of the personal memos which a concerned Geoff Aspin had sent to him over the last few months was quite incidental.

It was just as well these had gone through the shredder when the CID paid their unexpected visit to Aspin and Oakley's. Denis gave DS Lucy Blake his most winning smile and said that he was glad to see her again, hoping that DCI Peach would sense the unspoken rider that he was not at all glad to see him.

Peach showed no sign of being abashed. 'Our man has been out to the bank,' he announced breezily. 'Boring work, to my mind, but fortunately young DC Brendan Murphy is very thorough and conscientious.'

'I thought the details of personal finance were confidential,' said Denis Oakley sullenly.

'Not in a murder inquiry,' Percy explained cheerfully. 'Opens all the doors, does murder. Has its advantages that way. Not for the victim, of course.' He looked around the disarray in what had until last week been the victim's office. 'Having a clear-out, I see.'

'The world doesn't stand still. When we lose someone as important as Geoff Aspin, it's even more important that the rest of us roll up our sleeves and get on with things.'

'I expect it is, yes. And I expect you'll be using the firm's accounts to sort out your personal financial embarrassments, now that you're in sole charge.'

Denis glanced towards the door to the outer office, which he had shut firmly as his visitors came in. He hoped that the personal assistant at her desk out there wasn't able to hear any of this. She'd been very fond of Geoff Aspin, and she'd spoken to members of Peach's team earlier in the week. Denis wondered exactly what she had said about the relationship between the two partners who had driven the firm along for so long.

Denis said calmly, 'I do not own this firm, but I now have almost complete autonomy in the direction of it. That is the arrangement Geoff and I made many years ago, when we set up in business together, to cover the demise of either partner. I don't believe it was ever rescinded.' He spoke with the confidence of a man who had checked that out less than a month ago, when he first became aware that Pamela Williams was a serious presence in his partner's life.

Peach nodded. 'You have certain standing orders at the bank which are of a very personal nature.'

Denis beamed, first at Lucy Blake and then rather less affably at Peach. A winning frankness was clearly the order of the day, when they knew as much as they plainly did. 'I like women. That has been at once my pleasure and my cross over the years. I have certain obligatory payments – ex-wives do not come cheaply in these days of equality. There are also certain other less regular payments, which I feel obliged to make as a gentleman to certain ladies of my acquaintance.' He bestowed his most roguish grin upon DS Blake and said, 'There! I have made a clean breast of it. I wish I could say that I feel better for doing so, but I confess to feeling only a rather unmanly embarrassment.'

Peach gave him a conspiratorial, understanding smile, which made Oakley relax more than he should have done. Then the chief inspector's amusement vanished abruptly and he said, 'Your personal finances are in a mess, Mr Oakley. Your overdraft facilities have been curtailed. You wouldn't have been able to make these payments from the firm's coffers if Mr Aspin had been in this office today, would you?'

Denis mustered what protest he could. 'That is a matter of speculation, DCI Peach. I certainly have the authority to make these payments. Any irregularity will be a matter of discussion between me and the auditors at the end of the financial year. I do not anticipate any difficulties.'

Lucy Blake snapped shut the notebook in which she had made the briefest of entries. 'I think you have confirmed our views, Mr Oakley. We came here to hear from you what difference Mr Aspin's death had made to your personal situation: you have made that abundantly clear to us.'

It seemed clear even to Denis that the Oakley charm had made no impression on DS Blake. He sat down in the deserted office and pondered his position. It was a long time before he resumed work on the files.

It was the first time Lucy Blake could remember having all the windows open in Percy Peach's rackety, pebble-dashed, semi-detached house. On this sweltering July Lancashire evening, she did not even feel cold.

Even Percy's neglected and rather sorrowful back garden looked green and pleasant when gilded by the setting sun. They enjoyed a gin and tonic, perched a little precariously on chairs he had dug out of the garage for the occasion. 'I'm not much of a gardening man,' he understated thoughtfully. 'I always seem to be too busy. Perhaps things will change when I'm wed. Perhaps I'll do the traditional copper's thing and become a rose expert.'

Lucy instinctively shied away from the mention of marriage. They went inside and she sat in a battered moquette armchair and sipped her drink whilst Percy made a surprisingly competent job of dishing up the Marks and Spencer's food he had bought for them. She discussed the case with him over the meal: it was the one thing she could be sure would divert him from wedding dates.

At the conclusion of her thoughts, Percy said reflectively, 'He'd have been alive today, our Mr Aspin, if he hadn't planned a second marriage. Dangerous things, second wives.' He took an appreciative sip of his claret. 'That's what you'll be for me, of course. A second wife.'

'There's no hurry. I'm perfectly happy as we are.'

'Ah, but your mum isn't. And it would take a braver and a crueller man than me to disappoint Agnes Blake.'

Lucy could think of only one certain way to distract him now. She yawned extravagantly. 'It's been a tiring week and we're working over the weekend. I'm for an early night. At least it's warm, I won't have to shiver in your bathroom tonight.'

Percy brightened visibly. 'You're a shameless hussy, dragging me into my own bed like this. But your wish is my command, as always. I shall be putty in your hands.'

'Oh, I do hope not, Percy Peach.'

'Wash thee mouth out, lass. Or rather thee mind. And prepare to repel boarders.'

She liked it when he thee'd and thou'd her and switched into the Lancashire dialect. And she found it pleasantly warm in Percy's normally Arctic bathroom. It was even warmer in his bed, where Lucy's protestations of fatigue were emphatically forgotten.

Later, as they were lying on their backs and staring at Percy's invisible ceiling, she thought of what he had said earlier in the evening and surprised herself as well as her partner as she asked, 'Do you ever think of your first wife?'

It could have struck a jarring note, but it didn't. Percy said quietly and contentedly, 'Never! It didn't last long and fortunately there were no kids. It seems now to belong to another life entirely.'

There was a contented silence, even after he had put his arm tenderly around her and drawn her body against his. Lucy, stretching contentedly, decided he had gone to sleep. She was almost there herself when she heard him say drowsily, 'Tha can't 'ave me living over t' brush for ever, lass. We s'll 'ave to fix a date for us nuptials over t' weekend.'

Nineteen

At five o'clock on Saturday morning, the sun was already up. The western side of Pendle Hill is still in shade at that time of the day, but the clear light pours into the sleeping villages of the Ribble Valley.

A hundred years ago, at the height of the haymaking season, farmers would have been out at this hour, eyeing the skies anxiously, estimating the clouds, offering prayers for a few days without rain for the cut grass to lie in the meadows. They needed then to make the very most of the long summer days, even though they had worked until after nine on the previous evening.

In these days of silage towers and combine harvesters, both weather and time are of much less importance. Farmers can never be lazy, but in twenty-first-century summers they can afford to rise a little later. They operate their complex machinery with little assistance now, for the hundreds of farm labourers and migrant workers whom they used to pay to follow behind the horses and the cutters into the fields are no more.

On a Saturday morning, with the weekend stretching luxuriously before them, the Lancashire industrial towns are even more blanketed in silence than the country. Where once the clogs would have been preparing to clatter over the cobbles to the Saturday morning shift in the cotton mills, the denizens snore on after the excesses of Friday night drinking.

In town as in country, the dawn chorus of the birds is over now, so that even the sounds of blackbird and thrush are sporadic. The urban fox finds the security of modern wheelie bins as frustrating as his rural brother finds the netting round the few free-range hen coops which remain, but his sporadic barks do not disturb a sleeping Brunton. The rising sun illuminates more and more of the narrow this away from your husband and the children we might have a confession, you see. I'm an incurable optimist. I'm not saying that I want you to have done this, you understand. It's just that a confession from anyone would be a wonderful thing for overworked policemen like myself and DC Murphy to hear, you see. We could all go off and enjoy our weekend.'

'Well, I didn't kill my dad, much as you and the more sensational tabloids might wish I had. But I've been giving the matter thought, as you asked me to do. I think Pam Williams might have killed him.'

She had hoped for some reaction from Peach on this: even outrage or hilarity would have been more acceptable than his calm acceptance of her suggestion, as if it was exactly what he would have expected from her.

He merely nodded a couple of times and said, 'And why would you think that, Mrs Hawksworth?'

'She's got a record, hasn't she?'

This time Peach did smile, infuriatingly, as if he were indulgently correcting a headstrong girl. 'Not a record. She inherited some money from an older friend who died a few years ago. Perfectly legally.'

'Having cultivated him, as she was cultivating my father.'

Again that complacent, understanding smile: she knew now that he was enjoying riling her. 'Dangerous word, "cultivating", in this context. Lawyers wouldn't like it – that's one thing to be said for it, I suppose. But there is no evidence that Mrs Williams was doing anything other than responding to Mr Aspin's advances. A mutual friendship was developing between two people of almost the same age. Whereas Mrs Williams had been twenty-five years younger than this other gentleman you mention who left her money. It seems they're not really parallel cases, are they?'

She hadn't expected him to discuss her legacy allegation seriously. The police had obviously researched it and now knew more about it than she did. It made her nervous about what else they might have researched, what more they might know that she did not. Already she was regretting venturing into the lion's den like this: being shut up with two hostile men in this cramped little room put her at an additional disadvantage. 'Steve said Dad and Mrs Williams had a spat after

Saturday's party. More than a spat, perhaps. I thought Dad might have threatened to go back on his marriage promise and ditch her without a quid.'

It was nearer than she could have conceived to the truth. Surely she couldn't know about her father's promise to pay off Pam Williams's hefty mortgage and the suspicion that that promise might have been withdrawn?

Peach said cautiously, 'Our information is that it was Mrs Williams who was annoyed because your father announced his plans to wed her. She hadn't agreed to that previously and he hadn't consulted her about what he was going to say last Saturday.'

'She's claiming she didn't plan to marry him?'

'All I'm saying is that she thought he was being too precipitate. He hadn't discussed it with her and she wanted time to prepare the family for it.'

'That's what she says, I suppose.'

'It is. And as yet, we've no reason to doubt the truth of it. It would explain this sudden and unexpected row, when by everyone's account your dad was feeling pretty pleased with himself. No one has given us any reason to think that it was Mr Aspin who initiated the dispute.'

'And no one except her has given you any reason to think the facts are as she reported them.' She hoped that was true: she couldn't see why any of the family would have said anything favourable to the woman.

'But surely those facts argue that Mrs Williams would be the last person who would wish to see Mr Aspin dead? In view of the financial rewards which she could expect to follow marriage, she had every reason to keep him alive.'

'But you know now that she'd had this dispute with him when things broke up after the meal. And she was the last person with him before he died.' She didn't know where that last wild statement had come from. Desperation, she supposed: she hadn't intended to say it.

Peach raised the very black eyebrows beneath the very white bald head. 'Interesting theory, that. Your father didn't die immediately after the celebration at Marton Towers, Mrs Hawksworth.'

'You mean he was killed somewhere else, and then dumped

there?' She got the right degree of amazement into her voice, partly because she had surprised herself, not only by the idea but by the speed at which her brain was working.

'No. We think he was lured back to Marton Towers later in the evening, perhaps at dusk or even after nightfall, and killed by a man or a woman who had gone there for that very purpose.'

She noticed the evenness of his tone, the way he had carefully included both genders in his trawl, even the way the eager young man beside him leaned forward a fraction, in anticipation of her reply.

She said doggedly, 'That person could still be Pam Williams.'

'Indeed it could. It seems likely that your father would only have gone back there to meet someone he trusted. Probably the woman he planned to marry or one of his immediate family.'

He was watching her, she knew, studying the effect of this latest scarcely veiled suggestion about her own actions that night.

She tried hopelessly to divert him. 'It could have been a business colleague. Or even someone from another firm that he was trying to do a deal with. Dad never turned away a business opportunity.' Even as she said it, she was not sure that it was true.

'It's possible he might have met his partner, Mr Oakley, who had been at the meal earlier. Someone from another firm is hardly likely, at that hour on a Saturday night.'

'I suppose not.' She took a deep breath. 'Well, I was at home with my husband, Chief Inspector.'

'So we've been told, yes. I don't suppose you've thought of anyone else who can confirm that for us, have you? Suspicious coppers always like outside support for a husband-wife alibi, if it's possible.'

'No, I haven't. I spent an hour and a half with my children that night, putting them to bed and reading them stories. I don't want them brought into this.'

'And neither do we, Mrs Hawksworth. Courts don't like evidence from children.'

'Then you'll have to rely on Steve to authenticate my story that I was at home at the time when my father was killed, won't you?' She tried to pour contempt into each phrase, so as to underline quite how ridiculous it was that they should suspect her.

'What do you plan to do now, Mrs Hawksworth?'

'Now?' She was playing for time, thrown by his sudden switch.

'In the next few years, I should say. Your father's death will make you a rich woman.'

She wanted to tell him to go hang himself, that this was her business and not his. But she found that she wanted to outline her plans, to convince him of her innocence by her co-operation. 'We shall probably move to a bigger house, with a little more room for the children. We'll get the best possible schooling for Daisy and the best possible care for Michael.' She felt suddenly that she was being disloyal to Steve, making him seem like an inadequate provider for the family. 'We were thinking about doing this anyway. Steve earns quite a good wage. It's just that money from Dad's estate will make things a little easier, that's all.'

'Were you planning to get your father to help you with this, even when he was alive?'

She wished again that she had talked to Steve about this: she might then know just what he had said to them. It was no doubt her fault rather than his that they'd hardly spoken about these things since Dad had been killed. 'Yes, we were, as a matter of fact. Dad was a good granddad and I'm sure he'd have wanted the best for Daisy. And for Michael.'

Brendan Murphy, who had done nothing but listen and watch, picked up the tiny hesitation between the mentions of the two children. He said softly, 'How did your father react to having a Down's syndrome grandchild, Mrs Hawksworth? Was it a shock to him?'

A new attack, from a different quarter. Louise strove to switch her concentration towards this other, less threatening figure. Was this a trick? What did they know already?

She said dully, 'It wasn't a shock. I was told after scans during the pregnancy that a Down's baby was likely. My father wanted me to have a termination, but I refused.' There, it was out. If they'd thought they were going to trip her up on it, they'd failed.

Murphy's voice came softly to her, like a doctor's offering therapy. 'Was there a serious disagreement about this between the two of you?'

'Serious enough. It came between Dad and me, for a time.' She wanted to be honest now. This was Michael she was talking about, and she couldn't be dishonest about poor innocent, smiling, lovely Michael.

'And were you reconciled at the time of Mr Aspin's death?'

She returned to the real world with a physical start, which was so abrupt that it was painful. 'You're asking if I hated my father enough to kill him, aren't you?'

It was Peach who said with unexpected gentleness, 'We're probing your relationship with your father at the time of his death, Mrs Hawksworth, as we are probing the relationships of all those who had the opportunity for this murder. These things aren't pleasant, but murder is the vilest of all crimes.'

'All right. Perhaps Dad and I would never have been quite as close as we had been before I was married, but we'd made it up. Once Michael was around, Dad loved him. You couldn't help doing that: no one could help doing that.' For a moment, she was near to tears as she thought of her engaging, vulnerable, wonderful son. 'Dad was going to help to make life easier for Michael. Easier for all of us.'

For a moment she was out of that soulless interview room and playing on the carpet at home with Michael.

Then Peach said, almost reluctantly it seemed, 'So the advent of Mrs Williams upon the scene must have been an unwelcome development for you.'

She was weary of deceit, of trying to work out what Steve and Carol and all the others had said to them and what these men already knew. 'It was something we hadn't foreseen. Dad told me all plans would have to be put on hold for a little time until Pam was "part of the family". That was the phrase he used to me when I was telling him what we needed for Michael and for Daisy.'

'Was that a phrase you passed on to your sister and the rest of the family?'

'It may have been. I don't remember. In any case, the situation must have been obvious to everyone.' She looked up, saw Brendan Murphy making a note, wondered what exact words he was using. Then she said, as if it was important that he record things correctly, 'Dad's death has changed all that. We'll have the money to go ahead with things quite soon now.'

It was twenty minutes after Louise Hawksworth had left the station that DCI Peach had another visitor.

A slightly built man, who looked taller than he was because of that slimness; a man with a lined face and a mouth which was framed more for sourness than smiling; a man whose small, sharp nose was topped by grey eyes which were shrewd and observant. A man with a well-worn blue anorak over his arm, even with the temperature climbing into the seventies on this English summer day.

'Feel the cold, do you?' said Percy.

For a moment, his visitor was disconcerted. Then he looked down at the battered garment upon his arm and said, 'Force of habit. I spend a lot of time out of doors, hanging about. You get used to protecting yourself against the cold. I didn't realize the day would be as warm as this when I set out. Besides, I was expecting to feel the cold in Brunton. I was in Italy until last night.'

'Aye. Withholding information from a CID team engaged in a murder investigation. Since last Tuesday night at least.'

John Kirkby had expected a warmer welcome than this. He said huffily, 'I've come here of my own free will to offer information which I hope might be of use to you. I explained when I made my phone call from Lake Garda that it needed to be communicated in person to the officer in charge of the investigation.'

'Aye. And 'appen you thought there'd be brass in it for you, from those bastards who call themselves the fourth estate. Well, you can forget that. There's an embargo on any sensitive press releases, at present.'

Kirkby thought for an instant that he would assert his independence and declare pompously that he was an independent operator, not a police employee, so that no jumped-up DCI could tell him what deals he could do with the press. But only for an instant. Something about this bald-headed, pugnacious man told him that this was not a man to cross. He repeated the mantra of the private detective. 'It was Mr Aspin who was employing me and paying me. My first duty was and still is to him.'

'Your first duty is to see the law of the land observed.' Peach relaxed a little. 'In this case, that chimes with your duty to the man who employed you: you must surely wish to see his killer brought to justice.'

'I do. And I agree that your interests and mine are now the same. I'm ex-job, DCI Peach. I know how these things work. I wanted to report in person, not read things over the phone to some sergeant I'd never met. Coppers have been known to leak things to the press boys when there's something in it for them.'

'Not my coppers. Their feet wouldn't touch.' But Peach knew that the man was right. When the less scrupulous sections of the media were offering large sums for confidential information, there was an increasing tendency for police personnel to sell information, especially when they knew that with a big team the chances of detection were slight. 'So you were scared of some sod leaping in and selling what you hope to sell yourself.'

'Any contact I have with the press is legitimate. I'll only reveal what you sanction me to reveal.'

'Aye. Permit me a little cynicism about that, Mr Kirkby. Nothing personal, you understand. If you're ex-job as you say, you'll have seen how human nature responds to filthy lucre. Let's hear what you have to tell me about your work for Geoffrey Charles Aspin, your late employer.'

'Mr Aspin had asked me to look into the activities of his son-in-law, a man called Jemal Bilic.'

'Aye. We know Mr Bilic.'

'Then you may know about his activities.' Kirkby was suddenly disappointed.

'Tell me.'

'He's a villain. I can't give you all the evidence and the witnesses the Crown Prosecution Service would demand, but I know he's a villain.'

With the mention of the CPS, there was an immediate bond between copper and ex-copper. 'Never mind those buggers for the moment,' Peach said grimly. 'Tell me what you know about our friend Bilic.'

'He's bringing in illegal immigrants. Mainly young women but also a few young men from Eastern Europe.'

Trafficking in human misery; selling dreams which turn into nightmares. 'You can give us evidence?'

'I can't give you a court case, as I said. I haven't the resources: I'm basically a one-man band. But I can give you times and places. And a few names. Things you can easily follow up with your own team.'

Peach nodded. 'Customs and Immigration are already on to Bilic. I'll pass on your information to the senior officer involved. The situation has been complicated by the murder inquiry which has overtaken it. It's murder which is my concern, Mr Kirkby. When did you last report to Mr Aspin?'

'I last saw him six weeks before he died at his factory. But I'd been in frequent touch with him by phone in the weeks before he died. I was expecting him to phone me whilst I was in Italy. Then I read in a newspaper that he was dead and got in touch with you.'

Percy knew how these things worked. Kirkby had turned over a stone and found dangerous things beneath it. He was one man investigating vicious and ruthless men, without the vast resources of the police service behind him. Meetings with his employer would have been perilous for him; he would have been reluctant even to put things in writing for the man who was employing him, in case they fell into the wrong hands. He found himself filled with a reluctant admiration for this seedy figure with the stained anorak resting incongruously upon his forearm. 'Makes a change from divorce cases, I suppose.'

Kirkby gave him no more than a wry smile by way of reply.

'Do you think Bilic knew that Aspin was on to him?'

'Not through me, he didn't. I don't know what use he made of the information I gave to him. Sometimes people are inclined to think they can sort things out within the family. I'd warned Mr Aspin that it wouldn't work in this case. I'd told him the only safe way to handle it was to go to the police.'

'Which he might have been about to do at the time of his death. You'd better give me what you have.'

Kirkby hesitated for a moment: he felt a natural disinclination to hand over what his employer had paid him to gather to the police. It came hard to relinquish all this dangerously acquired information without any payment. But he knew that he had no choice. He was out of his league with murder and that was why he had come here. He produced a personal file from the pocket of his anorak and handed over four pages which were the only tangible evidence of months of work. The small, neat writing gave an account of dates and times and names which would be gold dust to those who were pursuing Jemal Bilic.

Peach glanced over these details, his silent admiration increasing with each phrase penned by this shabby figure with his own kind of stubborn, unlikely courage. He said brusquely, as if recognizing a weakness in himself, 'I'll pass these details on to the team from Customs and Immigration. You'll be due a payment from Aspin's estate, but you'll have to fight for that yourself. I'll try to make sure you're not eventually called as a Crown Court witness.'

Kirkby nodded. At least this stern CID man appreciated his situation. Private detectives did not like appearing in court. Their work dictated that they should remain as anonymous as possible. Nor did they make moral pronouncements upon those who employed them.

John Kirkby made an exception to that here. 'Geoffrey Aspin was a good man. I hope you get the bastard who throttled him.'

Pamela Williams seemed to her son to be amazingly calm.

Justin Williams had thought she would be very disturbed, in view of what he had read and what little she had told him on the phone about the murder inquiry into the death of Geoffrey Aspin. He had come into the house expecting to find her on edge and anxious to see him, but she appeared detached and calm.

'Sorry I couldn't get over until today. It's been a busy week,' he said, as he took her awkwardly into his arms.

'I didn't expect to see you. I'm surprised you've even come over today. I thought you'd be busy with the children on Saturday.'

'You're my priority, Mum, in a crisis,' Justin said determinedly.

'Crisis? Oh, you mean the hunt for Geoff's murderer. I expect they'll arrest the person responsible, eventually.'

'They're no nearer to getting him yet, then?'

'Him or her, dear. The CID made it very clear to me that they thought a woman might have done this.'

'They questioned you again, then?' Justin tried not to seem too anxious, tried not to see again the image of his children watching their grandmother being taken into the Crown Court which his wife had set dramatically before him last night.

'I'm a suspect. I was the last person seen with Geoff. We were having a hell of a row at the time. Of course I'm a suspect.' Her irritation with her son led to the first real animation she had shown since he came into the house.

'I understand that. But I thought they'd have cleared you by now, Mum.'

'I don't know what the police are thinking. They don't tell you that – I suppose you wouldn't expect them to. I had a motive. Geoff was clearing the mortgage on this place for me. He might have changed his mind about that, after the big row we had. That's obviously what they think anyway.'

'It's not a world I understand. I didn't think I'd ever be involved in a murder investigation.'

'You're not involved. It's me who's involved. You're safely on the other side of the Pennines.' She felt guilty with herself for her irritation with his lack of imagination; after all, he'd taken the trouble to come over those same Pennines to see her today. 'I'm sorry. I know you mean well, Justin. It's just that I've had nothing else but this to think about all week.'

'Do you want me to prescribe anything, Mum? You do look a little drawn.'

She wanted to yell at him that he should behave like a son, not a doctor, that he should just give her a real, prolonged hug and make words irrelevant. Instead, she said as calmly as she could, 'I don't need medication. I just need the police off my back. They know things about me from the past. They obviously think I might have been after Geoff's money.'

'That's ridiculous, Mum.' He tried to sound convincing.

'They can't seriously think you killed Geoffrey Aspin.' He sought feverishly for reasons, wanting to convince himself as much as her. 'Surely these people can see you wouldn't have had the strength to do it, for a start.'

'He was taken from behind and by surprise, apparently. No great strength was required. It could easily have been a woman.'

How cold and objective she seemed about it! Justin was alarmed rather than reassured by her composure and her apparent detachment when she should have been emotional. He took a deep breath. 'I think you should let me take you back with me, Mum. There's room in the house and I'm sure you'd be—'

'Thank you, but I shan't do that. The police would want to be informed of any movement outside the area and I don't want to draw attention to myself. I shall stay here until an arrest is made.'

She drew him on to other things, showed him what she had been doing in the garden, quizzed him about the doings of his family. He spent another two hours with her, without either of them mentioning Aspin's death again. It was she who made the conversational running, whilst he marvelled repeatedly at how laid back and unemotional she seemed.

As he drove home over the M62, Justin found himself hoping desperately that the arrest which must surely come soon would not be that of his mother.

If you want a dangerous man brought in, send a hard bastard. One of Percy Peach's axioms. Just common sense, in his view.

Detective Constable Clyde Northcott was a hard bastard. That was not the only reason why Peach had recruited the man to his CID team, but it was certainly one of them. He called in Northcott, who had been hoping to finish his Saturday stint at about midday, and gave his instructions. 'Take Brendan Murphy down there with you. If Jemal Bilic takes on two fit young lads like you, he's thicker than I think he is. If he doesn't want to come in to see Uncle Percy, arrest the bugger on suspicion of murder.' He went to the door of his office and called an afterthought down the corridor to the rapidly disappearing DC. 'Oh, and watch he doesn't pull a blade on you: he looks like that sort of joker to me!'

It wasn't the most pleasant of thoughts to carry in your head as you drove out of Brunton at lunchtime on a Saturday.

Northcott had once dealt a little in drugs and been a suspect in a murder case himself. Peach had spotted potential where others saw only brutishness, and had persuaded Northcott to join first the police and then, two years later, his own hand-picked team in CID.

Brendan Murphy went with him. He was softer-voiced, though he could handle himself well in any skirmish. Despite his name and his Irish ancestry, he was Brunton born and bred. He knew the history of the local-born villains better than some of them knew it themselves. He got on well with his contemporary Northcott, with whom he had a largely unspoken understanding. Despite the racial gibes which Northcott sometimes collected from drunks too far gone, he too was born in Lancashire.

They had driven for three miles before Northcott said, 'If he offers any resistance, we act tough. Right?'

Murphy glanced sideways at the speaker. It seemed odd to see Clyde Northcott behind the wheel of the police Mondeo; he was more used to seeing him astride his Yamaha 350, crouching almost horizontally over the fuel tank. Indeed, Brendan remembered one or two hair-raising journeys on the pillion of the gleaming machine which was Northcott's pride and joy.

Murphy said, 'You do the talking. Don't get closer than eight feet to him. If he does pull a knife, I'll go for it before he can even offer a threat.'

Northcott nodded, perfectly confident that his companion could do exactly what he promised. They didn't speak any more. The thought of a murder suspect with a knife caused a little tenseness, which they preferred to think of as concentration.

They parked between the high gateposts of the Edwardian house. They didn't intend to allow their quarry the chance, but if he chose to do a runner by car, he'd find their vehicle blocking his way. They stood for a moment looking up at the high, ivy-clad front elevation of the house, with its mellowed brick and York stone windows. It was the kind of house which they could never afford, from their side of the law, but there was no envy in their minds. Part of the training from Peach was to regard and treat all people as equals, whatever obeisance Tommy Bloody Tucker might pay to rank and wealth.

These two powerful young men were merely gathering their resources for the exchange to come.

Northcott half-expected a servant to open the big oak door above the stone steps. Instead, they were confronted by an unusually discomposed Carol Bilic, who asked them peremptorily what they wanted. They showed their warrant cards, which she inspected, as most people did not, and asked to see Mr Jemal Bilic.

She did not speak at first, but nodded two or three times, as if certain things were now falling into place for her. Then she said, 'He's not here.'

'Where is he, Mrs Bilic?'

'I don't know.'

Northcott began to tell her patiently that she would be unwise to conceal her husband's presence in the house from them, that he was wanted for questioning by the police on serious matters. Before he could get as far as the details of what being an accessory after the fact might imply, the woman standing above him said impatiently, 'I don't know where he is, you fool! He left this morning, before I was up. Look round the side of the house if you don't believe me. You'll see that his car's missing! And before you ask, I've not the faintest idea where he's gone!'

The two big men were almost as silent on their way back to the station as they had been on their outward journey.

It was not until they were turning into the car park that Brendan Murphy voiced the thought of both of them. 'Peach's not going to be pleased about this!'

Twenty

Agnes Blake was feeling very pleased with life. She was always delighted when Percy Peach was coming to tea. Or, as she had said when she was doing her morning shopping, when her daughter's fiancé was coming to tea.

'The only thing wrong with this is that you should be out there playing cricket,' she told Percy firmly as he came up the path to the old cottage. She gestured with a wide sweep of her arm towards the world beyond Pendle, towards the grounds of the Lancashire League towns, where Percy's dancing feet had until recently advanced down the wickets and driven boundaries off toiling bowlers.

'Anno Domini, Mrs B. It catches up with all of us,' said Percy with a sad shake of his head.

'You're thirty-nine, not seventy,' said Agnes with disgust. 'You could have played on for another three or four years at least with your skills! When you get to my age, you'll wish you had done.'

Percy had an uncomfortable feeling that she might be right. It was on days like this, when the sun blazed down and the wickets were hard and bowlers had to work hard for everything they got, that his fingers itched to pick up the bat from the corner of his garage and the battered blue cap from the back of his wardrobe.

'My eyes aren't as quick as they used to be,' he said sadly. Though when he saw some of the wayward bowling at a higher level on television, he still thought he could have flicked away a few fours and sixes. You were always a champion in your armchair.

He looked automatically at the colour photograph of himself with his cap pulled down jauntily towards his right eye and his bat raised towards the crowd's applause. It stood proudly beside the black and white one of Lucy's dead father on the mantelpiece. He realized with a shock that the photograph of himself had been changed, though the picture of Agnes's dead husband Bill climbing the steps with his sweater over his shoulder and looking shyly at the camera after taking six wickets was a fixed icon in this sitting room.

'You've changed my picture, Mrs B,' he said wonderingly.

'Aye. I've got several, now. Bought them from the *Evening Telegraph*.' She gave him the smug grin of a seventy-year-old who was delighted that she could still surprise the young. Then she added severely, 'I'd still be collecting new ones, if you hadn't retired much too early.'

'He's taken up golf,' said her daughter innocently, well aware of the reaction this would produce.

'*Golf!*' Neither Lucy nor Percy had ever heard so much contempt compressed into a single monosyllable. Consequently, they loved to trigger this supreme scorn from the cricket-loving Agnes.

'Some of the people at the station tell me he's now quite good at it,' added Lucy.

'Game for red-nosed colonels and pompous twits!' said Agnes with confident derision.

'That's an old-fashioned view of the game, Mum. All sorts of people play golf now. Look at Tiger Woods.'

'I do. And every time I see him, I think he should be playing cricket. Loose-limbed, that lad is, like Gary Sobers. Could have been opening both the batting and the bowling at test level like Gary, I reckon, if he hadn't been badly advised in his youth.'

'But Tiger is American, Mum,' protested Lucy mildly.

'*American!*' Her mother's performance on this word was less impressive than on golf only by virtue of the fact that this time she had four syllables into which to cram her disdain. 'Sex and violence. That's what we get from America!'

Lucy was tempted to point out that there wasn't a high incidence of those things in golf, but she'd had her fun. 'Why don't we eat outside? It's such a lovely day. Let's use your nice new patio.'

She had persuaded her mother to have the flags laid only

in the autumn of the previous year. Agnes looked at her darkly, then glanced up at the cloudless blue sky and relented. 'You'll have to help me bring stuff out, our Lucy.'

Peach and her daughter had the table set with the ham salad and the fruits of the older woman's baking with surprising speed. Some time later, when Agnes was pouring the tea into her best china cups, she said a little wistfully, 'I should have gone with you to Marton Towers last week, our Lucy. I didn't know I was going to miss a murder.'

Peach said breezily, 'You wouldn't have seen anything worthwhile, Mrs B. But with your powers of observation, you'd likely have picked up more than your daughter did.'

With fair colouring, dark red hair and a few freckles round the temples, it is difficult to do a good glower: you tend to turn red when you should be darkening thunderously. But Lucy Blake managed it: Percy decided it was a glower almost as good as Tommy Bloody Tucker at his most frustrated.

Lucy said with a fair degree of steel, 'I was enjoying a party to celebrate the sixtieth birthday of the father of my oldest friend. I had no idea at the time that it was going to end in homicide.'

'Ah, but if you'd been a proper detective, you'd have had a hunch, you see. People in books are always having hunches. Particularly people in American books.' He glanced sideways at Agnes Blake and was emboldened by the delight on her face at this latest slur on the special relationship. 'Useful things, hunches. Private eyes seem to rely almost exclusively upon them. My team seems to find them difficult to come by.'

'Perhaps because we know exactly what reaction we'd get, if we dared to produce anything as esoteric as a hunch for you.'

Percy smiled happily at the thought. 'A private eye came in to see me this morning at the station, Mrs B.' He delighted himself with the thought of how the shabby John Kirkby would have squirmed at that description.

Agnes Blake resisted the temptation to follow her favourite man down this fascinating byway. 'I hope you're not getting our Lucy into dangerous situations again, Percy Peach.'

'I'm doing my best to protect her, but you know how head-strong young women can be.' Percy professed the policeman's professional disdain for psychologists and psychiatrists, but his own knowledge of the way minds worked was surprisingly extensive. He knew, for instance, that women of twenty-nine are still young girls to their mothers and that all mothers like to think of their children as headstrong.

'Marriage will take her out of danger.'

'It will certainly be a large step in that direction, Mrs B.' Percy nodded sagely and closed his eyes in ecstasy as he bit into an Agnes Blake scone.

'You two are talking about me as if I'm not here again. You do it all the time,' said Lucy resentfully.

'It's high time we fixed a date for t'wedding. Now that we're all agreed it's going to happen,' said Agnes complacently.

'I agree, Mrs B. Forward planning is the secret of success. Superintendent Tucker tells me that frequently.'

'And we all know how much attention you pay to him,' said Lucy tartly.

Percy modestly accepted the slice of rich fruitcake which Agnes urged upon him. He looked at the sky, which was now darkening from the lighter shade of Wedgwood to the darker one, and said with relish, 'Our revered leader will be getting banged up for the night, any time now.'

Lucy and he were at last reconciled by the thought of the bewildered Tucker being locked away in a prison cell after a day of unsuccessful networking.

It was Agnes Blake who eventually broke the contented silence with a sally down an unexpected avenue. She said darkly, 'I told our Lucy that no good would come of it when Geoffrey Aspin began to dabble with women.'

'He wasn't "dabbling with women", Mum. His wife had been dead for nearly four years and he was a lonely man. He was developing a deep relationship with *one* woman, whom he planned to marry.'

Agnes considered it a mother's privilege to ignore logical arguments from her daughter when it suited her. She repeated stolidly, 'I said no good would come of it, and it didn't.'

Lucy thought of the picture of her beloved father in pride of place on the mantelpiece and wondered whether this was another statement of her mother's refusal to consider any other man for herself since Bill Blake's death over a decade ago. She said gently, 'Geoff Aspin might well be alive and well today if he hadn't decided upon a second marriage. But that doesn't mean that he was wrong to look for happiness.'

'You sound like a Mills and Boon, our Lucy,' said her mother with waspish satisfaction. She looked at Percy Peach for confirmation and found him sporting his widest beam of approval.

Lucy changed a subject where she was having scant success. 'Louise was looking very tired, Mum. She's got two children to look after, Daisy and Michael. Remember I told you that Michael has Down's syndrome.'

Agnes thought of the laughing teenager with flying hair and an infectious laugh who had once come frequently to her cottage. 'Life changes for all of us, love. How's her husband getting on?'

Lucy had forgotten that her mother had been at Louise's wedding, that she'd known Steve Hawksworth and liked him at that time. She hoped this wasn't going to be another oblique attack on her own unmarried state. 'He's all right, I think. I didn't get the chance to talk to him much at Marton Towers.'

And any talk since the murder was professional and confidential. Agnes Blake knew the rules. 'Has he got his own business yet? I know that was one of his ambitions when he'd only just started work.'

'No, he's still working as an accountant for Robinson's in Brunton. But he's doing well enough, I think. Not as well as Carol's husband, Jemal, though. They seem very prosperous but not very happy together.'

There was a silence, whilst Percy and Lucy wondered exactly where Jemal Bilic might be at this moment.

Agnes Blake said that she had never known the elder daughter very well and her husband not at all. She wanted to ask Lucy about the mysterious woman Pam Williams who had set all this off, but she knew that she must not trespass on to sensitive ground with a case in progress.

'They announced on Radio Lancashire this afternoon that Jemal Bilic had gone missing,' Agnes said. 'That he's wanted by the police for questioning.'

Percy shrugged. 'It will come out soon enough, Mrs B. He's been bringing in illegal immigrants.'

Agnes's eyes widened in horror. 'Like those poor Chinese cockle-pickers who were drowned in Morecambe Bay?'

The men who had been used as slave labour, undetected until they'd been caught by the treacherous tides and drowned. Twenty-three of them had died in 2004, though only twenty-one of the bodies had ever been retrieved. A few years ago now, but still vivid in the horrified minds of Lancastrians.

'Not cockle-pickers, but people like that, yes.'

'Those poor men.' Agnes shook her head a few times and the three were silent, dwelling for a moment on the depths of human misery and desperation, and the depths of human avarice which could trade upon such things.

'The people Bilic was bringing in are mostly from Eastern Europe, it seems, but they paid huge sums to get here and then were treated more or less as slaves when they arrived.'

It seemed from what he had heard from the investigation that most of the women were being forced to work as prostitutes. Peach sighed, looking up at the darkening sky: it was a naive thought, but at the end of days like this, it seemed even more amazing that there should be such depravity abroad. 'It's Customs and Immigration who are handling it. It's not our investigation, I'm glad to say. The private eye I mentioned had some valuable information, though, which has been passed on to them. Geoffrey Aspin had employed the man to find out just what his son-in-law was up to.'

'And now the man's killed him.'

Lucy glanced sharply at Peach, then said, 'We know Carol's husband is a wrong 'un, Mum. We don't know that he killed Geoff Aspin.'

That was a question Peach and Blake discussed more openly as midnight approached and they drove back to Brunton through the warm darkness. But it was not until well after dawn on Sunday morning, as he struggled into consciousness, that Peach thought he had the answer to it.

It was at that point that a chance remark from the previous

evening flicked the tiny connection in his brain which gave him the solution.

There was a watch on all major airports and departure ports for Jemal Bilic.

Twenty-first-century terrorism and the measures it has compelled have brought certain beneficial side effects. One of them is that it is less easy for wanted men to slip through cordons. Vigilance has now become a way of life for people who operate in such places.

Ironically, Bilic was arrested not at one of the outlets where hundreds of people had been alerted but at a small private airfield just south of Glasgow. It was known that he had flown in and out of the country from there before, so it was under discreet surveillance from the moment the news came through that he had fled from Brunton. In the end, it was something as mundane as the registration number on his Mercedes which alerted the watchers to his arrival there on Sunday morning.

There were a lot of police on the spot within twenty minutes, but they did not rush things. The more of the man's staff they could corner with him, the greater the chance of scuppering his vicious enterprise for ever. Jemal Bilic was preparing to board the small single-engined plane when the forces which had encircled the area moved in and arrested him.

His dark eyes flashed quickly to right and left as he was warned that it might prejudice his defence if he did not declare things he might later wish to use in court. He saw police everywhere: there was no escape and he knew it. He watched the handcuffs being clicked shut over his slim, steely wrists and delivered the ritual defiance which was all he had left to him: 'This is some ridiculous mistake and you will be made to pay for it. I shall say nothing until I have my lawyer here.'

The arresting officer was far too experienced to let his distaste for the man stray into verbal abuse. He spoke without emotion but with evident satisfaction as his prisoner was put into the back of the car. 'You are also wanted for questioning in connection with a murder in Brunton, Lancashire.'

*　　*　　*

Carol Bilic hesitated for a long time before she tapped in the number.

When her sister answered, Carol was uncharacteristically hesitant. She asked about Louise's children, hardly listened to the response, gave a few unremarkable details of the progress of her own older offspring.

When Louise asked her if Lisa was still as keen as ever on her horse, Carol's preoccupation did not permit her to reply. She cut through her sister's polite enquiries with a terse, 'Jemal's gone.'

'Gone?'

'Yes. Didn't you hear the radio or the television?' She was suddenly irritated by the innocence and ignorance of her sibling, as she had been when she was eighteen and Louise was eleven.

'We haven't had them on today. We took the children into the park for a while.' Not for the first time, Louise reflected how different her life was from that of her sister. She mouthed to Steve on the other side of the room that it was Carol. He went into the hall and picked up the other phone, coming back into the room with the instrument at his ear and his eyes anxiously upon his wife.

Carol rapped out a series of tense sentences. 'Well, Jemal's gone. I don't mean just that he's left me. He's fled from the police. He took his car and went early this morning before I was up. They've announced on the radio that they want to speak to him. That's what I meant when I said hadn't you heard.'

Louise did not know what to say. She managed a limp, 'I'm sorry!' which only made Carol more impatient on the other end of the line.

'Don't waste any sympathy on me! Still less on the bastard who was my husband. We were finished anyway, before all this blew up: I told you that. I'm sure he's going to deserve everything he gets!' Years of accumulated bitterness came out in the vehemence of this last sentiment.

Louise and Steve were looking with wide eyes at each other as the vitriol poured into their ears. Steve made a small, urgent gesture and his wife said tentatively, 'Carol, are you telling me Jemal murdered Dad?'

'I don't know, do I?' Her frustration burst out and she

heard the anger in the question herself. 'Sorry. I can't get my head round what's happening. All I know is that two plain clothes coppers came here looking for him yesterday and I had to tell them that he'd gone. And that I didn't know where he'd gone.' She heard her voice rising impatiently again: Carol was overtaken by a sudden, totally illogical, feeling that they should already know all this, that they shouldn't be delaying her with such banalities. 'They want him for other things. Serious things, I'm sure. I know now why the bastard never told me what he was up to.'

'But did he kill our dad, Carol?'

She hadn't heard Louise use that phrase 'our dad' for years. Not since they had lived under the family roof together, she thought. 'He may have done. I don't know, do I? The policemen didn't tell me what they wanted to speak to him about.'

From their more modest house, Steve Hawksworth then spoke to his sister-in-law. 'It's Steve here, Carol. I think Jemal might have murdered him. I'm afraid he probably did, if he's got other crimes on his hands. Perhaps your dad was on to him. Perhaps Jemal killed Geoff to prevent him telling the police what he knew.'

Carol Bilic was suddenly resentful that this man who had always seemed to her so timid should be using her dead father's first name like this. Her voice was brittle with emotion as she said, 'That's another thing I might have to face, isn't it?' She faltered into more words, then stopped abruptly and said, 'Look, can I come and see you? My kids are out for the day and—'

With the mention of children, Louise was suddenly firm and decisive. 'It had better be this evening. I'll get Daisy and Michael into bed and then we can have a proper, uninterrupted discussion.'

'Thank you. I'll come at about eight. I can arrange for my kids to do a stopover: they'll be better out of the house at present. I might have more news of Jemal and what's happening by then.'

Carol Bilic stared at the phone for a long moment when she had put it down, trying to sort out the issues in her teeming and uncharacteristically disordered mind.

*　　*　　*

Chief Superintendent Thomas Bulstrode Tucker cursed the prison service, the progressives who had landed him in the cell at Nottingham as part of their experiment, the Sunday train services which had left him on the platform at Manchester for half an hour.

He even cursed the perfect summer weather: why should the rest of the world have enjoyed two such balmy days whilst he had been incarcerated? He had glared up resentfully at the oblong of blue sky above the exercise yard as a hundred senior policemen paraded ridiculously round the cramped area during the forty minutes of exercise time they had been permitted on Saturday and Sunday.

He told himself that it was good to be out of that ridiculous prison uniform and back in his own clothes. What a disaster that had been! You couldn't even distinguish rank under that shabby grey denim. He'd spent twenty minutes cultivating some bloke from Brighton because he thought he was a chief constable, then found that he was no more than a humble inspector from the traffic section, who'd been sent on this pointless exercise to leave his seniors free to enjoy their weekends.

Chief Superintendent Tucker had queued with the man for that awful prison grub, sat talking about football with him at the table, endured all that drivel about the trials of the job at the seaside, where the population of the town could triple at a summer weekend, murmured his sympathy about the hardness of the beds in the cramped, overcrowded cells – and all for nothing.

All this was supposed to make you more understanding about the rest of the world, that pompous twit had said in his address at the end of the weekend. You were supposed to feel sympathy not only for the unfortunates who were locked away from the world in places like this but for those nearer to you in the hierarchy, those lesser ranks whose fate it was to be ordered about by you in their working lives.

Superintendent Tucker had listened and nodded his head dutifully and thoughtfully in all the right places, whilst his brain had told him what a load of pretentious codswallop this was. He'd show these lesser ranks what was what, when he was back in the station on Monday morning with this wasted weekend behind him. Brunton CID section had better be very careful indeed in the coming week, if it wished to avoid the wrath of its principal officer.

The train ran at last between the deserted platforms at Brunton. Only three people alighted from the thinly peopled carriages. Tucker stumped down the platform and out of the station. Not a taxi in sight. He had thought of ringing Barbara from Manchester to ask her to pick him up in the centre of Brunton, but had decided that he did not want to face her resentful countenance any earlier than was strictly necessary. Now that seemed the lesser of two evils.

Tucker stood with his suitcase and looked dolefully round the normally busy square in front of the station; apart from public transport, it was deserted at this hour on a baking Sunday evening. Wait for that elusive taxi: there was nothing else for it.

Then he had the first happening in several hours to relieve his pervading gloom. He glimpsed a maroon car he thought he recognized on the other side of the square. It disappeared behind two of the town's green corporation buses for a moment, but when it emerged, he was sure. Percy Peach! For once he was delighted to see his old adversary.

Then delight turned first to dismay and then to fury. Peach, his eyes determinedly and dutifully upon the deserted road ahead of him, ignored his chief's frantic gestures and accelerated straight past him.

It was fortunate that none of the church-going citizens of Brunton was within earshot of the head of its CID section that Sunday evening, for they would have heard a series of verbal obscenities which breached all decorum. Then, when it seemed the insufferable chief inspector was at the furthest point of the square and about to disappear, the maroon car swung in a wide arc and came slowly back towards the lone figure with the suitcase.

The window slid down and a beaming Peach said, 'Welcome home, sir! Can I offer you a lift?'

'I thought you'd missed me,' Tucker complained whiningly. He struggled into the back seat: he might have to accept a lift, but at least he would treat this minion as a taxi-driver.

'Didn't see you until the last minute, sir. Thought it must be safer to go round again, as the advanced driving manual advises us.'

Tucker, who had never read any such publication, brooded darkly for a moment, then said with what good grace he could manage, 'Anyway, I'm glad to see you, Peach. There was no sign of a taxi.'

'Thought Mrs Tucker might have been detailed to collect you,' said Peach, studying the road ahead and relishing the thought of Tucker attempting to 'detail' the formidable Barbara to do any such thing.

'I didn't want to worry her on a Sunday evening,' said Tucker. Then, because that didn't sound convincing even to him, he said, 'I'm on my way home from a most useful and instructive weekend.'

'Really, sir. You found slopping out a rewarding exercise, then?'

'I found the whole experience refreshing.' Tucker cudgelled his brain for some of the phrases that infuriating psychologist had used in his final address. 'It gave me an insight into the minds of people who lead very different lives from ours. It showed me how to understand the reactions to corrective regimes which the criminals we labour to incarcerate have to endure.'

'Really, sir. It sounds quite riveting.' Peach savoured the sight of two young women in summer dresses skipping across the zebra crossing in front of him. 'Got on well with the other poor sods there, did you?'

'It was good to be able to exchange notes with like-minded people from all over the country.'

'It must have been, sir. Did you get in any really useful creep . . . sorry, I mean did you enjoy the contact with minds as fine as your own, sir?'

'The object of the exercise was not personal aggrandisement, Peach. Do you realize that most of our criminal fraternity comes from the social groups D and E.'

'I think I was aware of that, yes. From my practical studies, you see, sir. I come face to face with rather a lot of the bastards. Survived all right on the iron rations, did you, sir?'

'I can handle Spartan regimes rather well, thank you, Peach.'

'Yes, sir. You were at public school, weren't you?'

'The aim of this weekend was to broaden our horizons, to increase our awareness of the philosophy behind corrective regimes.' Tucker sought desperately for the other phrases he had been striving for hours to reject. 'I don't mind admitting that I now feel a fuller and more rounded person. To be a senior officer in the modern police service, you need imagination and versatility, you know.'

Percy reflected that imagination and versatility were not qualities he would immediately associate with his chief. 'I'll tell the lads and lasses down below to expect an improvement in your philosophy, sir.'

The chief superintendent glared fiercely, but it had little effect on the back of a bald head. 'You need both to broaden your horizons and to increase your interests, Peach.'

Percy was tempted to dwell in detail upon the contours and physiology of DS Blake as embodying his interests. Instead, he said by way of a modest rejoinder, 'I do play a little golf, sir.'

Tucker was not so stupid that he did not recognize the need to veer away from a dangerous subject when it was broached. He said aggressively, 'Have you made an arrest in the Aspin murder case yet?'

'Getting near to one, I think, sir. Not many suspects in the D and E social classes, though. Perhaps I should have a rethink and find a more working-class suspect.'

Tucker looked through the window and saw that they were now within a mile of his home. There was no need for much more conversation with this odious underling who was doing him a good turn. He sighed and said with the air of a man who was a martyr to duty, 'Is there anything you wish to report to me?'

There wasn't really. But there might just be the opportunity to leave Tommy Bloody Tucker thoroughly confused and securely up a gum tree at the same time: Percy thought deeply for a moment and decided that this was not a mixed metaphor but two different concepts, each of them delightful. 'You won't have heard, sir, during your weekend on retreat. Jemal Bilic did a runner.'

'You've let him get away?'

You could always rely on a positive and encouraging response from Tommy Bloody Tucker. 'He was arrested this morning, sir, at an airport just south of Glasgow.'

'I always told you it would be him, you know.' Tucker was already conjecturing how he could incorporate this claim into his press conference.

'Mrs Williams still hasn't provided us with an alibi for the time of the murder.' Percy glanced into his rear-view mirror, saw his chief's bewilderment at the name and added helpfully, 'The woman Geoffrey Aspin was planning to marry, sir. The one who had the big row with him after the bunfight at Marton Towers.'

'Ah! *Cherchez les femmes*, Peach. An old-fashioned principle, but still a sound one in my view.'

'Yes, sir. It's interesting to see how much more broad-minded your attitude has become, as a result of your weekend in the can. And Mr Aspin's business partner, Denis Oakley, is now using the firm's money to relieve his private financial worries. A thing he wouldn't have been able to do before Mr Aspin's demise.'

Tucker's brow furrowed at this plethora of discoveries. 'This is the man you said wasn't a Freemason, isn't it?'

'I'm not sure I did, sir. But as far as I am aware, Mr Oakley is not a member of the Fraternity.'

'He may very well be your man at the end of the day. Financial desperation is often a motive for murder.'

'Is it really, sir? I must remember that. But here we are at your beautiful home. It's a pleasure to return you to the bosom of your family.'

Peach was pleased to see the bosom in question presented in the open doorway of the Edwardian house. Brünnhilde Barbara's bust was as impressive as ever, and a little way above it there loured a frown of pleasingly Wagnerian dimensions. He waved happily to this vision as he drove away.

It was always a pleasure to fire a few red herrings across Tommy Bloody Tucker's bow. This time that really was a mixed but totally satisfying metaphor.

Twenty-One

At half past eight that evening on the same Sunday, with the sun deepening towards crimson in the western sky behind her, Carol Bilic parked her car in the drive of her sister's house. She sat pensively behind the wheel for a full minute before climbing reluctantly out of the car and ringing the bell beside the front door.

Louise opened the door immediately and smiled a little nervously at her sister. 'Come in. The children are safely in bed.'

Carol was relieved to hear it. She always said she wasn't much good with children, except for her own. In truth, she was happy enough to chat to Louise's Daisy, who was a bright little girl, full of childish prattle. She found poor Michael – and she was well aware that Louise would have been outraged to hear her thinking of him as 'poor Michael' – quite difficult.

The boy smiled a lot, in a vacant, innocent, toddler's sort of way, but he hadn't any worthwhile language development yet, as far as Carol could see. She couldn't think of things to say to him, and when he interrupted his happy burbling to try to communicate with her, she couldn't tell what he was trying to say. She'd attempted to play with him, but it didn't help that he was so slow to pick things up; he seemed obstinately determined to ignore what you were trying to get him to do. It didn't help that Louise doted on the boy so and watched you when you were with him: it made you perpetually afraid of saying or doing the wrong thing.

She was pleased to see that Steve Hawksworth had cleared the children's toys and had a stiff gin and tonic ready for her when she went into the sitting room. The three of them sat quietly for a few minutes, sipping their drinks and appreciating this period immediately after the children were safe in bed. When Louise asked Carol about her own children, she said with sudden pugnacity, 'I want them to have the best education. I'm going to send them to boarding school.'

She had sensed that Louise wouldn't approve of her decision but she wasn't going to encourage any argument about her plans. Her sister said nothing for a moment, then asked, 'What does Jemal think of the idea?'

'Jemal is an irrelevance.' Once, in what now seemed another life, Carol had played Goneril in a production of *King Lear*. She remembered that formidable woman's dismissal of her marriage and her husband as 'an interlude'. That was how she would think of Jemal Bilic from now on. 'He will have no further part in my life or that of my children.'

'He'll at least have visiting rights, you know,' said Steve mildly.

Louise smiled a brittle smile. 'He'll find that difficult from inside a high-security prison, don't you think?' She saw the shock on their faces, exulted in the effects she was making, and added as casually as she could, 'They've caught him, by the way. He was arrested this morning. Some minor airfield in Scotland, apparently. He was trying to get out of the country.'

There was a little pause before Steve said, 'Do you know what they've charged him with?'

'I don't know and I don't care, frankly. I hope he's made to pay for whatever he's done. If that means a long stretch, so much the better. It will remove him from the children's life for good. I don't need his money any more, now that Dad's wealth is available to us.'

It was a shock to hear her speaking so brutally about her life. Louise sensed that there had been more suffering over the last few years than Carol's pride had allowed her to admit. She heard herself saying before she was aware that she had formed the thought, 'Carol, do you think Jemal killed Dad?'

Carol took so long to respond that they thought she was not going to speak. Then she said with apparent calm, 'I don't know, do I? We've been growing further apart for a year at least – probably longer than that when I look back from here. To be honest, I think now that I didn't want to know what he was doing, because I felt it would be something pretty awful and probably illegal. I suppose that makes me some kind of coward. What I can't deny is that I took his money and plenty of it for myself and the kids and the house. That certainly makes me a hypocrite.'

Steve Hawksworth gave her a sympathetic smile and replenished her gin and tonic. All three of them found the clink of the glasses and the sound of the liquid and his slow movements about the room soothing, as if the very ordinariness of his actions was a reassurance in this unnerving situation. As he resumed his seat, he said quietly, 'You may have to face up to the idea that Jemal killed your father, Carol. If they put out an alert on ports and airfields, he must have been involved in very serious crime. Statistically, it is the people already involved in crime who are most likely to go on and do even worse things. If you look round the people who were closest to Geoff, Jemal is overwhelmingly the most likely person to have killed him.'

Carol wanted to scream at him for his dullness and his logic and his talk of statistics. Typical bloody accountant! All head and no heart, all brain and no emotion! She watched her fingers whitening with her anger as they clenched her glass, told herself that the man meant well, that he was only trying to soften what he saw as the inevitable blow for her. She took a sip at her drink, swallowed, controlled her exasperation, and said calmly, 'You may well be right, Steve. What you say makes sense. It's what I was telling myself on my way here.'

Louise said, 'That's good, sis.' She had not used the diminutive for at least ten years, but it came back naturally to her at this time of stress. 'It's better to face up to it from the start rather than when it becomes public, I think.'

Carol could not take consolation from her younger sister: it was the first time in years that she had been offered it and she found that she could not stomach it.

She said with a sudden, startling vehemence, 'It might not have been Jemal! You're both talking as if it's established, when it isn't. It might have been that bloody Williams woman! It might have been Denis Oakley, who has his hand up every skirt which offers and some that don't!' She looked at the unbelieving faces and thrashed more wildly about her. 'It might even have been one of us!'

There was a pause, whilst all three of them listened to her breathing as it gradually slowed. Then Louise Hawksworth said quietly, as if trying to lower the temperature in the room, 'I went to see Pam Williams yesterday.'

'Why did you do that?' It was Steve, not her sister, who was in so quickly, wondering why she had done this unexpected thing without even mentioning her intentions to him.

'I thought it was time to bury the hatchet.' She wondered if that was the appropriate cliché, in these circumstances, but pressed on. 'We didn't behave very well to her, when you look back on it. We treated her with nothing but suspicion from the outset, because we all thought she was after Dad's money. Well, she can't have that now, can she? I thought it was time someone from the family made peace with her, so I did. She'll be coming to the funeral, when we're finally allowed to have it.'

Steve said accusingly, 'Louise, she might have murdered your dad. It was premature, to say the least.'

'She didn't kill Dad. She's as upset as any of us. She was very good with Michael. He liked her.'

No one cared to suggest that this was a non sequitur. Steve had been about to say that Pam Williams was probably upset because her meal ticket had been removed, but something in the set of his wife's face made him think better of it.

Steve threw in his own surprise instead. 'I went into your dad's factory on Friday. To see Denis Oakley.'

It wasn't the bombshell he had been half-hoping for.

Eventually, Carol Bilic looked at him coldly. 'Why did you do that?'

'I wanted to see the books. I wanted to see just what had been going on.'

'And did you do that?'

'No. He wouldn't let me see them. But he admitted that he was writing cheques on the firm to solve his personal financial difficulties. The police had just been to see him and he was pretty shaken.'

For a moment, Carol saw a wild, unlikely humour in the

situation, with the glib womaniser being confronted by this
dull, uxorious man who was professionally qualified to pick
out every financial irregularity in his conduct. She found
herself having to control a sudden impulse towards outright,
high-pitched, prolonged laughter, and realized in that moment
how near she was to hysteria. She made herself finish her
drink, stared for a moment at the melting ice and the slice
of lemon in the bottom of her glass, and said, 'So do you
think Oakley killed Dad?'

Steve resisted the impulse to rush in too strongly.

He said reflectively, 'He seems to me more like a serial
womaniser than a murderer. He may not be morally stain-
less, but there's a big step from philanderer to murderer.'

Louise was still seized by the notion that she must defend
Pam Williams from that charge, which meant finding someone
else to answer it. 'People get desperate, though, when they're
driven into corners. They do things which may not be charac-
teristic of their normal personalities. The police said something
on those lines to us, I think. We've all known Denis Oakley
for years, and yet we hardly know him at all. Dad was always
around here. Denis was always out on the road.'

Steve gestured towards Carol's glass, but she shook her
head and reminded him she had to drive home. He moved
across the sofa a little and put a reassuring hand on his wife's
arm. 'You're right, love. None of us really knows Denis. And
there's no doubt that Dad's death has been a boon to him.'

Louise resisted the inclination to shrug off his touch and
move away from him. Their natural, unthinking unity had
disintegrated since her dad's death; she was beginning to
wonder if they would ever regain it. Ten days ago, she would
never have gone to see Pam Williams without discussing it
with Steve first, and he would never have waltzed off to the
Aspin and Oakley factory without announcing his intentions
to her. She felt now that she was being disloyal to Steve as
she said dully, 'Denis Oakley's a womaniser, not a murderer.'

'Well, as I said, love, that was what I thought at first, but
I'm not quite so sure now.' Steve glanced quickly at Carol,
who was staring into the bottom of her glass again. 'But I'm
afraid we've got to face the fact that Jemal is overwhelmingly the most likely candidate.'

Carol felt a powerful urge to scream at this smug, self-satisfied man who was so happy to pile the blame on her husband. Despite him talking about a husband whom she had wanted rid of, a husband she now knew was a serious criminal at the very least. Perhaps she should have been glad that a man with a cool head like Steve should be taking over their thinking, should be directing them forward towards the paths on which their lives were going to develop. Instead, she felt a deep resentment that this man she had always dismissed as a dull and dutiful worm should be emerging as something much more dynamic since the death of her father.

She was saved from the outburst which was coming by the faint sound of a doorbell from somewhere far beyond the firmly shut door of the sitting room. The three of them looked at each other without speaking for a couple of seconds which seemed much longer.

Louise said, 'I'll get it. I don't want the children disturbed.'

The silence seemed to stretch after she had left the room. 'I don't know who it can be, at this hour on a Sunday night,' Steve said. 'We weren't expecting anyone.'

DCI Peach did not erupt into the room in his normal energetic manner. He came in quietly behind DS Blake. He looked round the room to see who was present, then watched Louise Hawksworth as she shut the door carefully behind her. She stood for a moment with her back against it before she moved into the centre of the room and stood very close to Lucy Blake.

Peach ignored her husband's gestured invitation to sit down and remained standing with Blake at his shoulder. He addressed himself first to Carol Bilic. 'I believe you have been informed that your husband was arrested this morning in Glasgow. I have to inform you that he has now been charged with serious offences under the Immigration Acts. In view of the nature of the charges, it is unlikely that he will be allowed bail. I must tell you that I expect him to be kept in custody until he comes to trial.'

'You have no need to be apologetic about that, Chief Inspector Peach. I should not want Jemal in my house if you released him. I hope that he will never set foot there again.'

Steve Hawksworth made a move to comfort her, but Carol shrugged his attentions angrily away.

It was Louise who voiced the question the three of them had in mind. 'Has Jemal been charged with the murder of my father?'

'No, Mrs Hawksworth, he has not. If he is found guilty of the charges brought against him, he will be in prison for a long time. But he will not be charged with murder.'

Louise glanced quickly at her sister, wondering how much the avoidance of this final horror would mean to her, but saw a face which might have been carved in stone. She had remained standing since she had ushered the CID pair into the room. It was Lucy Blake who now turned to her and set her old friend down not where she had been sitting on the sofa, but in an armchair beside the one occupied by her sister. Louise looked up at her with wide eyes, which were now filled not just with enquiry but also with fear.

Peach's dark-eyed, penetrating gaze ran round over the three very different faces which looked up towards his. He said, 'Jemal Bilic isn't the person who committed this vile act. That person is in this room.'

Steve Hawksworth looked at the horrified faces of the two women and said with his new-found authority, 'You had better be very certain of your ground here, Chief Inspector.'

Peach transferred his attention from husband to wife. 'Mrs Hawksworth, I know that you've already told us this once. But will you please recall to me in detail what happened in this house on the night of your father's death?'

Louise Hawksworth flicked her gaze from her husband to her sister and finally to her friend Lucy Blake, who gave her the slightest encouraging nod.

Louise's gaze transferred to the carpet, where it remained unwaveringly through an account she delivered almost like one in a trance. 'I came back here before Steve, because I didn't want to leave the children any longer than was necessary. They were fine, but a little overexcited, as I knew they would be. Michael in particular was on a bit of a high, almost feverish. I calmed them down a bit once I was on my own with them. They were going to be later than usual to bed, but I knew they wouldn't go down easily unless I let them wind down before they went. Steve came home a little later and helped me get them into bed.'

'What time was this, Louise?' The question came not from Peach but from Blake.

Louise looked up for a moment, not at her husband, but at her friend Lucy, whom she was surprised to see making notes. 'About half past eight. As I say, we usually have them in bed before that.' Correct domestic discipline suddenly seemed of pressing importance to her. 'Steve made sure Daisy had her bath and then got her into her pyjamas. I was still busy bathing Michael and trying to get him into his pyjamas – when he gets tired, his physical co-ordination isn't very good. Daisy was burbling happily enough in bed, so I said I'd read stories for both of them. Steve said he was pretty tired himself after his speech and the shock of Dad's news. He went down to get drinks for us ready for when I'd finished.'

'Time, Louise?' Lucy Blake's prompt came very quietly.

'Just after nine. I remember because the children hadn't been up so late since Christmas. It took me a long time to get Michael into his pyjamas and into bed. He wasn't very co-operative, but he couldn't help that, poor mite. He'd had a very long day. I read him a little story, but he was really past that. But I crooned little lullabies to him for quite a time and stroked his head, because I wanted to make sure he was asleep before I left him. I thought Daisy would have gone off by the time I was done with Michael, but she was still awake. I think she was determined to get her story. She's a lively little girl and once she's set her mind on something she doesn't let it escape her.' Her face shone with nostalgic pride as she recalled Michael's innocence and Daisy's mischievous will power.

'So what time did you get down here?'

Still she looked at Lucy with her small gold ball-pen poised over her notebook, not at Steve. 'It was just after half past ten. I remember saying to Steve that we'd be pushed to get half an hour to ourselves before we went up to bed.'

Peach had been silent, watching not the speaker but her husband's reactions to what she said. Now he said, 'And did Mr Hawksworth have that drink ready for you, after your marathon session with the children?'

For the first time, she faltered, as if this information had not been in her monologue. 'I – I don't think so. He poured me a gin and tonic when I slumped into a chair, I think.'

Peach looked at Hawksworth, who simply said, 'That's right, I think. It's difficult to remember details. None of us thought at the time that—'

'And where had you been whilst your wife was upstairs with the children, Mr Hawksworth?'

'Me? Oh, I'd been in this room, I think. I was pretty jaded after the day we'd had, as Louise told you. I was more mentally tired than—'

'Had you been out of the house?'

'Out of the house? No, certainly I hadn't. I might have gone to the kitchen perhaps, but certainly not out of the house.'

'Then why didn't you answer the phone?'

For the first time, something like panic flashed across the thin, alert features. 'There were no phone calls, I can assure you. I should certainly have answered them if there had been.'

'There was at least one phone call during that time. You did not answer it because it was made whilst you were out of the house.'

The two women as well as Hawksworth started at that bald, uncompromising statement. Steve repeated carefully, as if clarity could make it true, 'I wasn't out of the house at that time. There were no phone calls.'

Carol Bilic couldn't stand the tension any longer. She said, 'There was at least one call, Steve. I rang here during that time, but there was no answer, so I just left a message for you. I told them that on Thursday. I didn't think it mattered, at the time.'

Steve bathed her in the smile of his newly discovered urbanity. 'You're mistaken, Carol. We're all a little over-wrought, but that's hardly surprising. I'd have answered if you'd called. I was certainly here at that time.'

Peach kept his eyes firmly on his man as he said, 'Mrs Hawksworth, do you usually clear your messages?'

'No. I don't even listen to them every day, and when I do, I don't usually clear them. I'm a bit of a slut about that, I'm afraid!' Her brittle laughter rang like a knell around the quiet room.

Peach walked very deliberately across to the phone, his

eyes still upon Hawksworth. He tapped in the 1571 number and pressed the volume button so that everyone in the room could hear. The announcer's calm but slightly distorted voice said, 'You have six saved messages.'

The first one was a friend from the Down's Syndrome Association asking Louise to phone her back about an outing. The innocent words and the nervous social giggle at the end of the message played oddly against the tension in the room.

Then came the announcer's measured tones again. 'Second saved message. Message received on Saturday the thirtieth of June at nine fifty-eight p.m.' There was a click and a slightly distorted, metallic voice said, 'Louise, this is Carol. We need to talk about the Williams woman and Dad's announcement today. What can we do about it? Ring me back tomorrow.'

Peach put down the phone and came back to the centre of the room. 'Nine fifty-eight, Mr Hawksworth. Where were you at that time?'

'I – I must have dozed off. I told you, I was tired at the end of that Saturday.'

'You don't doze, Steve. And you're a light sleeper. You'd never have slept through the phone.' This was Louise, looking at him with her eyes widening in horror. 'You were out killing my dad.'

He looked at her for a moment as if she was Judas. Then his resistance crumbled. This was the woman he loved, being only her usual honest, uncomplicated self. A woman incapable of deceit: he'd always loved Louise for that. He said hopelessly, 'I did it for us. For Daisy and Michael. To give them a better life. I knew you wanted that.'

Louise looked at him as if he was a stranger in her husband's familiar skin. Was this the man she had slept with, whose children she had borne? The man with whom she had shared all kinds of aspirations, all kinds of intimacies over the years? Her voice was leaden as she said, 'Dad would have given us all of that. He was a good man, my dad.'

'He wouldn't, love. I saw him after his speech. You know he was going to set me up in my own firm.' He glanced guiltily at Carol: she hadn't known anything about his plans. 'Well, he said he couldn't make any commitments now.

That Pam had brought a new dimension to his life and he'd have to consult her about anything new. I knew what that meant.'

'You didn't know anything. He'd have done anything for me, my dad. And you were wrong about Pam Williams. We were all wrong. She wouldn't have stopped Dad helping you.'

He stared at her with the ultimate horror dawning for him. It must be so, if Louise said it was so. It had all been for nothing. It had all been unnecessary.

He looked at Peach. 'I'd arranged to meet Geoff at quarter to ten at Marton Towers. I knew it would be very quiet out there then. I don't think I intended to kill him when I arranged that meeting.'

'But you took a murder weapon with you.' This would all go into a statement later. It might be the difference between manslaughter and murder, when this came to court.

'I took a piece of cable from our garage, yes. You won't find it now, though.' For an instant his old pernickety pride in the detail of his performance came out. Louise gasped with horror, but this time he did not look at her. It was suddenly important to him that he had the minutiae of this out of the way without distractions.

As carefully as if he had been describing a minor road traffic accident, he said, 'Geoff still had various presents and souvenirs which people had given to him during the afternoon on the front passenger seat so I slid into the back of the car and talked to him from there.'

'And what did you say to him, Steve?' For the first time in the investigation, Peach used his forename: it was an acknowledgement that this was over now, that there was only the relief of confession left to him.

'I said that we needed money. That we'd planned a new house with all the things needed for the children, all the things needed to make life easy for Louise. He said all these things might still be achieved. At that moment, I thought everything might still be all right.'

'But it went wrong, Steve, didn't it? How did it go wrong?' Peach's voice was gentle as a therapist's. His attention was totally upon the man purging himself of his awful secret, and not at all upon the faces of the two appalled women who watched this tragic cameo.

Steve Hawksworth nodded, eager now to complete his tale and be honest and open again with his wife. 'I said he'd promised to set me up in my own business, that once I had that there would be no need for any more help from him. Geoff said that he'd never promised that, that it was an idea we had discussed but nothing more than that. He – he was very worried that night about Pam Williams. He said he'd upset her by what he'd said at the meal, that he needed to talk to her. He said that was far more important to him at that moment than any aspirations I might have for my own business. That's when I threw the cable round his neck.' He said it wonderingly, with a tiny smile, as if he could not believe that a man like him could have done anything so decisive.

'Did he struggle, Steve?'

'Not much, no. He told me not to be so ridiculous. I'm afraid that's when I lost it.' He might have been a man apologizing for spilling his tea. 'I tightened the cable around his neck, used both hands on it. I suddenly didn't want to hear any more words from him, you see.'

'And what then, Steve?'

'I realized he was dead, that I had to get out of there quickly. I'm not stupid, you see.' There was an awful bathos in this man sitting more alone in the world than he had ever been, protesting his efficiency as the man of action which he should never have tried to be. 'I'd worn gloves anyway, but I gave the door handle of Geoff's Jaguar a quick wipe before I left. Then I drove back here, as quickly as the law allowed.'

Everyone in the room save Hawksworth noted the awful irony of his care to observe driving decorum.

Peach said quietly, 'You were back before Louise came downstairs. But not quite in time to pour the drink you had promised her.'

'I was, you know. It slipped my mind, that's all. I suppose I was still preoccupied with what I had done.' He nodded a couple of times to himself, as if happy to have a rational explanation for his omission. He was cocooned now in that dreadful isolation which sometimes engulfs those who have set themselves apart from their fellows by the worst of all crimes.

Peach had remained standing through all of this. He now stepped across to Hawksworth and uttered the formal words of arrest. Lucy Blake made a small move towards the woman with whom she had shared so much in her school days, then thought better of it.

They did not handcuff their prisoner until he was outside the house, in deference to those who remained within it. The sisters stood as the bemused Steve Hawksworth was led from the room. He stopped for a moment in front of his wife, looking at her as if he had forgotten until that moment that she was there. 'I love you, Louise,' was all he said.

They left the two sisters clasped in each other's arms on the sofa, their shoulders shaking with the first soundless sobs of shock.